Tempting the Rival

Scandals and Spies, Book 3

Leighann Dobbs
Harmony Williams

This is a work of fiction.

None of it is real. All names, places, and events are products of the author's imagination. Any resemblance to real names, places, or events are purely coincidental, and should not be construed as being real.

Chapter One

London, England
October, 1806

If Gideon Graylocke were to envision being woken up in the middle of the night by a beautiful woman, it would not be by his sister-in-law. The moment he opened his eyes to see Philomena Graylocke, the Duchess of Tenwick standing over him with a serious expression on her impish face and her auburn hair hastily tied in a braid, he knew there was bad news to come.

He bolted up in bed, clutching the bedsheet to his chest to keep from exposing himself to her in the light of the candle pooling from the table next to his bed. Although the nights were cool, his bedroom, situated over the kitchens in the Tenwick townhouse, was always sweltering.

"Where's Morgan?" His voice was hoarse. Had something happened to his oldest brother?

"Here." Morgan slipped through the doorway leading to the corridor. The glow of candlelight barely stretched far enough to illuminate his silhouette. Like all the Graylocke brothers, he was over six feet tall and solidly built.

Her expression tight, Phil said, "There's been trouble. We need you down in the office."

Giddy nodded. He rubbed the sleep from his eyes with his free hand. Phil looked at him expectantly.

"Are you going to leave so I can dress?"

Scoffing, she turned her back. "As if I've never seen a naked man before." She rubbed her belly as she strode toward the door, where Morgan beckoned to her. The moment she nestled in the curve of his arm, he dropped his free hand to her belly, too.

The baby. They'd announced her pregnancy mere weeks ago. Surely this news wasn't so troublesome that it would endanger the baby?

No. Giddy forced himself to take a deep breath despite the sudden constriction around his chest. Any baby of Phil and Morgan's would inherit the Graylocke stubborn streak and Phil's fierce independence. Nothing short of an invasion would threaten that baby. If Morgan had thought for a second that it would, he would have kept the news from his wife and braved her displeasure later.

The thought didn't ease the trepidation gripping him. By the time he dressed and descended to the second floor, where his office resided, his palms were clammy. He wiped them on his shirt as he reached for the door handle.

Phil and Morgan weren't the only people in the room. The third was a short, stocky man with a shiny bald pate and a bit of a paunch. In public, he seemed an affable, carefree sort of fellow. Unfortunately, whenever Giddy had the misfortune of meeting Lord Strickland, it was usually because something dire had happened to warrant the concern of the Lord Commander of the British spy network. Tonight, Strickland stood as stiff as a statue in front of the sideboard, the grooves around his eyes and mouth intensified by the branch of candles resting next to the decanters of spirits. The fact that none of these was opened told Giddy that this situation went beyond the pale.

Although many of the Tenwick servants in London also served the spy network, Giddy shut the door to circumvent eavesdroppers. Phil, seated in the stuffed armchair in front of the desk with her slippers kicked off, ran her stocking-clad feet over the plush burgundy carpet. Standing, Morgan clutched her shoulder. His black hair was as disheveled as hers. Had the white streak at his temple grown?

Impossible. Giddy had seen him earlier that day. Or, given that it was past midnight, yesterday.

No one seemed to want to meet his gaze, despite the fact that they had summoned him from a solid sleep, the first he'd gotten in the months since his brother had recruited him into the spy network.

"What's happened?"

Phil and Morgan looked at Strickland to share the news, so Giddy turned his attention to the shorter man as well. Strickland clenched his fists so tight, the hair on his knuckles showed stark against his blanched skin.

"I can't dally long. There's a meeting between the generals in London at first light. I need to tell them that we're doing *something* on our end to mitigate this disaster."

Giddy gritted his teeth. He counted backward from twenty, not wanting to insult the Lord Commander by repeating the question. By his brother and Phil's grim expressions, they had already been informed of the situation.

Giddy, on the other hand, had been dreaming about the days when his only concern had been whether or not the glass in the orangery was sealed tight enough for his plants to withstand the elements.

Strickland ran his hand over his scalp. "Prussia has been defeated."

When his knees weakened, Giddy braced one hand against the door. "Impossible. We only joined forces with them last month." Napoleon couldn't have defeated Britain's new allies so quickly.

"They were... hell, they were bloody well decimated at Jena and Auerstedt yesterday. We just received word by semaphore." Strickland's voice and expression were bleak. His shoulders slumped in defeat. Meeting Giddy's gaze, he delivered the bald facts. "I have eyes on the Prussian king, I know the way he thinks. He'll pull Prussia's armies—what little haven't been slaughtered, captured, or fled—to regroup around Berlin, but he won't hold for long. He'll think first about the safety of his family and sign a bloody armistice."

Next to his wife, Morgan muttered, "That's if he doesn't annex his country to France." His voice was every bit as grim, to match the expressions of everyone in the room.

Throughout a long and tense armistice earlier in the year, Britain had clawed its way into some sort of upper hand in this bloody war. They'd achieved that by signing the treaty with Prussia. For the Prussian army to be beaten into submission a mere month after the coalition had been formed was a devastating blow to everyone involved.

Britain, especially. Without Prussia to hold Napoleon's attention, who was to stop him from invading the British Isles? Russia, Sweden? Their borders resided much farther from France.

"How can we help?" Giddy said weakly. "We're in London. Prussia is…" He swung his arm through the empty air. *Far away.*

Strickland's expression hardened. What little trace of joviality he had left dissipated in an instant. "Napoleon knew where to expect Prussia's forces. He knew exactly where and when to strike. His spies have infested some hole we don't know about and are privy to sensitive information between coalition members. It's my job to ensure that our leak is not in Britain."

Reflexively, Gideon glanced toward his brother. The duke looked away, his piercing gray eyes clouding over with doubt. As Strickland's second in command, Morgan trained the majority of the new recruits. He chose which men and women to trust with Britain's secrets. If one of their spies had turned against them…

"We have loyal men and women," Giddy said, his voice firm.

Although Strickland's eyebrows twitched, he did not look amused. "I'm sure France thought so, as well, but we managed to turn one of theirs."

"That was different," Phil piped up. "My brother never would have spied for the French if he hadn't been blackmailed. His loyalty has always been with Britain." She reached up, clasping Morgan's hand with a white-knuckled grip. Her stormy eyes narrowed on Strickland, accusing.

Frankly, Giddy was surprised the Lord Commander didn't apologize. Although any number of people might have filled the role of spy, there was only one brilliant inventor among them, and Phil was it. That her brother, Jared, also worked for the Crown in the precarious position of double agent was a sore spot to her. But Strickland turned his back on her in clear dismissal as he settled his gaze on Gideon.

Giddy reached to adjust a cravat he didn't currently wear, a nervous habit. "Why do I sense this is about me? I'm not selling British secrets!"

Lawks, he'd rather cut off his own arm than that. His family came from a long and prestigious line of loyal servants to the Crown.

In fact, all of the Graylocke brothers served in the war in some way, most as spies.

Morgan sighed, running his hand through his hair. "We know you aren't a traitor. We need your help discovering whether or not anyone is."

Giddy stood straighter, pushing himself away from the door. "Another mission?" Ever since he'd pledged his assistance to the cause, he'd been beset with assignments. One after another, without break. This was war; there was no end to the integral work that needed to be done. And, given the swiftness with which Gideon had grasped the essentials of spying, he had soon become one of Strickland's favorites to send out into the field, along with his second-oldest brother, Tristan.

Morgan gave a slight, surreptitious nod, though he didn't answer Giddy's inquiry. He left that for Strickland to do.

Turning his undivided attention to the spymaster, Gideon said, "This seems like a pivotal assignment. Why me and not Tristan? He has more experience."

Strickland squared his shoulders. "We don't need an experienced spy for this one. We need an experienced botanist."

Giddy's ears rang. He looked to his family for confirmation. Had he heard right...or was he dreaming? How in Zeus's name was a botanist supposed to help catch a traitor in the ranks?

All eyes remained fixed on him, steady as they read his reaction. By Jove, they were serious. He ran his hands through his hair.

"I feel as though I skipped a page. Perhaps you ought to go back. Why would you need my skills as a botanist?" Despite the level, cogent way he tried to deliver the words, they sounded disbelieving. He straightened and added, "Not that I'm not flattered. And more than willing to help. But this doesn't sound like the sort of thing a plant can fix."

Strickland raised a bushy eyebrow as if to say, *Are you quite done?*

Giddy snapped his mouth shut. He clenched his fists as he awaited the explanation.

Morgan squeezed his wife's shoulder one last time before he took a step forward. "You'll recall about five months ago, we captured Lady Whitewood and faked her disappearance."

Giddy nodded. It had been his first unofficial mission, and he'd provided a supportive role to Morgan and Phil, who had captured the French agent in order to liberate her brother from French influence. Not that it had worked out the way Phil had envisioned, considering that Jared had opted to remain a spy under British command. Lady Whitewood had been a piece in a puzzle that stemmed from Tristan's mission six months ago, which had ended with the known French ringmaster in London dead at the Tenwick ancestral estate. Tristan, Morgan, and Gideon had been searching for the ringleader's replacement ever since, an elusive Monsieur V. Lady Whitewood had reported directly to him, and was likely the only person of their acquaintance who knew his face. Everyone else, even Jared, dealt with the French spy's underlings.

"She can't have delivered this information, given that the coalition with Prussia hadn't even been formed at the time of her capture."

"She didn't," Strickland barked. "I have her under lock and key where no one has access to her."

Gideon rubbed his head. He sensed he was making a fool of himself by not putting this together sooner, but he had to ask, "Then how does she signify into Prussia's defeat?"

"She doesn't," Phil informed him, tucking her feet into her slippers once more. "At least, not directly."

Well, that was a relief. His mental faculties hadn't been softened by this incessant fieldwork, then.

With a brusque swipe of his hand through the air, Strickland said, "Forget Prussia for a moment. Our primary concern is to discover who Monsieur V is and whether he or his underlings have had access to sensitive British information regarding the positioning of troops on the continent. I've had my best interrogators working Lady Whitewood—"

Gideon wondered what, exactly, he meant by "working". He didn't peer too closely at Strickland's methods, but it was well known that he was a hard man who would not, under any circumstance, allow the French to get the upper hand on Britain.

"—Hell, I've even tried to break her myself. Neither she, nor any of the other low level French spies we've dared to capture have been willing to give up their employer. Either this Monsieur V inspires great loyalty, or unfathomable fear."

Giddy would lay his money on the latter.

He raised one shoulder in a half-shrug. "What do you want me to do about it, send him a bouquet of flowers?"

From the grim set of Strickland's mouth, he wasn't amused. "I need something to force her to talk. A truth serum."

Now Giddy knew he was definitely dreaming. Did his superior just ask him to conjure the impossible from thin air? Laughter bubbled in the back of his throat, but given the look on Strickland's face, he wasn't joking.

Gideon shook his head. Slowly, at first, trying to deny the reality of what they were asking him to create, but it gained more conviction the longer he thought about it. "It isn't possible. I wouldn't know where to start."

Phil sat straighter in the chair. "There has been chatter recently in some of the scientific journals that a plant from South America might hold the key to such a serum."

He knew of the plant in question. *Brugmansia,* commonly called angel's trumpets, and colloquially known as "*borracherro*" or the "get-you-drunk" tree. He also knew exactly who had been chattering in those scientific journals Phil had been reading.

A crackpot. Although there were sense-altering properties to the plant, that didn't mean the person who ingested it was guaranteed to tell the truth. It was a bloody plant, not magic.

Calmly, he pointed out, "That chatter has yet to be proven." And the author had been harping on the properties of that plant for well over two years now. If it was true, *someone* would have been able to produce a truth serum from it by now.

Strickland's face hardened. "So prove it." He strode directly for Giddy, looking like he might wring Gideon's neck if he refuted the possibility one more time.

When Giddy jumped to the side, Strickland yanked open the door. He paused in the threshold to say, "I need to attend my meeting. Tenwick, you can take it from here? I think it goes without speaking that you'll have every resource available." His voice was edged with weariness.

No more than Morgan's when he answered, "Yes, sir."

Gideon waited for the door to shut before he met his brother's gaze. The gray eyes that made enemies squirm had lost their sharp edge. As Phil stood, he wrapped his arm around his wife, tucking her into his side.

Over the past several months, Giddy had tried not to notice how content his two oldest brothers were to be married. Quiet moments like these weighed on him the most. It wasn't the wicked grins the married couples shared, or even the kisses when they thought no one was looking. It was the way Morgan drew strength from Phil's touch, as if he wasn't whole without her nearby. Moments like this made Giddy wonder if he was missing out on something unspeakably wonderful.

You don't have time to go hunting for a wife, he reminded himself. That was triply true now that he'd committed himself to the spy effort. Even so, a small part of him whispered that Tristan and Morgan hadn't had time to find wives, either. Somehow, in the course of their work, they'd found them anyway.

Hoping to banish the uncomfortable notion, Giddy ran his fingers through his hair again, as black as any other Graylocke sibling though he didn't sport the duke's white streak. He scrubbed his hand over the thick stubble lining his cheek. "I can't guarantee that I'll be able to do what you're asking, let alone in the time frame that Strickland seems to be expecting. I work with plants. I'm no chemist."

Morgan hid a yawn behind the back of his hand. "We know that. That's why we're bringing in help. The very best chemist to assist you. Between your knowledge of plants and theirs of serums, you should be able to come up with something."

Grimly, Giddy muttered, "I'll try."

This was what you wanted, wasn't it, a chance to dig in the dirt again and immerse yourself in a plant?

It was. It was also one of those moments when he was reminded to be careful what he wished for. He sensed this would be far from a holiday.

Wearily, he asked, "Who is my partner?" Over various missions, he'd been paired and re-paired, as the assignment necessitated. He'd even worked one or two with Tristan. Unfortunately, his brother was no chemist.

Phil answered, "F. Albright, the author of those papers I read on the plant."

Gideon groaned. He rubbed his suddenly throbbing temple. Anyone would have been better. Zeus, they could have paired him up with Monsieur V and he would have been more thrilled at the prospect.

When he opened his eyes, he found his brother glaring at him. "Is that going to be a problem?"

A problem, working with the F. Albright, the crackpot with whom he had been who had been in a public feud ever since Albright had made some unfounded corrections to a paper Giddy had published? "No, of course not." He managed to keep the sarcasm out of his voice when, in fact, the idea of being saddled with a whiny, arrogant chemist who had delusions of expanding outside his area of expertise was less then appealing.

Sullen, Gideon added, "He knows nothing about botany." Even if the fool wanted to pretend otherwise with his embarrassing, heated letters through the *Royal Botanical Gazette*.

Gideon couldn't help but be curious about Albright. With all the sparring back and forth in newspapers and journals, he'd never met the man, though he suspected F. Albright was actually Farnsworth Albright a somewhat reclusive scholar. An older gentleman, if what Gideon had heard was correct. Maybe he would tire easily and leave Gideon the room he needed to prove this crazy truth serum theory incorrect once and for all.

Morgan raised his eyebrows. "That's why we need you to take point on this one. Are you able to do this?"

Giddy gritted his teeth. "This is for Britain, isn't it?"

It was a rhetorical question, but his brother answered anyway.

"This is for us all."

Put that way, Gideon couldn't refuse. "I'll do it," he said, resigned.

Even if it meant that he had to work with his arch rival, F. Albright.

21

Chapter Two

Felicia Albright adjusted the bodice of her flamboyant red-and-indigo dress. Her skin puckered with goose bumps against the autumn chill clinging to the air. With the sun hiding behind clouds this morning, it would be a long while before she warmed up. Even so, she dismissed the notion of finding a shawl. More often than not, it was her feminine charms that attracted customers to her stall. Hence the reason her dress ended just high enough to display the curve of her ankle in her faded red, heeled shoes.

To keep herself warm, she busied herself around her stall. She stepped over her black mastiff, Chubs, who lounged with his eyes shut and his gangly legs stretched out to trip customers. After she adjusted the awning to ensure that her sign, *Felicia's Love Perfumes: Guaranteed to Attract the Man or Woman of Your Dreams!*, was visible from the far end of the market, she herded her dog closer to the wagon. Chubs groaned like an old man before he slinked closer to the wagon wall.

The gaudy, blue-and-gold covered wagon that doubled as her home shone like a beacon among the plain wood wagons parked along this row. With the harvest complete, farmers amassed on the northern edge of London in the hopes of selling their wares and stockpiling the other items they needed to survive the coming winter. They, like Felicia, parked on the half-frozen, churned mud. Some used their wagon beds as their stalls; others set up tables and awnings like Felicia. With the sky lightening to blue in between the wispy scraps of gray cloud, the city would soon be waking up to invade the market en masse. By noon, the ground would be thawed and thick with boot prints as men and women clogged the lanes in search of produce.

At this time of year, there were few stalls like Felicia's that sold wares other than agricultural. Fairs were more lucrative to her, but she hoped to take advantage of the farmers thinking about winter—and Christmas gifts. Yesterday, when she'd arrived from her tour of the northern counties, had been an encouraging day. Today, she hoped to be even better. After all, she had a winter to survive as well. October was often the last month she was able to remain open before she had to find shelter with thicker walls for the winter.

A young man wandered closer, empty-handed as he peered at the stalls. His brown hair fell over his forehead, all but obscuring his eyes as he cast glances toward her stall. The painted wagon tended to attract a lot of attention, which Felicia capitalized on by becoming an attraction, herself. Given the shabby quality of the clothes that hung on his thin frame, he had more likely come looking to rob someone than buy. Felicia wasn't worried; she had yet to encounter a thief that could outrun Chubs. However lazy he pretended to be, her dog knew that he only got fed if she got paid.

Toying with a lock of her curly red wig, Felicia strutted the length of her stall, keeping one eye on the thief. She tugged down her bodice to display the swells of her breasts to the cool air. Men always assumed two things about women: that they were weak and easily taken advantage of—hence the necessity of keeping Chubs close at hand—and that they were stupid. Felicia boasted a mind quicker than most scholars, but her ability to tally numbers and formulas in her head wouldn't put bread on the table. She'd learned early on that if she appeared to be the confident, intelligent woman she was and treated her clients with a businesslike demeanor, not only would they choose to believe her weak and stupid anyway, but they would often be off-put by her demeanor. As much as she'd like to change that, it was the way of the world. She wasn't above lowering herself to expectations in order to make ends meet—or, at the very least, pretend to.

The young man strolled closer. He tucked his thumbs into the waistband of his breeches, a deceptively casual pose. When he glanced in Felicia's direction, she twirled her finger around a lock of red hair and smiled, thrusting out her chest. Her figure wasn't as bountiful as some ladies', but it did the trick. His gaze meandered to the swell of her breasts.

Now...buy something or go away. She kept her smile in place by practice alone.

This close, she noticed the freckles on his cheeks beneath a smutch of dirt. At her guess, he was seventeen or eighteen years old—no older than she had been when she'd run away from home. Her flirtatious stance wilted as she recalled too many hungry nights before she'd been welcomed into the bosom of the circus she'd traveled with for the next few years. Maybe she should let him have a vial of her perfume, one of the more diluted ones.

She gritted her teeth. She couldn't afford to have sympathy for thieves or vagabonds. If she did, she would go hungry, too.

The young man slowed as he strolled past, paying more attention to her than to her wares. She followed him, shifting her attention from him to the table she'd set out beneath the awning. A cheap scarlet tablecloth that resembled velvet when not in bright light dripped over the sides of the rectangular table. Perfume bottles in small and medium sizes, hewn of translucent glass to showcase the pale amber liquid within, rested on the cloth by size. Although they looked the same, the formulas varied slightly. One contained ingredients to attract a woman; the other to attract a man. The ones on display were of the most diluted solutions—Felicia kept more condensed versions of the perfume in the wagon, contained in suitably expensive crystal bottles to reflect the quality.

Lightly, she brushed her fingertips over the tablecloth, straightening it as she ensured for the tenth time this morning that her wares were displayed to advantage. The young man moved on. Maybe she'd misjudged him.

"Ouch!"

A high-pitched squeal from behind made Felicia whirl to face the opposite end of her stall. On the far end of the table, a girl of about seven or eight writhed in pain as Felicia's mule sank his teeth into her arm. Still hitched to the front of the wagon, Rudolph shouldn't have been able to reach. In fact, he wouldn't have, if the girl hadn't backed away from the table after snatching one of the largest bottles. She clutched it in her free hand.

Felicia bunched her skirts and launched to help the girl. The instant she had the thief by the scruff of her scratchy, undyed shift, Felicia tugged on Rudolph's mane. "Let go, you brute. You're hurting the poor thing."

The thief, on cue, burst into tears.

Sweetheart, I was just like you, once. Albeit, about ten years older. Tears had earned her no sympathy. She hardened herself to the thief's plight and stuck out her hand. "I'll thank you to return that. You're much too young for it, anyway." Although she claimed that her perfumes induced true love, lust was a more accurate byproduct.

Rudolph stamped. He stretched out his neck, curling his lip up from over his blocky teeth as he tried to take a nip out of Felicia's skirts.

She steered herself and the girl out of reach with a scowl. "Eat your oats if you're hungry, you nag."

Rudolph twitched his tail.

As Felicia turned her full attention on the girl, she quivered beneath her palm. Tears jumped to the girl's eyes, making them as red as her nose. "Please don't hurt me, mum. I didn't mean nothing personal by it, I swear." Her voice was high-pitched and nasal with tears.

She almost had Felicia fooled. Against her better judgment, her hand relaxed and she nearly released the girl.

Until Chubs got to his feet, his hackles rising as he growled. But he didn't aim his snarl toward the thief in Felicia's hands—he advanced on the one at the other end of the stall. The young man had circled back and now had his hands poised over her wares.

Blast! If she pursued him, she would be leaving herself open for the girl to rob her instead.

The young man blanched the color of the wan clouds overhead, snatched as many bottles as his hands could carry, and turned to run. The glass clinked together. He stopped short as a tall man stepped into his path.

The man—an aristocrat by the tailored cut and quality of his coat, waistcoat, breeches, and boots—stood easily six feet tall. Broad in the shoulders, his build narrowed to lean hips. The confidence in his stance, more than his athletic build, made him formidable. When he swept the topper off his head, stopping the thief with no more than a palm on his shoulder, he uncovered black hair styled in a fashionable Brutus haircut with a white streak at one temple. His piercing gray eyes fixed on the young man.

"I suggest you return those." His voice, although temperate, send a chill down Felicia's spine. She was happy not be the focus of that unforgiving gaze.

The young man paled even further. He stammered an apology, blindly thrusting the bottles behind him onto the table once more. They bunched together in a haphazard fashion, more than one toppling onto its side. Fortunately, Felicia had sealed the vials herself and the stoppers allowed no leaks to escape.

Satisfied, the aristocrat produced a white card from his pocket. "Can you read?"

The young man drew himself up. Although he was taller than Felicia's five-foot-three, he didn't nearly match the supercilious lord for height.

"Of course I can."

A young woman around Felicia's height or shorter snorted as she came abreast. Like the aristocrat, she wore expensive fabrics—muslin, in her case, a dark netting over a forest green gown beneath. Her auburn hair was neatly styled, though she wore no bonnet to shield her from the sun. Given the sun-kissed cast to her skin, she didn't seem to care much for the standards of her peers. Her mouth curved in a secretive smile, made all the more mischievous by the sharp cast of her chin.

Felicia liked her on sight.

The lord shared a glance with the woman as he drawled, "No, then." He tucked the card in his pocket once more. "If you'd like gainful employment that will keep your belly full and keep you warm for the winter, take your companion and present yourselves at Lord Strickland's house. Tell him Tenwick sent you."

Tenwick, as in *the Duke of*?

The girl in Felicia's clutches twisted out of Felicia's slackened grip and scampered away. With a surly, guarded expression, the young man bowed and left as well. Given the look on his face, he didn't seem likely to obey the duke. A pity. If the duke's offer was genuine, it might be the best the pair could hope for this winter.

Could this be the duke standing in front of her? Felicia couldn't begin to fathom why he would be shopping in this market. Surely he had servants to do this sort of thing for him.

Better to err on the side of safety. After returning the bottle of perfume the girl had tried to steal to its rightful place, Felicia snapped her fingers. The sound silenced the low rumble in her dog's chest. She directed him to lie down next to the wagon. He laid his head back against his paws as he complied.

Good boy. You'll get a treat later, she silently promised. She didn't have time to praise him, not in front of a duke.

Spreading her skirts, she gave the aristocrat a smooth curtsey, adding a flourish to the end. Given the woman lingering next to him, Felicia opted not to show her cleavage too much. She didn't want to scare off a potential customer by making his wife or lover jealous.

"Thank you, your grace, for your assistance with those ne'er-do-wells. What can I do to repay you? Do you need some help wooing your lady, perchance?" She fixed a smile on them both, wavering between the couple so one didn't think she focused too much of her attention on the other. She could be wrong in her hunch—

they might only be friends, and have need of her potions.

With a wry smile and a glance toward the duke that crackled with amusement, the woman said, "I should think by now I'm sufficiently wooed."

The lady stepped forward, reaching for the bottles dumped onto Felicia's table. "Please, let me help you with those."

Felicia leaped to intercept her. "That's very kind, but far from necessary. It is my pleasure to arrange them myself."

As she hurried to upright the bottles to keep the well-bred lady from doing so, she noticed a gleaming diamond ring circled with sapphires on the woman's left hand. Married, then. And likely to the duke, given the protective way he hovered behind her.

Felicia leaned forward to whisper, "I know my sign claims that the perfume incites love, but in truth, it is closer to lust. You might find it...enhances your husband's performance in the bedroom."

Behind her, the duke stiffened. *Drat.* Felicia must have spoken too loudly and offended him.

The duchess, on the other hand, looked intrigued. "How does the perfume work?"

The duke muttered, "I do not have performance issues and you well know it."

Close up, the duchess stood an inch or two shorter than Felicia. She drew herself up to her full height as she twisted to meet her husband's gaze.

"You've been treating me like glass ever since you learned I was with child."

"I have not...and even if I have, I don't want to hurt the baby."

She rolled her eyes. "It's well protected, Morgan. It can't be hurt that way."

That sounded like a conversation Felicia should definitely stay out of. She smiled. "I have some better quality perfumes in the wagon. Why don't I fetch one for you and you can see if you like it?"

Before the pair answered her, she dipped a hasty curtsey and escaped. Chubs lumbered up after her as she dashed through the cramped interior to the small cupboard where she kept her bottled perfumes. She chose the best quality, a bottle-necked vial of intricately carved crystal that ended in a round bottom the size of her fist.

When she emerged into the crisp open air once more, the aristocrats hadn't moved on from her stall. That was encouraging.

Even if the duke said, "We do not need one of your perfumes."

The duchess snorted. "Speak for yourself." She leaned forward as Felicia broke the seal on the vial and removed the cork. The duchess leaned forward to sniff. She wrinkled her nose.

Felicia laughed. "I know, it smells potent in such a concentrated dose. You'll need only a dab on your neck, wrists, between your breasts... and anywhere else you'd like his attention." She stoppered the vial again, pressing her thumb against the wax seal to mold it in place and hopefully keep it from leaking if she tipped it accidentally. "I should warn that it will attract any man in the vicinity." She turned her attention to the duke. "If you want one to make your wife wild, that would be another formula. I do have those on hand, as well."

The duke rolled his eyes. "My wife is wild enough on her own, thank you."

In a smooth movement, the duchess elbowed her husband in the side. She shifted to stand in front of him, not that that blocked Felicia's view of his face.

"That's curious. How does it work?" the duchess asked.

"It's a complicated scientific reaction. Suffice it to say that it *will* work." She offered the vial on her palm, face up. "If you're unsatisfied, I will of course offer you a full refund."

Felicia didn't normally offer such a thing to her customers. Then again, she didn't normally sell to the likes of dukes, so if it would ensure a sale, she would make the offer. Word of mouth in that sphere could feed her all winter from a single day's purchases or commissions.

Narrowing her thickly lashed eyes, the duchess pursed her lips. "I am a scientist. I'll be able to follow along."

No, you aren't. Oh, the young woman—less than a handful of years younger than Felicia's age of twenty-nine, at a guess—might have an interest in science. She might even actively pursue the acquisition of knowledge in the fields that interested her. However, the science community, like every other, was dominated by men.

Scientists were doddery old men with weak chins and beady eyes that liked to think themselves above everyone else because they went to university. They respected women in such a sphere even less than they respected dogs. It was why Felicia had to publish her research papers under her initials rather than her name.

By force of will, she kept her smile in place as she took a deep breath, warding away the storm of resentment conjured by the knowledge of how the world worked.

None of this was the duchess's fault, of course, so Felicia tried not to take out her frustrations on a potential client. She'd thought she was immune to the disappointment by now, given that it had been twelve years since she'd learned the harsh truth of her future. But, seeing the beautiful scientist alongside a duke who seemed to indulge her every whim made the resentment fester in Felicia's chest once more.

She endeavored to ignore the feeling.

Before she pinched the precious crystal vial too hard and cracked it, she set it down on the table. "Are you familiar with pheromones?"

"I assume you mean the chemicals secreted in a mating sense."

So she did know science. Felicia nodded. "The perfume works on a similar principle. The chemicals are tailored to attract men or women, depending on the preference of the user. Since His Grace is already attracted to you, the perfume will make him lose the inhibitions that he has erected between you."

Tenwick sighed. "I'm standing right here."

"Yes, dear." His wife reached behind to absently pat him on the chest. To Felicia she asked, "How much do you want for it?"

"Five shillings," Felicia said, expecting to be haggled down.

Instead, the duchess opened the reticule on her wrist and produced the coins. "I'll take it."

Her husband sighed. "This isn't why we're here, Phil."

She shot him a wicked look. "I don't see why we can't do both."

Unwilling to lose such a high-paying customer, Felicia accepted the coins and exchanged them for the expensive bottle. "Remember, just a dab will do."

With a grin, the duchess tucked away her prize. Her husband sighed, fingering the white streak in his hair. They didn't leave.

Uncertain, Felicia asked, "Are you certain I can't offer you a vial to entice your wife?"

He straightened and dropped his hand, his expression impassive. "Indeed not. But you can offer me something else."

The only thing Felicia sold was her perfumes. Hesitantly, she dipped in another curtsey. She tried to hide her trepidation as she answered, "I am at Your Grace's service."

Still beaming from her purchase, the duchess asked, "You are the F. Albright who publishes in *Chemists Quarterly*?"

No one had ever accused Felicia of such a thing. In fact, the few times that Felicia had confessed that she was a respected chemist in her field, the men and sometimes even women involved in the exchange laughed at the idea. Slowly, Felicia answered, drawing out her words. "I am..."

The duchess turned to give her husband a triumphant look. "See, I told you it was the daughter. Women can practice the sciences as well as men. Sometimes better." She turned back to Felicia. "Though we did have quite a time tracking you down."

How *had* they found her? Everyone, including the publishers of the journals to which she sent her essays, believed her to be a man. Once or twice, someone had tried to track her down, only to settle on the surety that her scholar father was responsible for her papers as well as his own. After she'd been confronted by that mistaken notion, she'd stopped trying to correct people. Let her father deal with those who wanted to discuss or disparage her research. He was so absent-minded, she wouldn't put it past him to believe that he *had* written those essays and forgotten that she'd done so.

"I am the one, but I..." Felicia looked from duchess to duke. What, exactly, did they want with her?

His gray eyes piercing through her as if to read her inner turmoil, Tenwick said, "We'd like you to create the truth serum for us."

Chapter Three

He wanted the truth serum. *Her* truth serum.

It had to be some kind of jest. No one in the chemistry or botany fields believed her research to be solid. She'd railed against them for years. The science was sound. If only she had the funds and access to the right chemicals, she could prove them wrong.

Both the duke and duchess waited for her response.

She opened her mouth and shut it, gathering her thoughts before answering. Somehow, her clever response turned into, "You're serious?"

The duke nodded.

Felicia still didn't believe him. "*Why?*" He was a duke, for Heaven's sake! What could he possibly need with a truth serum?

"I like to be a patron of the sciences." He delivered the sentence with a calm, smooth tone of voice. Not a muscle twitched in his expression. He didn't look away from her eyes.

Perhaps it was that last that convinced her he must be lying. Liars liked to think that looking someone in the eye made them more believable, but in actuality, such unwavering attention usually meant that they were focusing too hard on hiding something. About then, Felicia would have given her left arm to have the truth serum completed and on hand, just so she could feed it to him and learn the truth.

You're smarter than that. This is a riddle.

As a child and young woman, she'd loved riddles. As an adult, she had no time for them. But maybe this one...

"I'll be paid, of course."

"And put up at my estate in the country for the duration of your research."

Outside of London, where she wouldn't have easy access to the chemicals she needed. It would cost more to have them shipped to a remote castle. Even more curious.

She tested him by stating, "I have this autumn's wares still to sell. I can make my way to your estate once I've finished with the market."

"I'll buy the lot of them."

A surge of satisfaction winked to life in her chest. She snuffed it out before it showed on her features. *I knew it.* He didn't want her to create the serum for him solely to be a patron of the arts. He wanted it done quickly, which meant that he had a purpose for the serum.

What could be so pressing? A lying servant? If his concern had been a cheating wife, the duchess would not have boldly accompanied him. She seemed like no fool, and knew exactly what he was about. Felicia studied her expression, trying to discern the truth from her, to no avail. They were good at hiding their intentions.

A duke built like a soldier. A duchess who openly claimed to be a scientist. Both somehow able to track her down despite her nomadic lifestyle and the fact that she, as a woman, was not affiliated with her work. This pair was far from what they seemed. Were they even nobility?

Spies. A war was being fought, not terribly far away, and a truth serum might infinitely come in handy to turn the tides.

Felicia narrowed her eyes. "Do you work for Britain?" She wasn't going to aid some foreign blackguards, not even for an exorbitant amount of money.

Shock showed on the woman's face. The man, on the other hand, remained impassive. "This isn't the place for discussion. May we go inside?"

Inside her wagon? It would be dreadfully cramped with three people. Could Felicia trust them? They could, after all, simply render her unconscious, kidnap her, and force her to work for them.

The moment the couple rounded her table, Chubs jumped to his feet. He didn't growl, but he stepped forward to lean against Felicia's thigh. He would never let something happen to her on his watch.

She glanced down the sparsely-populated lane of stalls and inwardly sighed. "Very well, but I'll need to bring my wares in."

The woman grinned. "I'll help. I'm Phil, by the way."

"Felicia." Her name slipped out, even though they obviously knew it already. Even if they hadn't sought her out, the sign hanging from her awning proclaimed it loud and clear.

Between the two women, they shortly stripped the stall of items. Phil piled the cloth and bottles into her husband's arms. Both she and Felicia carried the rest inside, clearing the stall in one trip whereas it had taken Felicia several to set the perfumes out.

She entered the wagon first. With only her and Chubs, the wagon often seemed crowded. She had only enough space for a seating area that doubled as her bed opposite a row of cupboards that rose to waist height, the tops cleared for her to use as a work bench. She slipped the perfumes into a crate in the far corner. Phil followed, handing off the rest of the bottles and finally the cloth, one by one. When Felicia stood, the wagon felt as tight as if she was in one of those bottles. Chubs was curled up in his usual corner, padded with spare blankets. The narrow space between the bed and the cupboards was eaten up by the duke's broad shoulders.

Felicia motioned to the bed, thanking her forethought for having straightened the sheets this morning. "Please sit, Your Grace."

Thankfully, neither of the aristocrats protested. Felicia leaned her rump against the work table as she faced the pair. Phil leaned against her husband, snuggling into his embrace. He encircled her with his arm. From the neutral expression on his face, he might not even notice he did so. It might be an unconscious gesture, needing and wanting her close.

Felicia buried a twinge of regret. If she hadn't run away from home, she might have had that.

Or she might have been miserable, forced to serve her husband's whims and denied the freedom to pursue her scientific research. At least now, she lived on her own terms. Marriage wasn't a part of her plans. At age thirty as of next month, she feared she was coming to the end of her childbearing years. She had made this choice, and she liked her freedom, even if she occasionally wondered, *"What if..."*

Right now, her only concern was: What if the duke and duchess weren't who they said they were?

She drew herself up, casting a glance toward Chubs to ensure that he was alert in case she needed him. He slinked off his blanket, slowly getting closer to the group. His body was so long that his rump could probably still touch his bed while his paws touched the duke's boots.

"You work for Britain?" She kept her voice light, despite the suspicion swirling inside her.

The duke raised an arched eyebrow. "We do. My family has been loyal to the crown since our nation's inception."

"Then you *are* the duke and duchess of Tenwick?"

Phil looked at Felicia with a quizzical expression. "Of course. He's a bit conspicuous to be disguised."

The duke clenched his jaw and shifted his arm around his wife. He said nothing.

Felicia pressed her lips together. "You want me to believe that a duke and duchess are Crown spies."

Tenwick's gray eyes snapped. "When did we say that?"

Heedless to her husband's displeasure, Phil leaned forward and answered over top of him. "Yes. In a support capacity, of course."

He made a face. "We don't know if we can trust her."

The duchess shot him a speaking look. "We'll have to trust her at some point, if she's to help us."

Felicia gnawed on her lower lip. "Perhaps you ought to tell me exactly why you want me to create this serum for you now." After all, she'd been publishing her research on the subject for years. The war with France was hardly new.

After a tense look exchanged between the aristocrats, the duke admitted, "We have a French spy in our midst and we're unable to discover who. Our one source who knows him refuses to give him up, even under duress. We need a sure thing, and... given the turn in the war, we need it as soon as possible."

His voice was stiff, formal, grim. What had happened in the war? Last Felicia had heard, the armistice with Napoleon was only just ending, what with Britain's new alliance with Prussia.

"Can you create the serum?" An edge of doubt entered Tenwick's voice.

Felicia drew herself up. "Of course I can." She had, after all, thoroughly researched that very thing. If she'd had the means to test her theory, she might have concocted such a serum already.

"Good." The duke stood. "Then you'll be working around the clock with our best botanist."

It was on the tip of Felicia's tongue to inquire after her pay for this endeavor, but the query dissolved beneath her curiosity. "Who?"

The duke's expression gentled. The corners of his lips twitched, almost an admission of amusement, or maybe pride. "My brother," he informed. "Gideon Graylocke."

Felicia bit the inside of her cheek to keep from laughing. Not the stubborn man who had been in a public row with her through the *Royal Botanical Gazette* over the past several months, simply because he refused to accept valid criticism. Oh, this was going to be more fun than she'd thought.

Although she tried to keep the amusement from her tone, it made her voice tight as she answered, "Perhaps it would be best if I meet with him first, to ensure he's willing to work with me."

She would even try not to nettle him too much in the process.

The duke raised his eyebrows in a haughty expression. "He's pledged himself to the Crown's service. He has no choice. But if you're willing to meet with him today, we'll discuss particulars then."

Felicia smiled. "Hanover Square. Three o'clock."

She could already imagine the expression on the botanist's face when he realized that the person with whom he'd been heatedly corresponding was a woman.

If he tried to underestimate her, she was going to prove to him exactly how poor an idea that was.

Chapter Four

The morning had been crisp and cold, chilly enough that opening the office window had been enough to rouse Gideon and allow him to brace himself for the coming day. By the time Morgan had sent him a note alerting him to the meeting with his rival that afternoon, Giddy had already scoured the library for books that might prove helpful with his coming assignment. He'd found and reviewed Mr. Albright's essays regarding this alleged truth serum.

Giddy still didn't believe it could be done, not to the effects stated by Mr. Albright. Liquor could loosen the tongue just as effectively. When intoxicated, it was more difficult to recall a lie, especially an elaborate one. It didn't guarantee the truth, which seemed to be what Mr. Albright proposed and what Strickland demanded.

Sweat clung to the back of Giddy's neck as he paced beneath the bright sun in Hanover Square. Towering brick-and-stucco townhouses ringed the square, each loftier than the last, and a neat, square garden replete with shrubs and trees occupied the center of the square. The carriages that rumbled past, clattering on the cobblestones, were hidden behind the bower on the other side as they turned the loop. Many retired to the mews at the north corner of the square. Although the air in this part of town smelled clean enough, every now and again, a breeze carried a whiff of the straw and manure scent of the stables.

When Giddy had arrived at precisely ten minutes to three of the afternoon, the garden had teemed with ladies young and old, as well as the occasional servant walking a dog. As the last vestiges of summer heat had returned with a vengeance, those ladies had retired to their townhouses, shielding themselves beneath bonnets and parasols. Giddy had no such luxury. He'd paced the edge of the garden by the gate, the heat in turn searing into his exposed skin and hidden beneath the dappled shade of an oak tree. After a time, when no gentleman presented himself, Giddy began to wonder if Mr. Albright awaited him at another corner of the square. At five minutes past three of the afternoon, he'd taken a circuit of the square; and again at a quarter past three.

Now, his pocket watch informed him that the hour drew close to half past three and he was still left alone to brood. Well, alone save for the woman seated on a stone bench in the shade of the oak tree, plying a handkerchief with her needle. She didn't appear as affected by the heat as the other ladies who had retired to their tea indoors.

He stood beneath the shade for a moment more, relishing the cool shadow over his heated cheeks. He had better things to do than wait until he expired for a man he didn't even like. A man he would be forced to work with for the next several weeks, if not months, until Strickland accepted that what he asked simply could not be done.

Meanwhile, Giddy had other problems to deal with. Although the Season had come to a close months ago, after a brief stint in the country, Mother had returned to Town to torment Giddy. Usually, he spent all his hours shut up in his orangery at the Tenwick ancestral estate. This was doubly true upon the Season's close, which allowed him the freedom to tend to his plants without remorse over neglecting social engagements. However, his engagements as a spy necessitated his remaining in London this year. As far as Mother was concerned, he might as well have stood on the roof of the house and threatened to jump. In her eyes, his decision not to tend to his plants was a cry for help.

A cry his younger sister, Lucy, was too happy to rectify. Between Mother, Lucy, and his co-sister-in-law, Charlie, he had never had to work so hard to convince someone that he was not, in fact, at death's door. At some point in the past month or two, Lucy had gotten it into her head that Giddy was jealous of his brothers' recent marriages. When he dragged himself home upon the completion of an exhausting night of spy work, the very last thing he wanted to do was fend off a grasping debutante who wanted to marry the brother of a duke. When he decided to marry, he wanted nothing less than the mutual respect and cooperation that Morgan had with his wife. He wanted someone he could work alongside, as equals. Despite what his mother and sister seemed to think, he didn't need to find such a woman now. He was only twenty-four, for Heaven's sake.

Unfortunately, despite his vociferous protests, Mother refused to believe that he wasn't lonely and pining for a wife. Since he couldn't possibly confess his affiliations with the British spy network, he had to endure her torturous efforts in silence. Mother, Lucy, and Charlie had already made the decision to accompany him when he returned, rather than staying in Town with Morgan and his newly pregnant wife. With Giddy's luck, his family would be smitten with Mr. Albright, and Giddy would spend the duration of his assignment fielding off comments of how much more polite and astute and congenial his rival was. Perhaps the poor man would wind up married into the family, thereby prolonging Giddy's suffering indefinitely.

Come to think of it, perhaps Giddy wasn't as irritated by Mr. Albright's tardiness after all. In fact, he now started to hope that the man had changed his mind and wouldn't show up.

"I don't think she's coming, tiger."

The woman's deep, musical voice, thick with amusement, shimmied down Giddy's spine. She spoke with the cultured accent of a gentlewoman, but there was an edge to her voice that warned she might not be as accustomed to doing so as her words suggested.

He turned, offering her a glance. "Are you speaking to me?"

They were the only two people in the square. Even the carriages had ceased their trundling, shut up in the mews to wait out the worst of the heat. The air all but shimmered from the glaring sun. Even so, the woman wore no bonnet. Although her skin was hidden from the sun's harmful rays beneath the boughs of the tree, her suntanned complexion bespoke that she commonly neglected to cover herself. Her black hair escaped its pins to coil around her head, wisps teasing the column of her neck. Her dress, a dark ochre in color, scooped low across her breasts to display her curves. She wore no necklace or earrings to accentuate her beauty, but she needed none. She attended her embroidery with an easy self-confidence radiating from her. Her nose and cheekbones were a bit sharp for conventional beauty, but that small flaw paled in the face of her self-assurance.

More curious than her attire and bearing was the fact that he couldn't name her. Hadn't his mother and sister dragged him to enough soirees by now for him to have met every gentlewoman in London? It seemed not.

Making another careful stitch, the woman answered him. "I see no one else waiting for a ladylove around here, do you?" A smile curved her lips.

He scowled. "I assure you, I am not awaiting a lover."

"Of course you aren't." Her thick black eyelashes veiled her eyes as she returned her focus to the handkerchief. Her delicate fingers, bare of gloves and just as tanned as her face, moved deftly in her work. That same knowing smile curved her lips.

He turned to pace, but some undeniable urge in his chest bid him to turn back. "It's the middle of the day. What kind of man meets a lover in the middle of the blasted day?"

Her mouth curved up in a quick hitch before she contained her amusement. When she stopped sewing long enough to raise her gaze to his, finally, the color of her eyes startled the breath from him. They weren't dark, as he would have assumed from her complexion, but rather a curious mix of green or gray. He couldn't tell from this distance. A sudden, burning desire to cross the waist-high iron fence to the other side seized him. Forget his assignment and Mr. Albright—he wanted to know the exact color of her eyes without the interference of the oak's shadow.

It was madness, folly. He served the Crown. He was about to embark on an assignment that would steal him away from London for a long time. He couldn't afford the distraction of a beautiful woman, and yet... something about her made him want to throw caution to the wind.

He reminded himself that, given that she must be near to Morgan's age, she must be married.

Her eyes dancing, she teased, "Your lover evidently thinks ill of you for suggesting to meet at such a time. Else you feel more strongly for her perhaps than she does for you?"

Giddy fought a frown. "I am not meeting with a lover." What else could he say to such buffoonery? To anyone who knew him, it was a ludicrous accusation. He wasn't as free with his affection as his brother, Tristan, had been prior to his marriage.

She leaned forward. For a dizzying moment, his gaze dropped to her décolletage. He forced his focus higher. He was no lecherous rake, to offer disrespect to a woman, no matter how alluring.

Her gaze twinkled with amusement. The expression seemed to make the shadowed color come to life. He wished for less space between them.

"Why else would you have waited nigh on forty minutes, if not for a lover?"

He glanced at his pocket watch, noting that he'd been waiting forty-five minutes by this point. No wonder his feet ached. He must have paced the length of the square twenty times over.

"I'll have you know I'm meeting my brother." And another, more infuriating man. Come to think of it, where was Morgan? It wasn't like him to be tardy. "Not every engagement has to do with courtship."

"No?" She made a few more stitches in the handkerchief as she adjusted her position.

Gideon had never been curious as to the creations his mother or sister made—especially the latter, given her wild imagination—but the careful way the woman plied her needle made him wonder what warranted so much of her attention. Was he jealous of a handkerchief? That would be the day.

"Then why would you wait so long?"

He gritted his teeth. "Perhaps it is a very important meeting that cannot be postponed."

She paused just long enough to shoot him a triumphant glance. "Your lover doesn't seem to think so."

"The day I make this man my lover is the day that pigs fly," Giddy snapped.

The moment his sharp tone left his lips, he regretted it. He colored up, and looked away for a moment to compose himself. He turned back, intending to apologize, only to be met with the woman's wide grin. She hadn't taken offense in the least. Had she been baiting him?

Two could play at that game. "You've been sitting here for just as long. Has your lover cast you aside?"

Blast. His tone lilted, more questioning than cutting. As if he probed to discover whether or not she had a lover.

He most certainly did not do that. In fact, he didn't care. In a matter of days, maybe even hours, he would be off to his ancestral home, where he would be spending the duration of his autumn and perhaps even winter. He didn't expect a speedy resolution to the problem Strickland wanted him to deal with.

His mission. Yes, it was safer to think of work than the bewitching woman behind the gate. Her wide lips parted to answer him, but at that moment, a man's voice sliced through the air.

"Giddy!"

Morgan. *Lud, thank you.* His brother had arrived at last. Had he brought Mr. Albright with him?

When Giddy turned, unfortunately he found his brother to be alone. The duke, his greatcoat hanging open to display a tawny tailcoat and breeches, strode forward with purpose. "Please forgive my tardiness. I hope you've made yourself well acquainted in the meantime."

Gideon frowned as Morgan stepped within hearing distance without having to raise his voice. "What do you mean?"

Ignoring him, his brother stepped toward the gate. He held it open for the woman to step out. Since she was their only witness and they were about to discuss the private business of the Crown, Giddy stepped aside to allow her to leave. It was then that he noticed a curious spark of amusement in his brother's eye.

What in the world?

To his astonishment, instead of the woman leaving, Morgan stepped forward and gripped her hand firmly. "Miss Albright, thank you so much for coming. Again, please do forgive my tardiness. I had a situation arise that required my attention."

"Think nothing of it. I occupied myself admirably." She wore a teasing smile, her eyelashes veiling her eyes once more.

Gideon's gaze riveted to the woman. Standing, she wasn't so imposing, at least a foot if not a full eighteen inches shorter than his six-and-a-half foot tall frame. The height, and her nearness, gave him the perfect opportunity to peek at the line of her bodice again.

He might have if his ears hadn't been ringing. Miss Albright? Had there been some mistake? She must be his rival's sister or cousin. She couldn't be—

Morgan swept his hand toward Giddy, his lips twitching at the corners. "May I formally present my brother, the honorable Lord Gideon Graylocke? Giddy, this is Miss Felicia Albright, the woman you'll be working with for the duration of your assigned project."

It *was* her. The arrogant, infuriating, argumentative F. Albright was a woman. Not just any woman, but potentially the most alluring woman Giddy had ever had the displeasure of looking upon.

How could he be expected to produce his best work alongside...*her?*

Chapter Five

Oh, dear. Lord Graylocke looked like he might faint. Perhaps Felicia had teased him a bit too much before his brother's arrival. Or perhaps the constant pacing he'd been engaged in for the better part of an hour had induced a heat stroke. Either way, the milk-white complexion that overcame his cheeks was not a good sign. It soured the feeling of triumph at shocking him.

In her defense, she hadn't expected him to be so young. The Gideon Graylocke well-respected for his botanical essays had been publishing them for... years. He must have begun while still in university, because he didn't look older than twenty-two or twenty-three at her guess.

When Felicia had run away from home at seventeen, she had been educated enough to publish essays on her research, so it shouldn't surprise her to find another brilliant young mind. What troubled her wasn't so much his age, but her reaction to him.

While sitting on the bench in the shadow of the oak, her eye had been drawn to his lanky build. His shoulders filled out his blue coat to advantage. As he'd paced, his tailcoat had shifted to give her glimpses of his muscular rear, shown in almost scandalous detail in the tight buckskin breeches he wore. His long legs led to the sort of shapely calves men padded themselves to obtain. Felicia had no doubt that Lord Graylocke wasn't the sort to pad his physique. He had an air about him that was at once absent and shrewd, as though such commonplace matters as his appearance couldn't concern him when he had more meaningful things to think about. As she'd teased him about his fictitious lover, he'd seemed to become grounded more in the moment—and focused on her. His full attention had stolen her breath.

From afar, he looked handsome in a devil-may-care way. Close up, even more so. His black hair, in disarray from running his fingers through it, curled onto his forehead. His square jaw held the barest shadow of stubble. And his eyes... Felicia had never seen eyes that shade of green before. It was as though the lush jungle foliage he studied so much was reflected in his gaze—and his eyes far outshone mere plants. But there was also a softness to his cheeks and mouth that bespoke of youth.

Felicia was nearly thirty and he was… young. Too young for her to be thinking of him in an attractive light. *He is a stubborn, arrogant scientist.* Better she focus on his undesirable qualities, the very qualities that had resulted in their bitter row by letter through the *Royal Botanical Gazette*. His appearance had nothing to do with the fact that he was unwilling to see reason. In fact, if she was to work with him, it was better he was off-balance.

She turned to the Duke of Tenwick. "You mentioned we would be working at your ancestral estate, Your Grace?"

"Indeed." Like when she'd met with him earlier in the day, he kept a neat appearance and didn't appear to be flustered. Neither did he treat her as most men of his station would treat a woman, even one whose services they wanted to engage. He spoke to her, not over her, and he didn't glance toward his brother even once. "But please, I insist you call me Morgan."

Pigs might fly before she addressed a duke with such familiarity, but she nodded and smiled to make him think that she would comply with his edict.

"If I'm to leave London, I'll need to make preparations. I won't be able to depart before Friday morning." After all, her wagon traveled slower than a carriage so she would need to send it on ahead, along with Chubs and Rudolph. Today, if at all possible. She had some contacts at a boarding house near the outskirts of London where she sometimes wintered. With luck, one of the landlady's sons would be willing to drive her wagon out to the Tenwick estate, for a price.

Morgan sighed. He fingered the white streak in his hair. "If Friday is as soon as you can be persuaded to leave, then Friday it will be."

"I cannot possibly leave sooner," she repeated. Something in his drawn expression made her add, "Is the situation so dire? Even once we reach your estate, I doubt we'll be able to magic the serum out of thin air. It will take time."

Next to her, Lord Graylocke snorted. The sound and the shift of his position drew her attention to him once more. She darted a glance toward him, but couldn't peek higher than his shoulder without him noticing the cant of her head. She endeavored to ignore him. After all, she knew exactly what he thought of her research. That he'd agreed to work with her was a cruel twist of fate.

Tenwick didn't twitch at his brother's outburst. Instead, the duke captured her gaze and held it. His gray eyes seemed to slice through her. "It is dire. This matter requires your undivided attention."

Felicia drew herself up, even though doing so didn't even bring her to the lofty height of Lord Graylocke's shoulder. "You will have it. I've devised a list of materials I'll need." She drew the neatly folded list out of her reticule. She'd had years to dream of the rare and expensive ingredients she might need to concoct her serum. Now that the day had finally come, her hand trembled as she handed the list over.

The duke, to his credit, pretended not to notice. "You shall have them."

Sandwiched between the two men, each over six feet tall though Lord Graylocke topped his brother by at least a hand, Felicia felt small and vulnerable. She shifted position, surreptitiously tugging at the line of her bodice to better reveal her cleavage. When men lusted after her form, she knew she had power over them.

Unfortunately, her charms seemed to have no effect on the duke whatsoever. She didn't dare glance toward his brother, the ornery man she would be working with for the foreseeable future.

"If at all possible, I'd like for the materials to be delivered to your estate before our arrival.

I've also included the fee for my services on that list."

Tenwick's mouth twitched. He raised one haughty eyebrow. "I assured you that you would be paid."

"So you did, but you neglected to discuss the particulars." She nodded to the list he now held in his hand. "I trust that you'll find my fee satisfactory, given that I am perhaps the only person who is able to perform the task you need." She craned her neck back, meeting the duke's gaze unflinchingly.

With an agonizingly slow movement, he unfolded the sheet of paper to peek at the figure she'd written within. His expression didn't alter. He folded it again. "Your price is satisfactory. You'll be put up in my estate for the duration of your assignment and paid upon its completion."

In other words, if she didn't present the serum the government craved so badly, she wouldn't be paid. A smart move, to ensure she didn't abscond with her payment and leave him dry. She'd expected him to haggle her down to a lower fee. Should she have asked for more money? With a slightly more exorbitant sum, she would have been able to purchase a cozy cottage to winter in.

She lifted her chin. Her neck was starting to ache from having to look up at him. All three of them stood closer than they might normally, so their voices didn't carry. "What of my dog and mule? Will they be included in my accommodations?"

"Certainly."

This was sounding better and better. It might take all winter before she struck upon the right concentration and ratio of ingredients for the serum. For once, she wouldn't have to worry about food or shelter or the well-being of her pets. The only downside was the man she would be forced to work with. That, she could overlook. Given the fact that he had yet to contribute to the conversation, she must have given him quite the shock upon revealing her identity. So long as she kept him in that state for the duration of their association, he would be easily molded to her desires.

Felicia banished the image of running her hands along him as if he was a piece of unworked clay. She kept her eyes firmly on his brother—who, although handsome, she didn't have the same reaction to. Perhaps because she'd already met his wife.

Was Lord Graylocke married? He was young... but then, at his age, Felicia would have been married for five years or more had she not taken her future in her own hands.

She thrust a hand out to the duke. "It sounds as though we have an arrangement, sir."

He gripped her firmly, not treating her like a wilting flower. "Good. As you have no prior connection to our organization, you will be under Giddy's command for the duration. I trust you can handle that?"

Was he baiting her? She drew herself up, sparing only a glance for the impossibly tall man at her side. Even that short glimpse sent her off-kilter. He'd regained his composure. In fact, he looked smug at the concept of being in charge of her.

Typical hot-blooded man.

She turned back to his brother and said, "I'm quite able to handle it, thank you."

That was all the duke was waiting to hear. The moment the words left her lips, he nodded to them and took his leave. "I'm afraid I can't linger. I need to follow up on the situation I had earlier. I'll leave you two to get to know each other better."

Felicia gritted her teeth. *I think I know him well enough.* A stubborn, arrogant lord too consumed with his own brilliance to consider the valid opinions of others—even when he thought his correspondent to be male. For all that he had fought her constructive criticism with such vehemence as to make it public, and therefore a matter of honor that she make her case, she couldn't deny that he was brilliant. When Tenwick offered her the best botanist to work with, he wasn't saying as much solely because Lord Graylocke was his brother.

Left alone with him, Felicia had no choice but to turn. From the steely look in his green eyes, he was far from happy at his new assignment, even if he might enjoy acting as her superior. She shifted her weight onto one foot, thrusting out one hip. The new position drew her dress tight over her breasts, waist, and hips. Triumph surged through her as his gaze dipped along her torso. He wasn't as immune to her as his brother was.

Good. That would make her association with him easier.

She held out her hand. "I trust we'll be able to set aside our differences for the duration of our assignment."

He raised an eyebrow even as he slid his palm into hers. Like her, he wore no gloves. His palm was warm and rough with callouses from gripping his tools. She retrieved her hand the moment he finished squeezing it.

"By our differences, would you be referring to the time you called me a stubborn baboon?"

She smiled. "No, that I stand by. I was referring to when you called my research on the truth serum to be foolhardy and...how did you put it, 'the obsession of a crackpot?'"

He grimaced. "I suppose we'll find out soon enough which of us is right. Where are you residing? I'll send a carriage for you promptly at eight of the morning on Friday."

Leaning forward, she brushed his sleeve with her hand. The hitch of his breath as he admired the line of her dress was reward in itself. "Actually," she said, lowering her voice to a purr. "I'll come to you. Meet me in front of your townhouse instead."

Without waiting for an answer, she lightly ran her fingers down his arm as she retreated. When she turned, she exaggerated the sway of her hips. She didn't need to turn around to know that he watched her. She felt his hot stare on her arse.

Yes, he should be easy enough to handle, stubborn scientist or not.

Chapter Six

On Friday morning, the sun beamed down behind a thin veil of clouds. Despite the brightness of the day, the sun did little as of yet to dispel the night chill from the air. Felicia's breath fogged in front of her face as she navigated the back gardens behind the row of townhouses. Her high-heeled ankle boots crunched on the frosted grass underfoot.

Every house in this line looked almost identical. The tall, narrow stone façade and slate roof loomed over groomed lawns, neat gardens in back housing decorative shrubs rather than vegetables or herbs, and trim fences in between. The latches on the side gates were simple enough to lift even when secured, if like Felicia you knew the trick. Dressed in a tawny brown travel dress that bared her ankles, she crossed the yards as close to the cold stone walls as possible, to avoid being seen by the servants. She counted down the row until she reached the townhouse in question that she searched for, the Graylocke residence.

The garden in this house was trim and neat, but no better tended than the others down the line, the plants wilted and shriveled. For a moment, Felicia wondered if she had the wrong house. Was a botanist in residence here?

She slipped along the narrow strip of lawn between the house and the fence separating it from the packed dirt alley between each of the homes on this street. Sticking to the shadow of the high wall, she approached the front, where a glimpse of the cobblestone street showed a waiting foursome of horses hitched to a closed carriage. At the corner was a large bush, mostly devoid of leaves though the thick tangle of thorny branches provided some cover for the young woman waiting there. Apparently, Felicia wasn't the only person who had thought to sneak up from the back of the house in order to observe Lord Graylocke.

The woman crouched, so it was difficult to tell whether she would be taller than Felicia or not if standing. Her hair was as ebony as the Graylocke brothers. It trailed down the back of her lavender dress in a single loose braid. She canted her head, trying to peek around the corner and onto the front street.

Biting back a smile, Felicia crouched as she crept closer to join the young woman. "What's happening?" she asked, her voice a whisper.

The young woman jumped. She clasped her gloved hand over her mouth, stifling an outcry as she twisted to look at Felicia. Now that she had announced her presence, Felicia thought that she would have to explain her presence in the house. To her surprise, the young woman didn't seem to care.

That, or she dismissed Felicia's plain attire as belonging to that of a servant. If the fine quality of her dress and the embroidery along its bodice, sleeves, and hem wasn't enough to announce her class, her features would have done so. Her eyes were a dark, velvety brown, but she strongly resembled her brothers. The set of her mouth and the shape of her chin was a touch more delicate and feminine than their rough, masculine features, but the family resemblance was clear.

Felicia settled herself onto the cold, half-frozen ground behind the bush, stealing a good vantage of the man pacing in front of it. Was he constantly in motion, or was it only the thought of meeting with her that made him nervous? He wore buckskins again today, though he paired it with an emerald jacket this time. His hair, for the moment, was tidy. Felicia didn't expect that to last for long, especially if she didn't reveal herself in the coming minutes as having arrived. Lord Graylocke, it seemed, was unfashionably prompt.

Then again, so was Felicia. Clients were far less likely to buy if she made them wait.

Craning her neck as she examined the road, Miss Graylocke—seventeen or eighteen at Felicia's guess—answered without sparing another glance at her new companion in the bushes. "My brother is meeting a woman. He's to bring her to our country estate."

Felicia laid a hand across her chest, feigning shock. "How scandalous!" Laughter bubbled in her throat, but she tamped it down.

The young woman sighed. With a speaking glance and a roll of the eyes, she said, "I wish. No, he claims she will be there for business, only. He's a botanist, you see."

Like many women her age, she seemed to be consumed with the thought of romance. Perhaps not for herself—Felicia had yet to make that determination—but certainly toward others, if her curiosity over her brother's meeting was any indication. The curiosity seemed good-natured, so Felicia decided to play along.

"If she is visiting for the purpose of business alone, then why are you spying?"

With a speaking look that Felicia was hard put not to giggle at, the young woman said, "Simply because he claims it is business does not mean there isn't something more. I want to see if there is more than friendship between them."

There was certainly something between Felicia and Lord Graylocke, but it wasn't friendship.

Cocking her chin, Miss Graylocke added, "Two of my brothers have recently married. I helped to pair them both. I know the signs."

Mirth warmed Felicia's chest as she confessed, "I can help with that." She tucked her fingers into her reticule and withdrew a small crystal vial of perfume. It was the most concentrated version, that she had hoped to persuade the duke to purchase, since his wife seemed so adamant over the idea. However, torturing Lord Graylocke—that seemed like an infinitely better use. Felicia pressed the vial into his sister's hand.

"What's this?"

"It's a cologne for men. I bought it at market, and was told by the seller that it's guaranteed to make someone fall in love with the man who wears it." She fought not to laugh as Miss Graylocke examined the amber liquid with interest. "If you sprinkle him with it, maybe this business partner he's come to meet will fall in love with him."

She won't. Felicia kept that thought to herself. She tried not to smile too wide and give the joke away.

The young woman's eyes brightened. "Oh! What a delightful idea." Curling her fingers around the vial, she clutched it to her chest and stood.

Felicia eased back to make room as Miss Graylocke sidled around the bush, arrowing for her brother. Lord Graylocke had his back to them at the moment, his jacket stretched tight across his shoulders as he paced toward the far corner of the townhouse. The horses stamped, picking up on his agitation and his sister's exuberance. The driver hopped down from his perch to settle the steeds.

"Giddy!"

Lord Graylocke turned at his sister's call. Trepidation crossed his face as he noticed her sprinting toward him, the hem of her dress draped over one arm. Her back was to Felicia, so she couldn't tell whether or not the vial of perfume would be visible to him. Would his sister give it to him and cajole him into wearing it?

No. Instead, she pretended to trip. As she fell against Lord Graylocke's chest, he caught her by the upper arms. "What the devil, Lucy!"

Felicia bit her tongue hard to keep silent. Lord Graylocke recoiled from his sister, backing away to show a dark splotch dripping over his beige waistcoat. Felicia wrapped her arms around herself, shaking with contained laughter. Her ribs ached. Even the pain didn't help to mitigate her amusement. His sister hadn't sprinkled the perfume on him—she'd upended the entire vial!

Even from feet away, Felicia smelled the musk. It wasn't the most pleasant of smells in such a concentrated dose, hence why she advised her customers that a little went a long way. Even with such a deep, earthy stench, the perfume performed its trick.

Three young debutantes newly out of the school room, at Felicia's guess, strolled along the street. The moment they reached the rear wheel of the carriage, a second after Lucy had poured the perfume onto her brother's chest, the young girls caught wind of the scent. They surrounded him, three girls his sister's age or younger, each dabbing vigorously at his person with their handkerchiefs while he tried adamantly to extract himself. He was so tall that his harried expression was unobscured even by the girls' bonnets.

Felicia lost the battle to keep quiet. She roared with laughter, leaning against the corner of the manor behind the bush.

The sound drew Lord Graylocke's attention to her. His expression darkened. "Miss Albright! What the devil did you direct her to spill on me?"

Felicia fought for breath. The rough stone snagged against her spencer as she slumped against the wall.

Miss Graylocke drew herself up, indignant. "What language, Giddy. There are ladies present!"

Indeed. And those ladies continued to attempt to clean him, gaggling all the while with demure tones that didn't carry. They didn't seem to notice or care for his disinterest. He snagged one woman's hand as she strayed too low for his comfort. My, she was a brazen one. Felicia liked her best. Not that she could tell the three apart, in equally pale, modest dresses and with bonnets covering their hair.

She wiped the moisture from her eyes. Her torso and cheeks ached from laughing. Even once she shut her eyes, she couldn't banish the image of Lord Graylocke's flustered expression. His voice tight, he apologized to the ladies and retreated inside with big, clomping steps.

A moment later, a shadow fell over her. She opened her eyes to Miss Graylocke's amused expression. "His business partner will fall in love with him, will she?"

Felicia smirked as she accepted the young woman's hand to rise. "Well, that was a bit of a stretch from the start. I'm afraid we don't much get along. But he has experience that I need and I have experience that he needs."

"What are you working on? He wouldn't say."

Standing, Felicia noticed that Miss Graylocke was a couple inches taller than her. The entire family were giants, it seemed. She offered the young lady a bland smile. "It has to do with a plant I've gotten in from South America. You likely wouldn't be interested, Miss Graylocke."

The young woman pursed her lips as she considered the statement, but she must have ruled in favor of agreement because all she said was, "Please, call me Lucy."

Felicia couldn't possibly address a duke with familiarity, but his sister was much more disarming. Not to mention over a decade younger. "Thank you. Then you must call me Felicia."

With a charming smile, Lucy linked arms with her and drew her toward the house. The debutantes lingered a bit as they strolled on their way, as if hoping Lord Graylocke would make an appearance again. Felicia battled another tide of laughter as Lucy craned her neck, staring after the trio.

"What was in that vial?"

Felicia laughed. "I didn't lie to you. It was a cologne for men."

"Designed to attract a woman to fall in love with him." Dubiousness entered Lucy's voice. Her delicately arched brows were pulled close over her eyes.

As they reached the steps, the younger woman released Felicia to allow her to mount them first. The Tenwick butler opened the door, stoically paying them no mind. Felicia suspected that he attended far more closely than he seemed to.

Lowering her voice, she admitted, "In a way. If you'll forgive the crass admission, it invites lust more than love. It has to do with a woman's chemical reaction to the smell. Though I asked you to put only a little. In high doses, the smell..."

Lucy wrinkled her nose. "Indeed. Does that actually work?"

Pausing on the top step, Felicia turned back to send the young woman an arch look. "Do young debutantes usually fall over themselves to touch your brother?"

"Maybe Tristan or Anthony," Lucy said with a laugh.

They entered the house, only for a screeching voice to announce, "Shut your gob, Lucy!"

With a sullen look, the young woman waved her hand toward a second, older woman and the blazing blue parrot perched on her arm. "*This* is why Giddy has no debutantes fighting over him."

Because of his bird or because of the stately woman serving as a perch? The outdoor sunlight cut off as the butler shut the door, leaving Felicia blinking rapidly to help her eyes adjust to the dimmer interior. Once she did, she noticed the resemblance between the two women immediately. Lady Graylocke had chestnut hair, instead of the ebony locks all her children seemed to share. Her eyes seemed a darker gray than her oldest son's, but similar in shape. With her delicate features, she looked to be an older version of her daughter. If she had been older than Lucy upon giving birth to her oldest son,

Felicia would eat her fist. The serene woman didn't appear more than fifteen or sixteen years older than Felicia, though perhaps she had aged well.

Confirming Felicia's suspicions, Lucy said, "This is my mother, Evelyn Graylocke."

Felicia curtsied. "Felicia Albright, my lady. It is a pleasure to meet you."

The woman waved her hand. "None of that formality, dear. I understand we're to live with each other for quite some time?" Her voice lilted, raising her calm statement into a question.

"Indeed, madam. I will be at the whim of your hospitality until your son and I complete our project." Inwardly, she added, *I hope it will take all winter.*

The bird on the dowager's arm turned its head sideways to inspect Felicia. Yellow markings around the large parrot's eye and black beak made it appear as if grinning. It squawked, bobbing its head up and down as it shifted position on the dowager's sleeve.

"That's Antonia," Lucy introduced.

The parrot half-opened her wings and pronounced, "Giddy!"

"She's giddy to meet you," Lucy informed, straight-faced.

Felicia gave the bird a flamboyant curtsey, the kind she sometimes used to attract customers. "The pleasure is all mine, Antonia."

"Giddy, giddy, giddy!"

Lucy added, "I named her after my brother, Anthony because he's so rarely at home."

"Oh?" Felicia offered a polite smile. "And why is that?"

It was the wrong thing to say. The dowager's polite expression turned hard and closed. Her lips thinned as she pressed them together.

Even Lucy's exuberance dulled as she explained, "He's a captain in the Royal Navy."

And thereby in the center of the war with France. Oh, dear. What could Felicia say to that? "He sounds very accomplished."

"All my children suffer from that particular affliction," Evelyn said, her voice tight.

Lucy laughed, though it sounded a bit strained. "Even Tristan?"

"Especially Tristan," her mother said. She stroked the bird's feathers, calming it and keeping it quiet for the moment. "He's been competing with Morgan from the moment he could walk."

Shaking her head with a fond smile, Lucy said, "I'm sure you're exaggerating, Mother."

"I am not. You weren't there. You don't know the trouble I had with those boys. All four of them."

"Even Lord Graylocke?" The man she'd been shown thus far had been studious and quiet, save for when she or his sister riled him.

Evelyn frowned. "To which Lord Graylocke are you referring? They all have titles, at least honorary ones."

Pinpricks of heat enflamed Felicia's cheeks. Did she have to refer to the ornery scientist so familiarly? She schooled her expression to one of mild disinterest that the *beau monde* seemed so fond to wear. "Lord Gideon."

The dowager's face blossomed into a broad smile. "He caused me the biggest fright. Every time I turned around, he had disappeared, off to explore or examine some plant or insect located on treacherous terrain. The quiet ones are always the worst. But please, if you stand on formality it will make the air at Tenwick Abbey dreadfully stiff. Call him Gideon or Giddy like we do."

She couldn't possibly. She smiled weakly. "Shouldn't that be something Lord Gideon invites me to use?"

"Nonsense. I'm his mother. If I say you can call him familiarly, then you must."

She said it in such a glib, matter-of-fact tone that Felicia almost believed her. Never mind that she was the daughter of an untitled gentleman—a fact that the dowager didn't even know. For all she knew, Felicia might have been raised by the circus folk she still called family. For all her absence from polite society these past thirteen years, she still retained the ability to speak with the refined accent of a peer. It no longer came as second nature to her, so she had to concentrate, but she had been from the moment she first engaged with Lucy. But sounding like an equal and treating a duke's family as equals were two very different things.

What sort of family was this, not to stand on the same ceremony every other haughty peer did?

Antonia saved Felicia the need to argue the point of familiarity with Lord Gideon when the bird squawked and shouted, "Giddy!" The screech punctured the air, making Felicia and the other two women wince.

Apparently, it could be heard above stairs, for the sound of loud footsteps on the staircase was accompanied by Lord Gideon's cry of, "I'm coming! No need to shout."

The person who first appeared at the top of the steps was not Lord Gideon, but a beautiful blond woman about Lucy's age. Her hair was dressed in ringlets, her cheeks as rosy as her dress. She wore a bleary, irritated expression.

As she reached the bottom of the steps, Lord Gideon directly behind her, she paused to yawn and mumble, "I don't see why we have to leave so blasted early in the morning. Don't you ever rise at a reasonable hour?"

The tall man behind her slipped around her form without comment, straightening his cravat. His hair was now in disarray from the task of changing. He wore a maroon coat matched with a dove-gray waistcoat. Both fit him to advantage, but Felicia couldn't help but feel disappointed over the fact that she wouldn't know whether or not the green coat emphasized his eyes.

Felicia lurched as Lucy linked arms with her and hauled her forward. "Charlie, this is Felicia Albright. Felicia, this is Charlotte Vale—or Charlie, to us. Isn't it wonderful, Charlie? Felicia will be staying with us for the foreseeable future."

Lucy snuck a smug glance toward her brother, who pulled at his cravat, knocking it askew. He didn't deign to contribute to the conversation. Instead he said, "I think we've been delayed long enough. Ladies, if you'll allow me to escort you to the carriage?"

Felicia was relieved to finally be underway. Although she was accustomed to drawing attention to herself, in this instance, she wouldn't mind a moment or two of respite. Even if she had to spend that time in Lord Gideon's company.

Chapter Seven

"I can't believe you don't have any luggage!"

Giddy gritted his teeth. If he hadn't heard the same exclamation fifteen or sixteen times since they'd all bundled into the closed carriage, he might not have been quite so annoyed at the proclamation.

The woman to his right, on the other hand, seemed perfectly in control of her emotions. If she resented the comment, she didn't show it. Her smile lit the interior of the carriage as she answered, yet again, "I have luggage, but I sent it on to the abbey."

"But we'll be stopping for the night," Lucy protested yet again. "You won't have a stitch to wear tomorrow!"

Giddy turned his gaze swiftly toward the tiny open window opposite the door. If he peered at Miss Albright, he might imagine her without a stitch on. He was acutely aware of her presence next to him as it was.

Confound it! Why did F. Albright have to be a woman? His manly instincts warred with his mind as his subconscious churned, trying to decide what to make of her. It didn't help that her moods were as changeable as the wind. She could be demure and polite one moment, and in an instant change to teasing and a bit lewd, considering the company. Unfortunately, just as he'd feared, his mother and sister had taken a shine to her. Charlie was curled in the corner of the carriage, asleep, and so hadn't had time to pass judgment.

Miss Albright leaned forward, that teasing side of her emerging once more. She'd unbuttoned her spencer, displaying the ample cleavage beneath. Seated so close to her, he couldn't avoid catching a glimpse or two of her charms.

With a teasing mien, she said, "Never you worry, Lucy. I promise not to come to the carriage wearing not a stitch."

Lud! Even staring at the passing terrain wasn't enough to banish that image.

The frustrating woman added, "What I'm wearing now will work quite nicely."

It would work nicely on the floor of his bedroom. Giddy gritted his teeth. He silently listed all of F. Albright's infuriating qualities alphabetically. It helped only moderately. After all, the woman was currently seated beside him. Whenever the carriage jolted along the road, her thigh pressed against his, a fleeting touch. When she batted a strand of hair over her shoulder, it brushed his sleeve. And she smelled…

Well, actually, he couldn't smell her at all. Even after changing clothes, the musk of that vial still clung to him. The noxious stench was the only thing keeping his attraction to her in check. Every time he inhaled, he was reminded of her machinations with Lucy. What *had* she poured onto him? Thus far, it hadn't had any adverse effects, but it was deuced irritating.

She toyed with a strand of her hair. Slowly, she trailed her fingers along its length, tracing the column of her neck at the same time. Did she realize she was doing it? Most likely it was yet another gesture meant to addle his brain. If not for the musk cloying to his person, it might have worked.

Perhaps he ought to bathe in the stench, just to ensure his thoughts of her remained hardened. In his defense, he hadn't expected F. Albright to be a woman, let alone a beautiful one.

A beautiful woman with a brilliant mind and an annoying personality.

Jolting him from his thoughts, Lucy said, "What will you wear to bed? Giddy, you must give her one of your nightshirts."

He was a foot and a half taller than Miss Albright. She would swim in any article of clothing he lent her. Not to mention, he didn't wear a nightshirt, so he had none to give.

He was loathe to admit that aloud, however. He didn't want Lucy to get even more alarming ideas. Instead, he arched an eyebrow and said, "If you're so adamant on her having one, why don't you offer one of your nightgowns?"

"I don't think she'd fit..."

Gideon frowned at his sister. Lucy was taller than Miss Albright and undoubtedly weighed more. Their figures were different, but Lucy's clothing would undoubtedly fit her better than anything Giddy offered. Not that he intended to offer anything at all.

"I am perfectly happy to sleep in my shift."

"It takes two days to reach Tenwick Abbey. We'll be sleeping overnight in an inn."

He had already mentioned this fact to Miss Albright, as had Lucy. Did she think repetition would change the irascible, obstinate Miss Albright's mind? The sky would rain shillings first.

Miss Albright hid any irritation with a demure expression and a calm statement. "I don't see how that signifies."

"It *signifies* because if you wear the same clothes and shift for two days, you'll smell."

Mother gasped. "Lucy! Don't be rude."

Antonia, perched on Mother's wrist, helpfully added, "Shut your gob, Lucy."

Ignoring the bird, his sister wrinkled her nose. "It's true. We'll be stuck in a coach with her."

"You're stuck in a coach with Lord Gideon and he smells," Miss Albright countered with a sweet smile. She glanced at him from the corner of her eye, the motion all but veiled by her thick eyelashes.

Giddy rolled his eyes and pretended to look out the window. "Don't think I've forgiven you for that, Miss Albright."

"Stop that, both of you," Mother said, drawing herself up. Unlike Gideon, who had to hunch in the carriage to avoid banging his head on every jolt, his mother still didn't near the solid roof. She offered her finger to Antonia, who traced the shape of her glove by taking the digit gently between her beak.

At the reprimand, Giddy felt heat climb up his neck. His ears burned. Would she make him apologize to Miss Albright? She was the one who had instructed Lucy to spill the chemical on him.

Instead of demanding an apology, Mother primly said, "I will not hear of this formality. You and Felicia will be under the same roof for weeks—"

Don't remind me.

"—I won't have you poisoning the air at home. Lud, you'd think we were at one of the *ton*'s stuffy balls..."

That was what had her so riled? "You want me to refer to her by her Christian name?"

Felicia didn't say a thing, but the purse of her lips was agreement enough for him. They couldn't possibly hope to conduct themselves in a professional manner if they were referring to each other as intimately as family. Just the thought of speaking her name aloud made him suppress a shiver. "Felicia" was a name to be whispered in bed, not snapped in anger or frustration over her comportment and antics.

Mother, unfortunately, had a different idea. She raised her eyebrows, looking even more imperious than Morgan did. More ducal, even, than Father had when he'd been alive. Giddy had only been fourteen when Father had died, but in that short time, he'd learned to cherish his father's praise over his superior schoolwork... and avoid his wrath. Mother had a quieter anger that had always made him shake like a leaf in the wind.

In a steely voice that belied her serene mien, she said, "I won't hear of anything else from the both of you."

Gideon exchanged a glance with the woman next to him. He offered her a weak smile. They could resume referring to each other properly once out of earshot. Most of their time together would be spent in the orangery, in any case.

Finished with her exploration of Mother's finger, Antonia lifted her head and pronounced, "Get off your rump, Lucy!"

As Giddy roared with laughter, his sister drew herself up.

"When on earth did she learn that?"

He laughed so hard, he couldn't breathe. The first time for Antonia to repeat that particular phrase couldn't have come at a more opportune time—it took the focus away from Giddy and Felicia.

Glaring daggers, Lucy groaned. "Giddy!" She kicked him in the shin. "This is your fault."

He wiped the moisture from his eyes and shifted to alleviate the sting in his leg. Turning to address Felicia, he said, "You should try to teach the bird a phrase or two while you stay with us. It's great fun."

Her eyes twinkled, but her voice was demure when she said, "I couldn't possibly settle on what phrase to teach her."

"Shorter is better," he advised.

Directly across from him, Charlie stirred, rubbing her eyes. "What's all the ruckus about? Are we stopping for lunch?"

"Not yet," Mother informed with a fond smile. She leaned forward to peer around her daughter, seated in the middle.

Lucy lamented, "Giddy taught Antonia another dreadful thing to say!"

The blonde pouted. "Why does Antonia recall all of his phrases but none of mine?"

He raised one eyebrow. "Perhaps because Antonia doesn't much care to ask Freddie to make her an aunt. I suggest you direct your inquiries to Tristan instead."

At Felicia's questioning look, he explained, "Tristan was married this spring to Charlie's sister, Frederica."

"I see."

Lucy crossed her arms, sullen. "You're turning my own pet against me."

The parrot had a keen interest in the conversation, for she shifted her position to groom one of her claws. In between nibbles, she offered, "Giddy smells like pickles."

The women rocked the carriage with their laughter. Gideon rolled his eyes. Although he didn't smell his best at the moment, it certainly wasn't reminiscent of pickles. "She obviously learned that from Phil's parrot." His words were overpowered by the raucous laughter. Mother's arm trembled from the force of her mirth. The movement offset the bird, who flapped her three-foot-wide wings for balance. Suddenly, the space in the coach was made much smaller.

"Here." Lucy, in the middle, accepted her pet once more and held her in a more open space until the parrot ceased panicking. As the laughter died down, his sister whispered, "I like you again. Say more things like that."

He stifled the urge to kick *her* in the shin.

Charlie, now awake, opened the reticule on her wrist and spilled the contents onto her lap. They consisted of a swathe of material, embroidery thread in various colors, and a needle. She selected the green thread and swiftly threaded the needle before holding the material taught between her index, middle finger, and thumb in lieu of an embroidery hoop.

"That's a fabulous idea," Felicia said. She unearthed the handkerchief she'd been embroidering when he'd met her, along with a length of blue thread.

Charlie smiled, trying to peer around the parrot. "You embroider?"

"From time to time," Felicia answered, her voice light.

He hadn't gotten a glimpse of the project when they'd first met. When he peeked over her shoulder to view the work in progress, he frowned. Along the edges of the handkerchief, Felicia worked on embroidering thin waves. The bulk of the handkerchief was complete, along with a yellow spiny creature along the bottom edge.

"Is that a sea serpent?"

A smile played along the edges of her mouth before she banished it. "It is," she said, her voice serene and devoid of any trace of mirth.

"It is…" Bizarre. Unique. Baffling. Quite like her, in fact. "… neatly done."

Mother leaned forward. "May I see, dear?"

Felicia handed over the handkerchief without complaint. Upon viewing the piece, Mother nodded. She stretched across Lucy to show it to the two women seated next to her. They all seemed duly impressed, no one bothered by the unorthodox subject matter.

"Very nice stitchery," Mother pronounced as she handed it back. "What a shame you aren't married yet. Men appreciate a woman with nimble fingers.”

Blast, why was she looking at him when she said that? Giddy couldn't care one way or another about a woman's nimble fingers. Unless she meant... No, his mother could *not* be implying that he might appreciate Felicia's talents in the marriage bed.

He turned his head to peer out the small window. Unfortunately, the rolling green landscape, dotted with trees, looked much the same as it had an hour ago. “How long until we reach the inn for luncheon?”

“Not far now, I imagine,” Mother answered. “Perhaps an hour or two longer.”

Antonia squawked and pronounced herself giddy for pickles.

Felicia shifted her position, her body brushing against his and igniting an unwelcome burn. From the sidelong look she gave him, he wasn't the only one affected by their nearness.

He suffered knowing looks from Mother and Lucy.

The inn was not close enough.

***

That blasted, bloody, bewitching perfume! In the closed carriage, squashed next to Lord Gideon, Felicia couldn't escape it. The musky scent might be overwhelming, but the effects were no less potent for the dousing. Every time he adjusted his long legs or stretched his neck and shoulders, her attention arrowed to him once more. The heat of his body seeped through her clothes until it seemed to warm her, too. More than warm her, it made her burn. Goose bumps coalesced over her skin at inopportune times. If it wasn't for the long sleeves of her spencer, she would have been helpless to conceal her reaction to him.

Not to him—her reaction to the perfume. There was no fighting it with logic. The ingredients were designed to burrow under her skin and elicit a chemical response in her body. If she'd ever doubted her own work, she did no longer. Had she been alone with him...

Perhaps it was best that she not contemplate that eventuality. With the less-than-subtle comments from his sister and mother, they would be only too happy to arrange such a thing. Although Felicia had initially been shocked and pleased at their disregard for what others of the *ton* would consider propriety, at the moment, she could do with a bit more stiffness. At least that way, she wouldn't suspect that they might encourage things that had best be left for the marriage bed—his, not hers.

Felicia was no prude. She was no virgin, either. When she'd walked away from her life as a gentleman's daughter, she'd realized that she could leave the constraints of society in the past as well. So long as she chose bed partners of a like mind and was careful not to become enceinte, she took her pleasure where she found it.

Albeit, in recent months, that was nowhere. Her last lover had gotten too serious, wanting to marry her when Felicia desired nothing of the sort. She was an independent woman, a scientist unfettered by the constraints placed upon her gender, and she intended to stay that way. Even if that meant giving up the yearning she had for children and a family, it was worthwhile in the end. That yearning was entirely biological, anyway.

Just like her attraction to the young, handsome Lord Gideon. If she could resist her body's urge to create a child, she could damn well resist the urge to create that child with him.

Once the perfume washed off his person, she would be able to think more clearly. And then she would remember what a stubborn man he was. It was a difficult thing to recall when he barely spoke a word throughout the carriage ride, except to return the quips shot to him by his sister.

The carriage jolted, throwing her against Gideon as the horses veered off the road. Her left side was pressed against him, her body quivering from the intimate contact. The moment she regained her balance, she shoved as far away from him as possible.

The abrupt movement roused Antonia, who exclaimed, "Let's go for a walk!"

Lucy groaned, rolling her neck as the carriage slowed and stopped. "That isn't a terrible idea. I feel as though I've been shut away in here for centuries."

Although she'd taken turns with her mother in carrying the overlarge bird, her arms must be in agony from serving as Antonia's perch. The blanket covering the women's legs had seen better days, now littered with the parrot's droppings. At the very least, the blanket had saved their skirts.

The dowager disembarked from the carriage first, accepting the driver's hand as he assisted her down the steps. Light from a lantern glowed golden, beckoning beyond the blazing red light of the sunset. After handing Antonia out the door to her mother, Lucy staggered out of the carriage. Charlie, bright-eyed now that it was no longer morning, followed after her, leaving Felicia and Gideon alone.

When Felicia slid along the seat to the door, Gideon transferred his weight to the opposite bench. The thick, earthy scent of perfume cloying to him lightened somewhat with the distance. The carriage would have to be aired out, if Felicia hoped for the smallest pinprick of sanity tomorrow. Gideon thrust his leg out, barring her path to the door.

"Allow me," he said, his words clipped. "I'll help you out."

"The other ladies managed perfectly well on their own. I think I'll be able to do so as well."

When she tried to shove him out of the way, he stood—as much as the carriage would allow. A man of Gideon's pronounced height had to bend nearly double. The position looked uncomfortable, and brought him entirely too close for her peace of mind. She eased back as irritation crossed his face.

"Forgive me for treating you like a lady."

Although the light was dim and he blocked out most of it, Felicia leaned forward, bracing her elbows against her knees. Her spencer gaped open to show her cleavage. The irritation melted off his face as his gaze dipped downward. Gideon, for all his quick mind, was just as fallible as any other man to the display of skin.

She tucked away a smile. "I don't look like a lady to you?"

Her voice was huskier than she intended, but she told herself that was all the better to tease him. A man like Gideon was evidently not accustomed to being teased, for color infused his cheeks and he averted his gaze.

"A gentlewoman, then," he said, his voice clipped.

Apparently, he'd forgotten all about disembarking from the carriage, because he remained rooted in place, blocking the exit. Getting to her feet, Felicia brushed against him as she squeezed past. She meant for the contact to torture him, but it had the same effect on her.

The evening air was cool against her skin, raising goose bumps and dousing her desire. She buttoned her spencer with a businesslike mien and looked around for the other ladies. Although there was another carriage in the packed dirt courtyard with a pair of older women slipping out, the Graylocke family was nowhere to be seen.

"Where did the ladies go?" Felicia asked the driver, laying a hand on his arm.

He was a portly man with stiff, bristle-like sideburns. Although he was far from a callow youth, her touch raised color in his cheeks. "They went to warm themselves inside, Miss. If you'll forgive my boldness, you should do the same. Don't want to be catching a chill."

The warmth of the day had flattened into a brisk autumn chill. The temperature seemed to plummet along with the light of the sun the longer she stood out in the courtyard. The grand, four-story edifice overlooking the courtyard loomed, a large shadow. Light pooled from a lantern hung beside the door. More streamed from the two-story stable to the left.

Felicia took a step toward the inn before she realized that Gideon still hadn't emerged from the carriage. Had she given him an apoplexy? With a smirk, she turned to rouse him, just as he emerged into the open air.

He looked in no better a mood now than he had in the carriage, so she spun on her heel without a word and strode for the inn. His long-legged stride carried him to meet her before she reached the door. He offered his arm to her.

She battled a smile. "Do I look incapable of walking on my own, my lord?"

He gritted his teeth with such force, the sound was nearly audible. "Will you let me act the gentleman, please?" His voice was tight. The light next to the door didn't quite reach far enough to illuminate his expression.

"Would you offer your arm to your business partner had he been male?"

"No, of course not."

She lifted her chin. "Then I will thank you to treat me no differently."

He grumbled under his breath but clasped his hands behind his back.

She preceded him into the inn. At first, the light from the fire in the hearth was blinding. The fire chuckled, spitting sparks as a log shifted. The sparks landed harmlessly on a floor worn smooth by time and use. The tables, although rough-hewn and pockmarked from mishaps, were clean and polished. Patrons filled the common room nearly halfway. Evelyn, Lucy, and Charlie stood at the dark wood bar, speaking to a portly man with a thick mustache who was presumably the owner. Next to them, the lofty pair of older ladies from the other carriage waited. The taller woman, with steely gray hair and a tightly buttoned spencer that tickled the bottom of her chin, adjusted her glasses and clasped her hands primly in front of her thin form. Her shorter, curvier friend exclaimed, leaning forward, "But that can't be!"

As Felicia approached with Gideon behind her, the innkeeper nodded. "I'm afraid so, madam. These fine ladies have commandeered the other four rooms available."

"We are old women," said the taller lady, her voice pinched. "Surely you wouldn't have us reduced."

The dowager drew herself up. Although she'd acted serene and approachable to Felicia, at the moment, she looked every inch the duchess. "Mrs. Biddleford, surely you aren't suggesting that I, the former Duchess of Tenwick, share a bed? My daughter is already sharing with her friend, and you can't expect Miss Albright to share with my son."

Gideon made a choking sound. Felicia's smile wavered, but she pinned it in place.

The stork-like Mrs. Biddleford to whom the ladies spoke made a face. "Indeed not, Lady Graylocke."

Her companion sighed. As her shoulders drooped forward, her low-cut bodice gaped over the top of her large breasts. "I suppose we'll be sharing a room, Theodosia."

As she turned, noticing Felicia and Gideon standing a mere foot away, her expression turned from haggard to interested. "Though I don't know why Miss Albright would protest sharing a room with a well-formed man like Lord Gideon. I certainly wouldn't mind."

Felicia choked down her laughter as Gideon clamped his palms over her shoulder, maneuvering her squarely between him and the sprightly lady. Since Felicia was nearly a foot and a half shorter than Gideon, the position didn't save him from being ogled. She bit into her bottom lip hard. The perfume must still have an effect. At least she wasn't the only woman to react to Gideon's attractive form. In fact, she might even be one of the few able to contain herself.

Mrs. Biddleford, only a couple inches shorter than Gideon, somehow managed to look down her nose at him in a saucy way. "I don't believe he's offering, Hester. Not very gentlemanly, if you ask me."

Gideon's hands tightened as he made a strangled sound. Apparently he'd lost his voice. Felicia bit hard into her cheek to keep from laughing at the poor man.

Taking pity on him, she said, "If our rooms are ready, perhaps someone would be so kind as to direct us? I'd like to freshen up before dinner."

"Dinner," the short Hester exclaimed. "What a fabulous idea! Let's take it together in one of the private rooms. What do you say?"

Although Felicia expected Evelyn to act coldly toward the old women after the blatant ogling of her son, she was as composed as ever as she said, "A grand idea, Miss Maize. Shall we meet in half an hour?"

"No," Gideon said, his voice strained. Given his nearness to Felicia and the low pitch of his protest, she doubted anyone else heard.

"Splendid," Mrs. Biddleford said. She linked arms with her companion, Miss Maize, and drew her aside as the owner slipped around the corner of the counter to show them to their rooms.

Although Felicia had suggested they retire, she hung back to allow the other ladies to pass before she stepped forward. Gideon still gripped her like a shield between himself and the older women. With a smirk, Felicia glanced over her shoulder as she pulled free.

"Do you mean to tell me that you don't enjoy the attentions of older women?"

His cheeks turned a pronounced shade of pink. "I prefer not to entertain women older than my mother."

She grinned. "It's good to know that you have standards."

When he shifted on his feet, uncomfortable, she took pity on him and patted his arm. "It's the perfume," she informed.

He scoffed. "That, I doubt very much."

Turning to follow the procession of women, she tucked away a smile. He judged the perfume based on the smell, not realizing it worked like an aphrodisiac on females. For now, she chose not to enlighten him.

It was more fun this way.

Chapter Eight

Judging by the strained look on Gideon's face, he was in agony. Were it not for Gideon's obvious discomfort, Felicia would be in misery as well. The private dining room was much smaller than she'd anticipated; with seven people, the table was crammed. Felicia pressed against Gideon's right side, able to feel every shift of his arm as he applied himself to the mutton on his plate. On his other side, Miss Maize pressed just as close to him, despite the fact that she sat on the corner and could spare the room. From time to time, her hand disappeared beneath the table and Gideon's body stiffened before he attended to the problem. Felicia found it hard not to laugh.

"Business partners," Mrs. Biddleford said in disgust. No wonder she was so thin. she'd hardly touched the food on her plate as she'd led the conversation through a merry chase of topics. Ending, unfortunately for Felicia, on the subject of her visit to Tenwick Abbey.

Miss Maize shook her head. Her coif was a bit unsecure and wobbled toward Gideon.

Alarm crossed his face as he shifted toward Felicia, as though he feared it might fall off.

"Back in my day," Miss Maize said, stabbing her mutton violently, "if a woman wanted to attract a man, she found a way into his bed, not into his orangery."

Gideon turned as red as the wine in his cup. He took a healthy gulp and wiggled his index finger beneath his cravat to loosen it.

Felicia's hands knotted in her napkin. In as glib a tone as she could manage, she said, "I'm afraid your imagination is running wild. We'll be conducting a few experiments on a plant discovered in South America called *brugmansia*." Seeing as the plant wasn't well-circulated, only a botanist or chemist might be able to connect it with her essays on the potential serum it might create, and only then a select few. With a bland smile, she continued, "Have you heard of the plant? Most delightful specimen. It is a shrub or a small tree with alternate leaves along the stem. The stems, you see, usually grow about so large—" Felicia widened the space between her hands, though she wasn't particularly interested in maintaining accuracy, only in turning the topic of conversation.

That, she accomplished handily. Mrs. Biddleford cleared her throat, interrupting. "It sounds like quite the fascinating project."

For a moment, blissful silence fell as they ate. Antonia was above in the room Lucy and Charlie shared, so there was no one to interrupt. As Felicia loosened her death grip on her napkin, Gideon's hand found hers and squeezed, a gesture of gratitude. He didn't look at her as he lifted his wine glass to his lips at the same time. Felicia's skin burned from his hot touch. Her gloves proved little barrier. To hide her reaction, she speared one of the green beans on the edge of her plate.

Her fork was halfway to her mouth when Mrs. Biddleford regained the use of her tongue.

"A beautiful woman like you is wasted on business. It is your duty to marry and raise children."

Felicia didn't see what her appearance had to do with her life choices. Not to mention that they sat at the table with a spinster much longer in the tooth than Felicia. Did Mrs. Biddleford mean to imply that she did not find her own companion comely enough to have ensnared a man? From the old woman's composed countenance, Felicia couldn't tell.

Slowly, she lowered her fork to her plate once more. She held the utensil in a punishing grip. Luckily, her white gloves prevented the busybody from seeing her white-knuckled grasp. Somehow, she managed to keep her voice even when she answered. "I am also gifted with a quick mind. It is my duty to put it to good use." Venom laced her words despite her attempt to hide it. She hadn't taken well to people demanding she marry when she was seventeen, and she didn't take well to the intrusion now, either.

"Well then, the answer is clear." The older lady arched her thin eyebrows. "You must marry a man who will help you perform that duty." She glanced pointedly at Gideon.

Although she enjoyed seeing him squirm, when her future was involved in the discussion, her enjoyment soured.

Leaning forward, Miss Maize added, "Even better if he has enough money to ensure your time won't be spent chasing after the children to the exclusion of all else." She waggled her eyebrows.

Felicia's stomach swished, threatening to turn itself inside out. She didn't want to contemplate such a future, with Gideon or with anyone else. She'd long ago resigned herself to the fact that she wouldn't have children. It was the price she had to pay in order to maintain her independence. Seeing as she barely kept herself from starving some winters, she couldn't stomach bringing a child into the life she led.

Pushing the morose thoughts from her head, Felicia wadded her napkin and set it on the table. "If you'll forgive me, it's been a long day of travel. I fear I must rest before we begin again tomorrow."

She expected the others to agree with her—for Gideon to agree, at the very least—but she was disappointed. Instead, Lucy said with dismay, "You're retiring so soon? The night is young! We've barely had the chance to speak."

She offered Lucy a slim smile. "I imagine we'll have plenty of time to speak at Tenwick Abbey, never you fear."

As Lucy opened her mouth again, the dowager laid a hand on her arm. To Felicia, she said, "Goodnight, dear. Sleep well."

"Thank you." Felicia nearly curtsied before she recalled that the dowager didn't care for such formality. Instead, she inclined her head. "I wish you the same."

She spared the slimmest glance for Gideon before she turned toward the door. Apprehension lined his face and lingered in his green eyes, dark with the light from the sharp-smelling oil lamp that lit the room. Turning away, Felicia nearly collided with a buxom blonde serving girl. She apologized quickly and stepped aside for the woman to pass.

The woman, a few years older than Felicia at her guess, sashayed straight to Gideon and bent so low over his arm to collect Felicia's plate that her breasts brushed his shoulder. Biting her cheek to contain her mirth, Felicia hurried from the room. The woman attracted to him this time was certainly younger than his mother. Perhaps her advances would be more agreeable to him.

Judging by the alarm edging his expression when she'd left, he wasn't the least bit happy to have another admirer.

The inn was worn and plain, from the walls to the floorboards, but a sense of security underlined the simple abode. It had stood long before Felicia had been born and would likely remain until long after she was dead. She mounted the smooth steps to the second floor, where her room resided. With every step, the clamor from the common room faded along with the tension between her shoulders. She had work to do, but for tonight, she could relax and sleep.

In her room—a square space devoured by the bed, a dressing screen, a small desk wedged into one corner, and a pedestal and basin of water— she loosened the enclosures to her placket-front dress and slipped out of it. She draped the material over the desk, trying not to look at the other, closed door in the room. As she dipped her handkerchief into the lukewarm basin of sweet-smelling water and dabbed along her hairline and neck, her gaze remained locked on that plain wooden door. The adjoining door to Gideon's room, as she'd discovered earlier.

She'd also learned that it had no lock.

He is a gentleman, or he fancies himself one. Felicia didn't for a second believe that he would enter her chambers, invited or otherwise. He'd made that clear in his gallant attempt to take her arm earlier. But would she be able to resist the lure of entering his chambers?

She brushed the thought aside like an errant lock of hair. Of course she would. Her reaction to him was purely chemical, aided by the pheromones in the perfume. When not in close proximity, her head was clear of temptation.

Finished washing away the sweat of the day, she opened her reticule and found the small comb she'd brought with her. One by one, she pulled the pins free from her hair and arranged them neatly on the desk next to her dress. She combed out her hair with slow strokes, counting to one hundred.

Around sixty strokes, she heard movement in the other room. Gideon must have returned.

At seventy-nine strokes, more movement. Gideon cried out. "What the devil?" His voice was high and sharp with alarm.

Felicia didn't think twice. She barreled through the connecting door armed with the sharp teeth of her comb. Her heart pounded in her throat as she searched the room for danger.

The room was identical to hers, with two exceptions—first, the buxom blond serving girl reclined on the bed with her skirts yanked up over her knees and her bodice yanked down to display her naked breasts. The second was Gideon clad only in his trousers, bare from the waist up. He pressed his back against the door to the hall, as far from her as he could possibly get, an expression close to panic on his face.

"What in bloody Hell are you doing in my room?"

Gideon rubbed his hand across his mouth. Although he'd changed out of his travel clothes for dinner, he hadn't shaved. The dark shadow of his stubble looked even thicker next to his suddenly waxen skin. It covered his jaw and the upper part of his throat, fading into smooth-looking skin a shade paler than his face and hands. His shoulders and chest looked even wider without the constraint of his jacket. Dark hair on his chest narrowed to an arrow disappearing below the waistband of his breeches. He was so consumed in staring, mouth agape, at the woman on the bed that he didn't appear to notice Felicia's entrance, nor recall his nudity. The rest of his clothes were discarded next to the desk.

Felicia was no prude, but apparently, Gideon was. He stared at the maid in his bed with what looked to be bald horror. Didn't he get propositioned on a regular basis? Aside from being handsome in a heady, absent-minded, brilliant mind kind of way, he was also the son of a duke. That in itself ought to attract a few giggling debutantes or lonely widows.

Laughter bubbled up in Felicia's throat before she tamped it down. Tears streamed from her eyes as she clasped the door frame for support. The comb bit into her palm. Blindly, she tossed it behind her into her room. It clattered to the floor.

The serving maid shifted on the bed, jiggling her breasts as she said, "Don't be shy. I don't mind if she joins us."

At the alarm that flashed across his face, Felicia roared with laughter. He lunged for his jacket and tossed it onto the bed. "Cover yourself, madam."

Her lips plumping in a pout, the woman used his jacket as a screen while she tugged her bodice into place once more.

Gideon rounded on Felicia. He angled himself so he didn't take his attention off the woman on the bed while he did so. "This is no laughing matter."

"It is." She wiped at the moisture on her cheeks. "The look on your face—" She pressed her bare hand tight to her mouth to keep from breaking into guffaws again.

He glared at her, but the color rose in his cheeks. "I'd thank you to get out."

The blonde swung her legs over the side of the bed, making the mattress sway a bit on its ropes. His jacket slipped to the floor by her feet. "You heard him, luv. Leave us be."

Felicia bit hard into her lower lip to keep from laughing aloud. When she had herself under control, she managed to say, "I believe he was talking to you, *love*."

"I most certainly was. Get out." He stepped aside, providing quick access to the door.

Disgust mottled the woman's face as she rose and stomped toward him. Gideon shrunk back, as if afraid she might strike him. Instead, the woman gentled her expression and movements as she came near, brushing against his body as she reached for the latch on the door.

"Are you sure I can't change your mind, my lord?"

His expression hardened. He must have learned that look from his brother. "Very sure. I'm not looking for company tonight."

"No." The woman shot Felicia a dirty look. "It seems as though you already have all the company you need." Leaning forward, the woman whispered something that made Gideon turn as red as a tomato.

"Good day, madam," he said stiffly. He didn't move an inch as the serving maid opened the door and left.

The moment the door reunited with the frame, he lunged for his jacket and dug through the pockets until he found the key to the door. He locked it.

Felicia took a step back, intending to return to her room and leave him in peace. When he tilted his head toward the ceiling, his eyes screwed tight as if in pain, pity surged in her chest. She couldn't leave him so obviously distraught by the ordeal. For a stubborn, dominant man in all other respects, he'd reacted to her like a boy. In fact, Felicia was astounded he'd managed to find the mettle to force his admirer to leave.

Without departing from the threshold of the connecting door, Felicia offered, "It's the perfume."

He opened his eyes. His irises appeared greener than ever with an emotion she couldn't name. "What is?"

She gestured to the shut door. "The women, throwing themselves at you."

He rolled his eyes. "No other cologne I've had the misfortune of using has had that effect."

"Well, they weren't brewed by me, were they?" She propped her hands on her hips. "It's a perfume designed to attract the opposite sex. I sell them at market."

"Lawks!" He raised his hand as if to claw away his shirt, only to realize that he had already begun undressing. His cheeks turned pink again. He crossed his arms, not that that hid his torso overmuch. "How do I make it stop?"

Felicia bit the inside of her cheek to stifle a laugh. "Soap and water will do the trick."

He crossed to the basin, only to stop short. "I haven't any soap."

"There was some in my room. Wait a moment."

It smelled soft and floral, clearly only added to her room because she traveled with the Dowager Duchess of Tenwick, but it would serve Gideon well enough. By the time she returned with the small square of soap, he stood over the basin, splashing water on himself with his hands. He didn't even have a rag or handkerchief. With a sigh, she turned on her heel and found one.

She dipped it in the water and lathered the soap. "Where did Lucy spill the perfume?"

He looked away and muttered, "Where didn't she?"

"I'd rather not have to smell various parts of your chest to find out."

The look he gave her was mixed alarm and something else. His eyes darkened. She focused on his bare chest, though that didn't help her sanity much. The musky scent of the perfume swirled around her. She dabbed at his skin.

He raised his hand, tracing out a large circle of skin on his left side. "Here." His voice was husky. It sent a shiver down her spine.

Pressing her lips together, she fought not to show a reaction. She applied the wet handkerchief to his skin, rinsed it, lathered it with more soap, and continued. The musky scent lightened, but only marginally.

"I'm not a virgin," he blurted. "I have made love to a woman."

A quick glance to his face showed his jaw clenched as he looked away from her. He flew his colors.

A woman. He probably wasn't as sexually experienced as her, but he wasn't as old as her, either. Her breasts ached as an unwanted thought flashed across her mind. What would it be like to teach him more of the pleasures between a man and a woman? She bet he'd be a quick study.

She bit the inside of her cheek and continued her ministrations. "I believe you."

Damn! Was her voice as husky as his? It was the perfume's effect. This close to him, she had difficulty ignoring it. She'd never had to test her own product in such a way before.

His palm wrapped around her shoulder. The short sleeve of her chemise muted his touch, but not enough. Warmth seeped into her skin through the thin material.

"I have."

His muscles bunched beneath her hand and handkerchief. A droplet of water snaked down his torso and beneath the breeches covering his navel. Felicia licked her lips, battling the urge to trace its path.

The perfume. The knowledge of what it was doing to her was little balm to her frayed resistance.

"I said I believe you."

"So you said, but I don't think that you do." His grip on her shoulder tightened. The edge of his hand grazed her bare skin beneath the sleeve. That small brush of his skin branded her.

She swallowed and licked her lips. Her hand tightened on the wet handkerchief. "What does it matter whether I believe you?"

"It matters," he said, his expression intense. He lowered his mouth to hers.

He had to bend to meld their mouths. He had plenty of time and opportunity to think better of the action—and so did she. Lust clouded her judgment due to the perfume still clinging to his skin. What was *his* excuse?

The moment his mouth brushed hers, desire surged and obliterated the small measure of control she still had left. She lifted onto her tiptoes, wrapping her arms around his neck as she opened her mouth. He took full advantage, conquering her and pressing her closer.

He touched her everywhere, like he couldn't get enough. Between her shoulder blades, over her hip, palming her breast through her chemise. Until he touched bare skin above her knee, she hadn't realized that her legs were bare. Her chemise didn't extend to the floor. Had she been half-naked in front of him this entire time?

A stupid question. Of course she had. She broke the kiss, gulping for air as clarity returned. Raising his hand to cup her cheek, he stroked her bottom lip with his thumb.

Felicia knew the exact moment his senses returned, because alarm spiked across his expression. He released her with alacrity.

"I think it's best that you leave."

She'd already turned her back. Bolting for the adjoining door mere steps away, she shut it hard. Her hand still on the cold metal latch, she battled for breath. Her body tingled, ignited from his touch.

That blasted perfume. It was going to be a long, sleepless night.

Chapter Nine

Voices, muffled by the wall and door between them. Felicia held her breath, straining her ears. She shut her eyes against the thin morning light streaming through the window, the better to catch the words—or, at the very least, the identity of those who spoke next door. No luck. Her heart thumped too loudly in her ears for her to hear.

The only reason she had kissed the pigheaded Lord Gideon Graylocke last night was because of the pheromones in the perfume. But that didn't mean she wanted to be caught alone in his presence. The easiest way to ensure that would be to wait until everyone else had entered the carriage. She paced her room again, waiting for the voices to stop and for him to leave his room. Hers overlooked the courtyard, an excellent vantage point that had afforded her a glimpse of the coach as it was readied and brought around, not to mention the two ebony-haired heads and one blonde who had disappeared within not two minutes ago. Gideon was the last.

She didn't have to await him long; in a moment, the voices ceased and the opening and closing of the door indicated that he had gone below stairs. She straightened her shoulders. As she was to be ensconced in a closed carriage with him for the next several hours, she couldn't avoid him entirely. Nor did she want to. She'd done nothing wrong.

After all, *he* had kissed her. She'd only responded because of the perfume.

Even armed with that consolation, she waited until the footsteps retreated down the stairs before she slipped out of her room, leaving the key on the desk for retrieval. The moment she shut the door behind her, the door to Gideon's room opened. He froze in the threshold.

"I thought you'd gone down already."

Blast, why had she said that?

In a distant, even tone, he answered, "The driver came to collect my trunk."

Of course. How bacon-brained of her not to consider it! Simply because she chose to travel light did not mean that the Graylocke family did the same.

Gideon's hair was a mess this morning, looking as though he'd tried to finger-comb it flat. He'd shaved, but the lack of stubble only emphasized the shape and softness of his mouth. He was dressed to the nines in a soft-looking brown jacket, paired with dark breeches. His cravat was tied in a simple knot, slightly askew. From the way it gaped away from his collar, he'd already attempted to adjust it this morning.

Coldly, he shut the door and motioned for her to precede him. "Ladies first, Miss Albright."

Oh, so she was Miss Albright again, was she? Not that he'd uttered her Christian name aloud, but sometime during the carriage ride yesterday, the atmosphere had softened to one of informality. He certainly hadn't been thinking of her as Miss Albright while he'd been kissing her.

She narrowed her eyes. If he was determined to ignore the passion that had ignited between them, she would prove to him just how impossible that task could be.

Although she'd donned her spencer to brace against the autumn chill outdoors, she hadn't buttoned it yet. She was glad for that now. Leaning forward, she offered him a better view of her low cut gown and asked, "Aren't you going to offer to escort me down?"

He spluttered. His mouth flapped like a fish. Open, closed, open again, mimicking the fists at his sides. His gaze strayed from her décolletage to search her face. "Yesterday, you said…"

She sidled closer, emphasizing the sway of her hips. He took small, measured steps back. Did he realize he was doing it? She smirked. "I know what I said yesterday."

While battling laughter, she couldn't quite manage a husky purr. But she must have come close, because alarm flashed over Gideon's face.

Leaning up on her tiptoes—not that it drew her any closer—she whispered, "I also know what I did yesterday."

"I—uh—" He dashed his fingers through his hair, mussing it further.

Laughter welled in her throat. Her cheeks ached as her smile grew. She turned on her heel before he realized she was laughing at his lack of composure. A stoic, controlled man like Gideon was never out of his element. Except with her.

As she sashayed to the stairs, she thought, *The ride today ought to be a delight.*

***

The ride was not a delight. At first, it amused her to keep him off balance. The graze of her arm against his or her fingertips over his thigh, making him jump. Leaning forward at just the right angle to remind him of her feminine form. When his family shot her disapproving looks—or worse, sly ones—the game soon grew tiresome. Gideon's cheeks were perpetually ruddy. He shifted position twice a minute as he stared out the window, not contributing to the conversation at all.

Although she'd expected the aroma of the perfume to be gone today, it continued to cling to him. She only caught a whiff of the musk when she leaned in to tease him, but that small scent was enough to alert her to the fact that it continued to wreak havoc on her body. After washing, the residual perfume left clinging to him was probably close to the recommended dose. From the moment she realized that, she kept to the corner of the coach, trying to put as much distance between herself and that perfume as possible. It had already made her do something that she regretted; better not add to it. Though flustering him was fun, it lost much of his allure with the suspicious narrowing of his mother and sister's eyes.

Did they suspect that Felicia had kissed him? She applied herself to embroidery for much of the ride to Tenwick Abbey.

As they rattled through a small village, identical to several others they'd traversed, Lucy straightened. She handed Antonia, asleep with her head tucked under her wing, to Evelyn.

"Look, it's Locksley village!" She clasped Charlie's arm. "We're almost home."

Curious, Felicia glanced out the window, ignoring Gideon and focusing on the passing of the wooden houses. Within a minute, they had reached the village limits and driven free again.

Trees enclosed the road, their bare branches clawing at the gray sky. Felicia moved back, though she kept one eye on the narrow window, hoping for a view of the abbey before they arrived.

She wasn't disappointed. Within ten minutes, they passed a whitewashed church with a tall steeple. Trees bordered the road, not quite blotting out the view of the steeple rising above them. The carriage ambled for another two or three minutes before it turned into a long drive lined with neatly-trimmed box hedges.

The drive was a road in itself. In the distance, a hill loomed with a tall tree cresting it. The tree was barely visible over the opulent abbey.

Tenwick Abbey was ancient. That much was clear even before they neared the sprawling edifice. The dark stone rose from the dry, off-color grass around it as though it had risen from the ground, fully erect. One part in the north corner, the loftiest spire, appeared to be in disrepair. The rest of the mansion was magnificent. At least four stories high, and as long as a London city block. What could one family possibly do with so much space? Felicia couldn't fathom it.

The drive ended in a circle. One side led to the entrance to the abbey—the other, to the stables. At the crest of the circle, her colorful wagon awaited. Although Rudolph wasn't hitched to it, Chubs sat in front of the door, guarding the entrance. Felicia grinned. The Graylockes were home and now, so was she.

"What's that?" Lucy asked.

Felicia barely heard her. She hummed with joy over the thought of seeing her pets again. Although three days hadn't seemed like such a prodigiously long time, in actuality, it had been. She'd missed having Chubs sit near her ankles as she ate, inching closer and closer as if she couldn't see an eleven-stone dog. She'd missed the way Rudolph lipped at her hand when she scratched the coarse whiskers on his chin. With the lumpy mattress she'd slept on last night, she'd even missed her narrow cot.

Home. She was lucky to be able to bring it with her wherever she went.

The second the carriage stopped, she bolted out the door. Her wagon was twenty feet away from where they'd stopped, but Chubs noticed her immediately. He stood from his guard position, his tail wagging madly.

"Come here, boy."

Chubs thundered over the packed dirt. His pink tongue flopped out the side of his mouth, flapping with each of his steps along with his ears. To keep him from jumping, Felicia lowered herself onto her knees and opened her arms wide in welcome. He barreled into her and knocked her to the ground, squeezing the air from her lungs as he planted his paws on her shoulders and cleaned her face.

She turned her face to the side, giggling. "I missed you too, Chubs, but you've been sneaking too many snacks while I was away. You're heavy!"

When she tried to ease him off of her, she nearly got a tongue in her mouth for her troubles. She clamped her lips and her eyes shut and squirmed until she could roll onto her side. When she opened one eye into the barest slit, she looked directly into a large, black dog nose.

"Sit."

The ground vibrated as Chubs dropped his bottom onto it. His tail thumped the ground with vigor.

"I take it this is your beast." Gideon's voice was laced with sarcasm as he exited the carriage and helped the eager ladies out after him.

Felicia grinned. "Well he certainly isn't going to win any prizes for beauty."

With a whine, the mastiff clawed at her with his heavy paw. One thing she hadn't missed was feeling that paw in her face first thing in the morning when he had to make water. Cooing under her breath, she scratched him behind his ears.

He was a mangy thing. Bigger in the paws than he was around the legs. She fed him as much as she could, but for all her quips he could probably use a few more meals. His ribs weren't poking out the way they were when she'd met him, but she could still see them against his glossy black coat.

Parts of his body betrayed his less than gentlemanly past. Bald patches of skin over scars on his rump, side, and ear. One of his ears was a bit misshapen, likely from a fight with a cat in a nasty mood. For all that, he didn't seem to realize that he wasn't quite to the caliber of breeding as a lord's dog might be. He sat as tall and proud as if he'd been awarded Dog of the Year. His tongue hung from the side of his mouth. Felicia leaned forward and gave him a kiss on his long snout. He tried to reciprocate, but she pulled away faster, still rubbing his ears. As her thumbs dipped inside, his eyes shut in ecstasy.

She'd probably been caught in the Dog Petting trap, never to be able to stop again, but she didn't mind. She *had* missed him, after all. She waved Gideon closer.

"This is Chubs. Why don't you meet him, so he doesn't accidentally tear you to shreds if you approach the wagon?"

A dubious expression crossed his face as he tentatively stepped closer. When he offered his hand, Chubs licked it and rolled onto the ground, belly up. Gideon crouched to scratch the dog's barrel chest.

"This is your guard dog?"

She laughed. "He's much different when he's on protective duty, I assure you."

"If you say so..." His voice was laden with disbelief.

She turned her face, only then realizing how close she was to him. Her smile slipped. Only inches separated them. Far too close. She had to get away from that blasted perfume. She stood, wiping the palms of her gloves on her skirt. She buttoned up one more button on her spencer, just to be safe. It was cool, but not as much as it had been this morning. The sun, hiding behind the clouds at the moment, had chased away a lot of the autumn chill.

At the carriage, a clamor started at the door, a testament to Lucy's excitement to get out into the open air. Unfortunately, she was laden with an uncooperative parrot who didn't want to close her wings enough to safely fit through the carriage door.

"Stop it, you blasted bird. You can't stay in here forever."

Evelyn hiked her skirt over her ankle and mounted the bottom step of the carriage. The driver hovered at her elbow, ready to offer his assistance if need be.

"Let me take her." When Evelyn reached out her hands, Antonia quieted. She made a cooing sort of sound and stepped, meek as a dove, from Lucy's arm onto Evelyn's.

Lucy scowled. "Why does she like you better than me?"

"You're very excitable, dear. You have to be calm or she'll pick up on your agitation."

Had Lucy ever been calm? She was filled with such energy, mischief, and enthusiasm that

Felicia suspected the only peaceful mood she had was while asleep.

She clomped down the stairs. Antonia flapped her wings and screeched, "Get off your rump!"

Lucy scowled. "That's what I'm doing now, isn't it?"

The dowager petted the bird with light, steady strokes. "She's a parrot, dear. She doesn't know what she's saying."

Lucy glowered. "She knows..."

Felicia pressed her lips together to keep from laughing. It wouldn't help.

The moment Charlie stepped to the ground, stretching her legs and groaning, Gideon stopped scratching the mastiff's belly and glanced over his shoulder. Without the distraction, Chubs noticed the large blue bird. He rolled onto his feet, slobber flying as he barked. The parrot dug her claws into Evelyn's arm through her glove—painfully, judging by her expression and the way she tried to wheedle her hand in between.

"Pudding-house," Antonia screamed.

Chubs barked. He danced around the dowager and the bird, his tail wagging like mad, as he tried to decide on the best angle to greet his new friend.

"Pickle," cried the bird. "Giddy, pickle, pickle!"

Apparently, Antonia had a limited vocabulary. Though Felicia had to admit, there was a time or two when she ran out of words to say when Chubs frustrated her, too.

This time, the word was easy. "Chubs, *no*. Sit."

The dog sat, drumming his tail on the ground. His haunches coiled to jump.

"No!"

Felicia lunged for his collar, falling half on top of him. Gideon had the same idea. They collided in midair, cracking their heads together and falling to the hard ground in a tangle of limbs. Felicia groaned as she struggled to get her feet beneath her.

"Not there." Gideon's words were strained, little more than a hiss, but his fingers clamped over her hips to still her was anything but. The grip was unyielding. She could barely wiggle against him, let alone gain any more traction.

"Let me up."

"Carefully," he spat between gritted teeth.

Only then did she realize how close her knee had come to injuring his manhood. "Forgive me," she muttered as she straightened out her leg.

The movement freed him from danger, but did little to help her rise. In fact, she was pressed even more fully against him, her breasts crushed to his chest and his mouth so close to hers that his warm breath played over her cheek. He smelled incredible. Too good. Even knowing her reaction to him was chemical did little to keep it from happening.

And judging by the bulge against her pelvis, he couldn't help his reaction to her, either. She met his gaze, stilling and waiting for the reaction to subside. She couldn't stand and expose it, could she?

Better that than encourage him. The moment their eyes met, his a deep, crystal green, a shiver coursed through her. She rolled off of him, onto the packed dirt. This time, he let her. He rolled in the opposite direction, away from his family.

Fortunately, Chubs and Antonia occupied their attention. Evelyn held the bird as high as her trembling arm could support while Antonia whistled provocatively, called Chubs a bizarre series of insults, and flicked her tail feather at him. Chubs was slathering at the mouth as he dreamt of what parrot feathers would taste like when licked. It took both Charlie and Lucy, tugging on his collar, to keep him on the ground.

With a tense expression, sweat beading on her forehead, Lucy struggled to make herself heard above the dog's puncturing barks. "Take her inside!"

Although it took more than one try before her meaning was clear, the dowager soon balanced the agitated bird while rounding the carriage and hurrying up the broad, stone steps to a massive set of double doors. They were opened from within as she approached and she disappeared without issue.

Chubs continued to strain against the young women restraining him. Felicia straightened, put on her most imposing dog owner voice, and said, "Quiet, Chubs. Lay down."

Whimpering, the dog lowered onto his front legs. His rear end was poised partially into the air wriggling as if he hoped to escape and run after the bird. He glanced over his shoulder at Felicia, his brown eyes limpid pools of wretchedness.

What an actor he was. Shaking her head, Felicia approached and laid her hand on his rump. "You can let him go. He won't run. He may lick you, however, so beware."

The girls set upon him with admiring words and scratches.

"Is he yours?" Lucy asked. "I didn't know you had a dog. We could have taken him with us."

Gideon, now on his feet and in a less embarrassing state, brushed off his breeches as he grumbled, "Lord save us if we put this fellow and Antonia in an enclosed space together."

Felicia grinned. He had a point. "I needed him to guard the wagon while I was away. That is the reason I adopted him, after all."

Lucy cooed. "What a smart dog you are, to save us from that dangerous parrot."

Laughing, Felicia could barely force out the words, "I thought Antonia was your pet."

"Oh, she is. That doesn't mean she isn't dangerous."

Gideon offered a bland smile. "She fits in with the rest of the family."

Lucy's dark eyebrows snapped down over her eyes, her expression hostile. "What is that supposed to mean?"

"Nothing at all," Gideon said, his tone and expression innocent. "It's cold out here. Why don't we go warm ourselves inside and continue the conversation there?"

"A splendid idea," Felicia said.

She rose, snapping her fingers to get her dog's attention. Groaning, he straightened to his full height. You'd think she asked him to walk over a bed of hot coals.

Absently, she added, "I won't be long. Back before supper, to be sure. Come, boy." She turned toward the stables.

Gideon's mouth dropped open as she strode past him. A moment later, he turned and trotted at her heels. "Back?"

Lucy hiked up her skirts and sprinted to Felicia's side. "Where are you going? What's in the wagon? Why do you have it? Do you usually travel that way?"

Throughout the barrage of questions, Gideon repeated his statement in the same disbelieving tone. "Back?"

She ignored him.

When Lucy took a breath, Felicia informed her and the young blonde trotting behind, "I'm going into town. The wagon is my home and holds my belongings. Do you remember when you spilled that vial on Gideon? Well, I created that perfume, I didn't buy it. Actually, I sell it at market. It's how I'm able to sustain my style of living. And yes, I've been all over Britain in that sturdy wagon."

She reached the doors of the stables. Lucy asked more questions—about how she sold her perfumes, the places that she'd been, what kind of clientele she attracted. Felicia walked down the row of stalls, searching for her mule and found him, happily munching away at some hay. He seemed reluctant to see her, as if he knew it meant more exertion. Shaking her head, she gave his nose a pat and grabbed hold of his halter to guide him out.

As she strode back toward her wagon, she answered as many of Lucy's questions as she could before the slim young woman asked more. Lucy pulled a small notebook from her reticule, no bigger than her hand, and jotted down Felicia's answers. Although Felicia sought to give the most simple answer and thus end the tirade, Lucy's questions were endless. Felicia managed to hitch Rudolph to the wagon while talking. She opened the wagon door to let Chubs take his usual roost inside, and climbed aboard the front driver's seat.

Although the seat was high off the ground, it was only at the level of Gideon's shoulders. He brushed past his sister and Charlie and met her gaze. "We just arrived. Surely you don't mean to leave again."

"That I do."

She flicked the reins and Rudolph started forward with a groan. For all his leisure and reluctance in reaching the wagon, he seemed to sense that there was a better chance of being fed if they arrived at their destination quickly. The wheels creaked a bit as they found traction on the packed earth, and they were away. Felicia waved her hand and called, "I'll be back again soon!"

The ladies waved to her, then linked arms to retreat into the abbey. Gideon, on the other hand, stood in the middle of the drive, flabbergasted. Felicia faced forward, but even then she seemed to feel his gaze.

She savored the moment she turned from the long drive onto the road. She was alone again, without the company of the Graylockes. Not that, as a whole, they were poor travel companions, but pressed up against Gideon for the entire ride had proven trying. She breathed deep the cool, crisp air. Before long, she wished she'd stopped to find a cloak or pelisse in her wagon. Seeing as she recalled the town as being so near to the abbey, she didn't bother stopping but continued to drive.

One mule moved slower than four matched horses, and it took her over five minutes before the steeple of the church came into view. The lofty white edifice served as a beacon to her. It looked in good repair as she ambled past. A woman in a plain gray cloak carrying a basket slipped from between the doors as the wagon passed. Felicia waved.

A half an hour later, she reached the village. The trees dropped away, giving rise to squat, sturdy houses built mostly of wood. One, near to the edge of the village, sported a swinging sign that proclaimed it, *The Golden Goose.* A tavern or inn, by her guess. There was a small stable in the back, barely large enough to house five or six horses. The Golden Goose was a square building three stories high. It dwarfed the smaller homes and shops nearby, but didn't look spacious, especially with the steep slant to the roof.

The hour was just after lunch, and patrons trickled from the tavern's doors. Since it seemed to be a popular building for the area, Felicia parked her wagon in the flat area across from it. Not close enough to be associated with the tavern and risk the enmity of the owner, but close enough that the patrons emerging into the gray daylight immediately set eyes upon her wagon.

The moment she drew to a stop, she leaped off the hard driver's seat and looped Rudolph's reins around a hook in the corner. If he decided to amble forward, the bit would tighten uncomfortably in his mouth and it would prompt him to stop. Not that she thought he would decide to move of his own volition. Rudolph was the laziest mule she'd ever met.

However, he was spurred by his stomach, so as a reward she found a carrot inside the wagon as she let Chubs out. "Guard," she told the dog. She fed the carrot to Rudolph while Chubs sat on his haunches and kept watch.

The men and women exiting the Golden Goose slowed, staring at her wagon. With the ease of long practice, she unfurled the awning and propped it on two posts. *Felicia's Love Perfumes* billowed a bit in the breeze, but it was legible enough for those who could read. Those who couldn't would be attracted by the sign and the gaudy colors of her wagon.

When she exited the wagon with the table that she hastily unfolded, she'd gathered a crowd of about six. She smiled and waved, and returned to the wagon to fetch the tablecloth and her wares. The most diluted samples, as this didn't appear to be a prosperous crowd, for all their proximity to the Duke of Tenwick's estate.

When she returned outside, the crowd had swelled to seven people, three men and four women. She beckoned them closer as she laid out her wares, probing them for information about their love lives. Despite the chill, she unbuttoned her plain spencer to show more of her tawny dress and wished it was more colorful. The flashier she looked, the more people she enticed to peruse her wares and listen to their effect.

Donning her saleswoman persona was like slipping into a second skin. Her troubles melted away beneath the onslaught of her efforts to be entertaining and charming. Not too alluring, so that she wasn't branded a trollop and eschewed by the women, but enough to catch the eyes of the men with a flirtatious smile or the glimpse of her ankle as she paced the length of her table. A couple of young women seemed interested in her wares, but didn't have the pin money on hand to purchase a vial and so had to run home to their fathers to beg for money. A pair of men older than Felicia joked about attracting their wives' attentions once more. She tried to sell to them, but they shook their heads and sauntered off. Most other patrons kept to the outskirts of the group, listened to what she had to say, but didn't make eye contact. After spending so long on the road, Felicia was used to deciphering a patron's mood from their expressions. These were proper, God-fearing villagers. She saw some interest in the eyes of an older matron or two, clearly hoping to marry off a daughter that they hadn't had any luck with as of yet. They might still return. As for the others... it was a lucky thing that Felicia was staying with the Graylockes, because otherwise, this would have been a lean village to pander her wares.

A young man with longish, caramel-brown hair flirted with her as he quizzed her about her wares. She answered his questions halfheartedly, gifting him with just enough of a smile so that he wouldn't feel slighted. To her surprise, he bought a vial of the perfume.

The moment they concluded the deal, Felicia handed over his chosen bottle. "You don't need to douse yourself in the perfume. A dab or two on your pulse points will do."

Pulling out the stopper, he poured a splash onto his palm and rubbed it over his neck and wrists. "Like this?"

"Exactly so."

Once he plugged the bottle and tucked it into his pocket, he leaned forward. "What is your verdict, fair Felicia? Do you find me irresistible?"

I didn't mean for you to use it on me!

She resisted the urge to rub her suddenly-throbbing temple or worse, smack the smug expression off his face. Although she skimmed the crowd for an ally, their expressions were closed off. Farther into town, more villagers marched on their business. A few glanced at her stall, but they either couldn't read or weren't interested in what she had to sell. One young woman, in a sky-blue dress and straw bonnet, caught Felicia's eye. She lingered two houses down, staring at the stall with an expression that was unreadable at this distance.

Felicia returned her gaze to the flirtatious pest. His eyes danced as he awaited an answer. Either she had to admit to finding him attractive or she would lose the business of the town once word got out that her wares didn't work.

"It takes more than a second to take hold," she told him, which was true. Ideally, the wearer had to be in enclosed spaces with the object of their affection for a prodigious length of time. A day seated next to a man in a closed carriage did the trick, for instance. It took no more than ten or fifteen minutes. Felicia held her breath, not wanting to find herself inconveniently attracted to this rogue, if she could help it.

"Perhaps I can convince you to have a warm cup of cider with me at the Golden Goose."

Only in your dreams. She turned her smile to one of regret. "I'm afraid I have to work, sir."

"Call me James. I insist."

Over my dead body. If she was reluctant to call Gideon by his Christian name, when they were to work intimately for the next several weeks until they completed the task set for them by the Crown, she certainly wouldn't call a stranger by such a familiar term. Especially not one who seemed bent on seducing her.

Felicia didn't mind a little seduction now and again, but now was not the time, and he was not the man. She dug her fingernails into her palm to keep the image at bay of the man she might prefer for bed sport. She suspected she knew the answer her mind dredged up and would not be happy with it.

"Without selling my wares, I won't be able to eat." She batted her eyelashes, but not too many times. She didn't want to encourage him too much.

"I'll buy your dinner," he declared.

Although she would love to say no, she didn't dare. If she gave him the cut direct, he would regret his purchase. An unhappy customer was never a good thing, let alone in a town she had yet to make her mark in. So instead she fixed him with her best smile and said, "Perhaps another time. I cannot shirk my work. Surely you understand."

A flash of sky blue caught her eye. The young woman! Felicia had suspected that the young woman might prove a customer. The woman, about Felicia's age, must have been able to read, for she stood a few feet away with a hesitant expression on her face as she beheld Felicia's banner. As Felicia turned her attention to the new arrival, thankful for the excuse to end her conversation with the young man, the woman firmed her chin and stepped closer. She'd made her decision.

Felicia might have a genuine customer, if she played the game right. She approached the woman with a broad smile.

"Hello, there! I am Felicia. Do you have a beau, perhaps? Someone whose wandering eye you'd like to attract?"

The woman had the look of a spinster. The neckline of her dress flirted with her collarbone. Her bonnet was trimmed with matching ribbon, likely by her own hand. She wore no gloves, revealing that no rings adorned her fingers. Hence, unmarried. From the pensive and hesitant way she'd approached the stall, she was undoubtedly unlucky in love and looking to do anything she could to change that. At their age, women were considered to be firmly on the shelf and not considered of marriageable age anymore. What poppycock.

The woman brushed a slim lock of brown hair beneath her bonnet once more. She had a handful of freckles across her nose, so light they were barely noticeable against her pale skin. A pretty woman, though with her mousy demeanor she might never be called a diamond of the first water. But her skin was unblemished, her teeth weren't too crooked, and her figure was trim. With the help of Felicia's perfume, she shouldn't have trouble attracting the man of her heart, so long as she finagled her way into his presence.

"Your perfumes," she said, her voice soft. "How do they work? Not—" She lowered her voice further as she added, "—witchcraft?"

Felicia was accused of that enough times in particularly pious towns to know how to handle it. "Certainly not, Miss. My perfumes work by science. If you have a grounding in chemistry or human physiology, I'd be happy to explain it to you."

"Thank you, that won't be necessary." She seemed appeased, but lingered over the bottles, not asking how much they were.

Felicia offered the information. The young woman nodded. She didn't speak and avoided eye contact. Drat! Felicia would lose the sale if she didn't find a means of convincing her.

"Do you have your eye on a man a bit hesitant to commit?"

She raised her gaze to Felicia's. Her eyes were a light blue that matched her dress and made her look innocent and younger than the light grooves etched around her nose and between her eyebrows suggested.

"In a manner of speaking. Until recently, I would have said the entire family was hesitant to choose wives, but his brothers have recently done so."

Felicia nodded. "Men can be peculiar. Sometimes all they need is the slightest nudge for their resolve to crumble into dust."

"Feli—*Miss* Albright!"

Gideon's angry bellow rent the air. Felicia jumped. She turned her gaze to the road leading to Tenwick Abbey. There he was, dressed in the same clothes he'd worn to travel. Since he didn't lead a horse, she assumed he'd followed on foot. He must have been motivated in order to reach the village so soon on her heels.

She offered the young woman a slim smile and said, "If you'll excuse me but a moment."

The young man, James, shrunk back at Gideon's arrival. At least the blasted botanist was good for that much. With luck, the young flirt would return to his work and wouldn't think of her until long after she'd returned to Tenwick Abbey.

Squaring her shoulders, she turned to face Gideon. She raised her eyebrows, folding her arms over her chest as she waited for him to approach within hearing distance without her yelling.

"Yes, Lord Gideon? How may I help you? I daresay you haven't come to purchase one of my perfumes."

He rolled his eyes. "Hardly." Running his hands through his hair, stuck up at all angles and a bit damp from sweating during the exertion of his walk, he added, "What in blazes do you think you're doing?"

"I'm selling off my stock. You can hardly expect me to neglect my work while I'm here."

He jabbed a finger through the air, but stopped several inches short of making contact with her. "Your *work* while you're here is to assist me."

"Oh?" She raised her eyebrows. "And here it was my impression that *you* were to assist *me*."

Judging by the irritated expression that crossed his face, he couldn't refute that. Instead, the infuriating man attacked her livelihood. He motioned toward her sole customer.

"Are you poisoning poor Miss Merewether with your blasted spiel over these perfumes?

She's a good, proper young woman. Unlike *some* I know."

Felicia leaned closer to him. He'd stepped closer as he loosed his tirade, so close that her breasts came dangerously close to brushing his coat when she gave him a look at her cleavage. As expected, his gaze dropped. Was he thinking of their kiss? Wondering what madness had consumed him to do it, perhaps? Well, she'd known exactly what had consumed her, and it was nothing more than chemistry. It wouldn't happen again, at least not on her part.

From the color rising in his cheeks, he was much less secure in that knowledge than she was.

"I've never pretended to be proper," she said, lowering her voice to a husky murmur. After all, proper was what had been expected of her when she was seventeen. Proper was constricting and boring. She'd rather be eccentric, be labeled a hoyden even, so long as it meant that she could be herself.

He clenched his jaw. "No, you haven't."

She swatted him on the arm. At the brief touch, he stepped away, his cheeks turning even pinker. "Why are you attacking my perfumes? You, of all people, know their effect."

He didn't quite meet her gaze as he muttered, "That I do. I doubt she would be happy to find an unwanted man in her bed. Leave the poor woman alone."

Because he'd ordered such a thing, she did the opposite. She turned to Miss Merewether with a sunny smile. "What will it be, miss? It might be just the push you need."

Gideon ran his hand through his hair again. "Just the push you need to hurl your sanity off a cliff."

Felicia doubted that his words were loud enough to meet the young woman's ears. She had to strain hers in order to hear them.

Miss Merewether bought the perfume. Her gaze lingered on Gideon for a long moment, as if she hoped for his forgiveness or sought his condemnation. He gave neither, his expression impassive.

The moment Felicia slid the coins into the reticule on her wrist, Gideon clutched her by the elbow. He towed her a pace or two away from her table. She didn't have any other customers, so she let him guide her away for the time being. Chubs rose onto all four feet. From the way he danced, he didn't understand why his new friend who had so recently rubbed his belly was now manhandling Felicia.

Gideon dropped his hold the moment they stepped closer to the wagon wall. "There. You've sold your perfume. Now, will you return home?"

"Why?" She leaned forward, fluttering her eyelashes. "Are you that anxious to find yourself in my company again?"

He fumbled with the knot of his cravat as he took a healthy step back. "Hardly."

"Then do you propose we start work the very afternoon we arrive?"

"No..." He drew out the word, as if wondering if it was truly the answer he wished to give.

"In that case, I'll return to the abbey in an hour or two, once I've peddled what I can."

He ground the heel of his palms against his eyes. "The materials you requested have been delivered."

"Excellent!" She grinned. She hadn't expected the duke to be able to secure them so fast, let alone transport them to Tenwick Abbey. The Crown must be desperate for this truth serum, after all. "Don't touch the bottles. It would be too easy for you to mix them up, with disastrous results. I'll unpack them once I return to the abbey."

He opened his mouth, most likely to argue, but she cut in.

"Where will we be working?"

"In the orangery, of course. It is where I keep all of my tools."

"Wonderful. I'll unpack my supplies in the orangery, then. Please ensure there is a workbench free for my supplies."

A tick started in his jaw. He rubbed at it. Under his breath, he grumbled, "I don't know why you refuse to stop this madness. No one will take you seriously as a scientist if you sell perfumes that purportedly make people fall in love." He refused to meet her gaze.

She crossed her arms again. "Not purportedly. They work, as you've discovered yourself. I provide a public service."

He snorted.

"Well," she amended, lowering her voice. "They make people fall in lust more so than love, but it often amounts to the same thing."

"Which is?" He mirrored her stance.

"Marriage, of course."

Shaking his head, he informed, "Trust me, the very last thing I contemplated was the notion of stepping into the parson's mouse trap. In fact, I was trying to avoid it."

"Of course you were." She dropped her hands to her hips. "*You* were the one wearing the perfume, not the one impacted by it. I assure you, those young debutantes who tried to get your attention were certainly thinking of you as a matrimonial match."

His green eyes glinted with amusement. A sly smile turned up one corner of his mouth. "Is that so?" He leaned closer. "And were you thinking of marriage, Miss Albright?"

Was he trying to tease her? Two could play that game, and she was much more experienced at it. She leaned forward, batting her eyelashes at him. "Why, Lord Gideon, are you wishing that I had?"

When she brushed her hand over his sleeve, he jerked away and stumbled back. He looked as white as a sheet. "No. Of course not. I only meant—"

Given the baffled look on his face, he didn't know what he meant. She took pity on him. "Go home, my lord. I won't be long."

As she turned away, noticing that Miss Merewether had lingered by the table with her purchase clutched in her hand, Gideon captured her arm. He turned Felicia to face him once more. The intensity in his eyes belied his stony expression.

"Don't you give a whit about people taking you seriously as a scientist?"

Felicia laughed. Gideon's long fingers raised goose bumps beneath the sleeves of her dress as he released her with aching slowness. She wiped at her eyes, shaking her head as she battled her mirth. With her situation, if she didn't laugh, she would cry.

"I'm a woman, Gideon. No one takes me seriously as a scientist no matter what I do."

He withdrew, his face hard. "They should. For all that you're a crackpot, you are a brilliant one."

Turning on his heel, he strode away from the village. Felicia gaped after him. What did he mean by that? Could he...respect her?

No. It was ludicrous. Felicia had met with fellow scientists before, even ones less stubborn and arrogant than Gideon Graylocke. They humored her, but they left no doubt that they didn't consider her to have an original thought in her head. If she tried to prove her knowledge, she was well-read or repeating the research of her father. Men didn't believe she was as capable as them.

Gideon had to be the same. If not... If he admired and respected her mind she couldn't consider the notion of actually coming to *like* him. Or a future in which she craved his kiss for reasons other than the effects brought on by the perfume. She was so much older than him, in both age and experience. Not to mention, she'd relinquished her right to claim that life when she'd run away from her arranged marriage.

No, Gideon Graylocke was like all other men. And her reaction to him was purely chemical. For her own sanity, it had to be so.

Chapter Ten

Giddy stormed away from the garish painted wagon and its infuriating owner. He balled his fists as he strode away, battling the urge to look back. If she didn't want to make an effort to earn the respect of the scientific community... he stopped in the shadow of the Golden Goose and rubbed his forehead.

Therein lay the rub. She *was* respected in the scientific community... as F. Albright, presumed male. If it was widely known that she was female, her prestige would likely plummet. She was right, blast it all, and he couldn't stomach the thought. She should at least attempt to cultivate the same respect as a woman as she would be offered were she a man.

Footsteps thwacked against the packed dirt road behind him. Giddy stiffened his shoulders, refusing to turn to see whether Felicia had chased after him. The footsteps mounted, drilling into his clenched teeth and giving him a headache. He marched down the road leading to his family's ancestral estate.

Someone a good deal taller than Felicia thumped Giddy on the shoulder and slowed to match his pace. Gideon glanced sideways into the knowing grin of his best friend, Edgar Catterson III.

Catt, his blue eyes dancing as he fixed Giddy with his best in-the-cream smile, teased, "Lover's quarrel?"

Blast. He'd seen the entire damn exchange with Felicia. Giddy had hoped to evade notice. He should have known better than to think he could keep something from Catt. Even if he hadn't mentioned Felicia or the friction between them, Catt would have learned from Rocky—Joy Rockwood, Gideon's other best friend, and the woman who happened to be employed by the Graylocke family as their gardener. Catt, Rocky, and Gideon all shared a passion for plants. In the case of Rocky and Catt, gossip was also on the list of favorite hobbies, at least insofar as it came to outdoing one another. They loved to lord secret knowledge over one another.

"Felicia is not my lover."

Catt waggled his pale eyebrows, a shade lighter than his strawberry blond hair. After the sunny summer and the time he'd spent outdoors, his hair was more blond than strawberry at the moment. "Oh? You call her Felicia, do you?"

Gideon could practically see the spittle foaming in the corner of his mouth as he thought about relaying the information to Rocky. Or rather, taunting Rocky until she squeezed the gossip from him.

Gideon waved a hand behind him to indicate the wagon. It was too far away to read the banner without squinting, though Felicia's form was easy to spot as she strutted along the length of her stall. He turned his face away from the spectacle.

"I know you can read."

"And I know you can lie better than that."

Giddy wrinkled his nose. He quickened his step, hoping to outpace the shorter man. Unfortunately, although Gideon did have a longer stride, his friend was only a few inches shorter than him and matched him easily.

Catt persisted. "This looked like more than a conflict between a vendor and a customer."

"Why do you say that?" Giddy asked, keeping his voice carefully blasé.

Cutting in front of him, Catt forced Gideon to make an abrupt stop or else bowl him over. When Giddy tried to step around his friend, Catt moved to block him. Gideon didn't like the glint in the other botanist's eyes.

"You have no reason to concern yourself with someone who sets up shop on the edge of Locksley."

With a shrug, Giddy countered, "My family owns Tenwick Abbey and the surrounding area. We own most of the village. I'd say it's very much my business."

Catt raised his eyebrows. As pale as they were, they stood out against his milk-white skin. For all the time he spent outdoors, the sun refused to bronze him.

"That would make it your brother's business."

"My brother is not at home. I am currently the man of the house."

Catt snorted. "Please. Your sister is more man than you when it comes to village affairs."

"Shall I tell her you said so?"

His friend's smile slipped. "Please don't."

For all that she was six years younger than him, Catt was intimidated by Lucy. She had that effect on many people who eventually came to call her a friend. Although she knew to act demure in public, outside of the soirees and balls of the Season, she chose not to. If someone had valuable knowledge she needed to complete her ever-growing book, nothing could stand in the way of her learning it. At the moment, he thought it was about a princess-turned-swashbuckling-pirate who invented her own guns and had a parrot sidekick, but he couldn't be sure. Now that she'd met Felicia, there would probably be a bloody love perfume involved, too.

Since Catt was the closest of friends, Giddy resorted to blackmail. "I won't tell Lucy what you said provided you cease to comment about what you think you observed between me and the lady."

Catt's chin firmed. He nodded. "Agreed."

They continued to walk. The air between them lifted from strained to companionable as they meandered down the lane. Catt, who let a room in Locksley village, visited Tenwick Abbey on a daily basis when the family was in residence. They both knew the path by rote.

The wind picked up. It rattled the naked branches of the trees on either side of the road and chased a chill down Gideon's neck. He pulled his greatcoat closer to his body.

No more than two minutes passed before Catt said conversationally, "So you do know her last name..."

"Catt," Gideon said, lacing the word with warning.

His friend flashed him a cheery smile. "Your deal was not to speak of the incident which never occurred, not to avoid speaking of her. Are you planning on telling me who she is?"

Gideon took a deep breath, then another. He raised his gaze to the frothy gray sky. When he answered, only two short words emerged. "F. Albright."

He walked ten paces before he realized that Catt was no longer beside him. When Gideon turned, he found his friend standing between two wagon ruts, his jaw slack.

"F. Albright, the fellow who's been nettling you all year about our orchid research?"

"The same." Gideon sighed.

"Wasn't that the chem—*oh*." His ginger hair flopped into his eyes as he glanced over his shoulder, back the way they'd come. Thankfully, they'd walked far enough that the edge of the village—and therefore the wagon—was no longer visible. "What was she selling?"

"Perfumes," Gideon said, his voice flat. He shooed his friend into motion once more.

Although he said nothing more on the subject, Catt nodded. They walked another minute or two in silence. The back of Giddy's throat burned.

"*Love* perfumes," he clarified to the empty air.

Catt made a strangled sound. Either he was trying not to laugh or he was choking on his own tongue. His lean shoulders shook. "You're jesting."

"I wish." If word got out that he was working with a chemist who specialized in love perfumes...

He rubbed at his throbbing forehead. Word wouldn't get out. They were working together for the Crown, after all, in a secret capacity.

"She's a crackpot!"

Giddy couldn't disagree with that.

"So that's what your row was about, her presence in Locksley?"

If only. Gideon sighed. He ran his hand through his hair. "No, her presence is to be expected. She'll be staying at Tenwick Abbey for the foreseeable future."

Catt's eyebrows soared. Although the interest was written plain on his face, he didn't speak another word. Unfortunately, Giddy knew his friend better than to think he would remain in that state for the duration of the walk.

His throat closed as he was about to reveal the real reason she was in the country. He couldn't. He hadn't seen his closest friend in six months, and everything in his life had changed. After all, six months ago, Giddy hadn't been a British spy.

In London, compartmentalizing his secret life was easy. His missions never occurred in his house, so he simply informed his family that he was going to the club, and removed himself from their speculative gazes. Even better when Morgan or Tristan left with him, because it cut short their suspicions that he was meeting with a lover. He'd dodged one too many of Mother's disapproving glances over the summer. In her eyes, he was probably following in the debauched footsteps of his brothers. The assumption, at the very least, kept her from directly asking him where he was at night. He tried to make up for his absence by being the devoted son and irritating brother while he was at home, as if nothing had changed.

Now, his two worlds were entangling in ways he hadn't expected. He was returning to the work he craved, the work he knew best, but it came at a cost—namely that he had to work with his rival. Even worse, he had to do it inside his own home. That meant exposing his family to the mission while simultaneously trying to keep his true purpose a secret.

Why had he thought this would be easy?

Knowing that his best friend would be able to call him on a lie, he said, "We're working together on a project." That was true.

Catt's mouth dropped open. "She asked you for help?"

Not exactly. Gideon grimaced. He swiped his palm over his chin, feeling the rough stubble that had accumulated during his travels. "You might say that I asked her."

In a roundabout way. Morgan had brought Felicia into the spy ring chiefly to help Giddy with this project, after all.

His lanky friend stopped short. Giddy glanced at the white steeple soaring above the tree line. So close, and yet so far.

"*You* asked *her* for help?"

Gideon walked away. If Catt needed clarification on the conversation, he wasn't listening. After less than ten steps, he heard the rapid thumps of Catt's footfalls as his friend jogged to catch up.

"Why would you do such a thing? You hate her. You fret yourself to shreds every time she calls you out in the *Royal Botanical Gazette*."

He had—but that had been before they'd met. Surely now that they were working together, she wouldn't disparage his work. He'd prove to her that he knew best when it came to botany.

"Please tell me you aren't going to take her advice regarding the orchid."

Catt had a right to be concerned. He and Giddy had been working on attempting to transplant a foreign orchid into British soil. The breadth of the botanical community was attempting to do the very same thing, to take advantage of the flower's natural beauty and monetary value if it could be grown in a hothouse. However, it had been well over a year since the plant had been discovered in the jungle of South America, and no one had been able to coax it to bloom. When Gideon had published an essay on their work with the plant thus far, he had been publicly torn to shreds by Felicia as she tried to correct his research.

That would be a blow to the ego, had he made a mistake. But he hadn't. Her hypothesis about the acidity of the soil affecting the grafting process was as nonsensical as her insistence about being able to create a truth serum. At the very least, he would soon discover the truth of that second point.

"We're working on a new joint project. She isn't touching our orchid."

That seemed to mollify his friend somewhat, at least until Catt narrowed his eyes. "You met her in London?"

"I did." Giddy drew out the words, wondering what his friend found significant about this fact.

"How long did you know her before you invited her help?"

He released a gusty breath. "Not long." After all, Morgan had asked Felicia for her help before Giddy had even met her.

"I knew it."

He probably didn't want to know what had Catt sounding so smug. He quickened his step, trying to outpace the forbidding feeling creeping up his spine. Catt lengthened his stride, matching him.

"You didn't realize she was a woman," his friend crowed.

Giddy glared at him. "Neither did you."

"Maybe, but I don't seem to find her as beguiling as you do."

Lud, please tell him the conversation wasn't about to veer in *that* direction. He measured the length of the road with his gaze, trying to gage the distance to the church and the shortcut through the woods behind it. Not close enough.

As if his hint wasn't enough comment, Catt added, "You invited her to work with you because you find her attractive. Admit it."

"I will never admit that."

It had been beyond his control, after all.

His reaction to her, when she'd been wearing the gauzy chemise that covered little and hid less, was an entirely different story. The vision of her scantily-clad body haunted him along with the memory of her kiss. She was no wilting flower to pretend at demure behavior. If she wanted something, the devil take anyone who stood in her way.

That fact would have been enough to console him—*if* she'd been the one to initiate the kiss. Apparently her blasted perfume was supposed to entice her to kiss him, unless she was somehow immune. But no, he'd been the one to lose his inhibitions.

The same way he'd lost himself in one simple, earth-shaking kiss.

Catt wore a devilish smirk. "You're blushing. I'm right, aren't I? You only asked to work with her because she's a beautiful woman."

"That is not why I am working with her. She's a brilliant chemist."

Catt laughed. "And you're a botanist. What use do you have for a chemist in your research?"

Rubbing the back of his neck, Giddy muttered, "More than I'd care to admit."

"Of course."

Gideon could have lived without his friend's sarcasm. They strode along in silence for nearly a full minute.

"It has nothing to do with the way she looks in a dress."

It would be wrong to darken his friend's daylights. Giddy jammed his fists into the pockets of his greatcoat.

"She is here because of her mind, not because of her body."

There. That ought to put the subject to rest.

It did not. Catt nudged him with an elbow. "Ah, but finding yourself in the company of such beauty doesn't hurt, does it?"

Giddy rubbed at his tight, aching forehead. "Actually, it does," he muttered under his breath.

"Aha! I knew you were drawn to her."

"I am not drawn to her." Although Gideon forced out the words, the lie burned his throat. It likely imprinted itself on his cheeks, too.

"No?" Catt's smile infused his sly voice with warmth. "Then why did I witness quite so much touching during your... exchange a few minutes ago?"

The cold wind slapped against Giddy's burning cheeks, but it did little to squelch the heat in his face. "If you recall, she touched me. I made no move to reciprocate."

His friend laughed, the rascal. Giddy pulled the collar of his greatcoat closer to his neck to hide the growing flush of his skin. *Mark my words, when you're next beguiled by a woman...*

No. Gideon was *not* beguiled by Miss Felicia Albright. She was a partner for this one assignment, nothing more. Once they ruled the mission impossible, she would be on her merry way.

Unfortunately, that could take months before Strickland was satisfied with the lack of results.

Under his breath, Giddy added, "If anything, that indicates her interest in me, not the other way around."

He clamped his lips shut before he confessed to kissing her. He still couldn't believe that he'd succumbed to temptation—let alone admit to how tempted he still was at the thought.

Catt lifted his shoulder in a half-shrug. "You're the son of a duke. Of course she's interested in you. Aren't all young women?"

No. At least, not while Giddy's brothers had still been eligible for marriage. Now that he was the only unmarried Graylocke brother on solid land, he had to contend with much more interest from the matrons with marriageable daughters. And, often as not, the matrons themselves, for a different reason. It was one reason why he'd been glad to hide behind his spy work and not have to field off the advances of women who, six months ago, hadn't remembered his existence.

"This is strictly business," he told Catt. "I'll thank you to drop the subject."

Judging by his friend's slim smile, he would do nothing of the sort. For the moment, however, Giddy managed to earn himself a hope of peace as the church loomed on the left-hand side of the road. He and Catt crossed to the trail behind the edifice and returned to Tenwick Abbey inside ten minutes.

His stomach shrank with every step. It wouldn't be long before Felicia returned and they set about their task. How was he supposed to work with her when her demeanor defied professionalism?

He would have to find a way. By this point, it was far too late to back down.

Chapter Eleven

Felicia sold three other perfumes that afternoon. With each, the tight feeling in her chest lightened. *Take that, Gideon.*

By the time an hour had passed, Chubs was dancing on his feet, whining. The wind whipped stray strands of her hair, chilling her to the bone. She peeked from beneath her awning at the sky, churning with clouds. A storm was on its way, and if she didn't care to be caught in it, she had best pack up and return to the safe, solid walls of the abbey.

With her lips pressed tightly together, she set about the task. She fed Rudolph another carrot to keep him from growing agitated as she boxed her perfumes and cradled them in the tablecloth to keep them from rattling and breaking. After putting away her awning and table, she whistled Chubs into the wagon and leaped onto the driver's seat.

Rudolph didn't need encouragement to remove himself from the spot. Not only had he chomped the brittle grasses around him to a nub, but the only thing he hated worse than going hungry was enduring a storm. He hauled the wagon with vigor. The road, a bit soft in places, was as a whole tightly packed half-frozen dirt. She held her breath every time Rudolph strained at the harness, but the wheels never remained stuck for more than a moment.

By the time Tenwick Abbey came into view, her lips were chapped from cold and her eyes streamed tears from the wind. She squinted, hunching her shoulders to keep herself warm. Her numb fingers fumbled with the reins as she directed Rudolph around the arcing circle to the place where her wagon had been parked when she'd arrived. The moment she hauled Rudolph to a stop, she crumbled to her mastiff's whining and opened the door for him to join her. Antsy, he loped in a circle around the wagon, barked next to Rudolph's ear and nearly earned himself a kick in return, and tangled himself in her skirts. Felicia splayed her palm against the cold wood of her wagon to steady herself as Chubs ran another few laps around the wagon.

His help in herding Rudolph to the stables was not appreciated. When they reached the door and he risked scaring the other horses, she raised her voice and commanded him to sit. He flopped to the ground in dejection, his ears pressed tight to his skull and his eyes large and pitiful.

After she handed her mule into his assigned stall, brushed him and ensured he had enough food and water—to the objections of the hostlers, who assured her they would look after him—she smiled and waved and returned outside. The bite of the wind cut through her dress. Chubs, with his thick fur coat, didn't appear to be affected. He whined and slithered on his belly to her feet. With a sigh, she crouched to scratch him.

"You aren't in trouble. I know I've been away for some time. Come on, you have to return to the wagon now." She very much doubted that a ducal family like the Graylockes would welcome an eleven-stone mastiff into their home.

When they reached the wagon door and Chubs realized that she wasn't about to enter with him, he cried and raised his paw to get her attention. Her chest ached at the thought of leaving him out in the storm. He cowered from thunder and lightning. Perhaps the Graylockes wouldn't mind if she cried off tonight and spent the night with him out in the wagon.

"Felicia!"

The wind nearly whipped away the hollered words. Pinning her hair away from her face with one hand, she turned to the abbey to spy the caller. Lucy and Charlie huddled in the partially-open doorway to the massive stone edifice. Both women had changed from their travel clothes into more colorful dresses. Lucy beckoned Felicia closer with broad sweeping motions of her arm.

Felicia eyed her dog. He tilted his head, his ears flopping to one side with the motion. "Guard," she commanded.

He melded his rump to the ground and straightened regally. From the resentful way he met her gaze, he wasn't happy with the command.

I'll be back in just a second, she promised silently. Picking up a fistful of her skirt in each hand, she jogged across the drive to the wide stone steps leading to the double doors.

Lucy looked past her, a small frown on her face as she viewed the wagon. "Aren't you going to bring Chubs inside? The weather doesn't bode well."

Can I? Felicia glanced over her shoulder. Chubs was out of guard position, scratching his ear with a hind leg. She didn't want to leave him out of doors.

Hesitantly, she said, "I didn't want to intrude. He is large and not used to spending time in a kennel with other dogs."

"What kennel?" Lucy asked with a shrug. "Bring him inside. So long as he knows to do his business outside, it will be fine."

"He does," Felicia assured. It was one of the first things she ensured that he knew how to do, given that they shared very small quarters and she didn't care for the smell or mess.

"Then bring him in."

Pursing her lips, she glanced in her dog's direction again. He sat upright again, but not directly in front of the wagon. He tested the limits of her command. She battled the urge to shake her head. Two days away from him, and he'd already learned bad habits. Not that she was the strictest taskmistress. In fact, she'd never spent a night away from him before. They shared the wagon, or the tight accommodations she chose for the winter.

"Only during the storm," she acceded. She couldn't see him left out, afraid, not even in the safety of the wagon. "The moment it passes, he'll have to guard the wagon again."

"Why?" Charlie asked, her eyes wide. "No one will touch it."

With a nod, Lucy added, "Our family estate is secure and our servants are trustworthy. Your wagon will be fine."

The moment Felicia lifted her fingers to her lips to whistle, Chubs charged across the circular drive toward them. He slowed as he reached the steps, tail wagging. Felicia started to lift her knee, afraid he would jump, but he remembered his manners. He vigorously sniffed the ladies' skirts instead. Cooing, they leaned down to scratch his ears.

Smiling to herself, Felicia shook her head.

The moment she stepped into Tenwick Abbey, her smile slipped. It was like walking into a palace. The main antechamber was bigger than most London townhouses. Marble floors glistened in the light streaming through narrow cathedral windows set high in the stone wall. On the left side of the chamber, a balcony with a mahogany railing overlooked the vaulting chamber. Her footsteps echoed off the floor as she entered.

You don't belong here. Her stomach shrank to the size of a pea. Once upon a time, she was a humble scholar's daughter and had lived in a house perhaps half the size of this one room. Now she lived out of a wagon a fraction of the size. This room—this house—was a place for princes.

Or dukes.

Lucy didn't appear to notice the grandeur, or Felicia's reaction to it. She grinned as she passed, Chubs trotting at her heels as they traversed the length. Felicia took slow, plodding steps.

When a hand ghosted over her elbow, she jumped. Charlie gave her a kind smile. "It's a sight to behold, isn't it? You'll get used to it before long."

That, Felicia doubted she ever would. She was a pauper in a palace.

As they reached the end of the antechamber, where Lucy lingered in the doorway to what appeared to be a corridor, Felicia forced a smile. "It looks easy to get lost in here. Is there a room laid aside for me?" She prayed it was close to the servants, someone closer to her ilk.

"Of course. We put you in the guest wing next to Charlie and Mrs. Vale." Stepping into the opulent corridor, she crossed the scarlet runner and purloined one of several tallow candles on a low table. Aside from the unlit candles, the table also held a delicate-looking vase patterned in gold paint that shimmered in the light of a single lit candle. After Lucy lit the candle, she jammed it in a narrow candlestick holder and offered it to Felicia.

"You'll want to carry a candle. We don't light the breadth of the abbey unless guests are in attendance."

Felicia would hope not. Lighting a single room would cost a fortune. She accepted the candlestick and clucked her tongue to Chubs. "Heel." Aside from the vase, fragile decorations lined the corridor in both directions. Statuettes, busts, gilt-framed mirrors and priceless paintings on the walls. If her boisterous dog knocked one of them down, she couldn't hope to be able to repay the cost. Better he stick close.

He obeyed her without question as Lucy led the way. "I'll give you a proper tour after I show you to your room," she said over her shoulder. As she went, she pointed out several parlors used for different occasions, an informal dining room, and the corridor toward a ballroom and what she deemed the ancestor's hall beyond. Felicia was grateful to reach the wide marble staircase and followed mutely to the second level.

At the top, Lucy turned right. Over her shoulder, she said, "The guest wing begins here and lasts until the far staircase at the end of the wing. During our annual house party in the spring, we situated the women on this side of the hall." She turned to indicate the left side with an idle wave of her hand. "The men are assigned rooms over there. Your room is next to Charlie's."

Three doors down the opulent hall, Lucy opened a closed door and glided inside. Hesitantly, Felicia followed. She stopped short in the threshold of a room bigger than her wagon. The bed alone could have devoured half the space she usually lived in. The spacious bed, the main fixture in the room, sported four intricately carved wooden posters and gauzy blue drapes. The drapes on the windows, of a heavier quality, matched the color, as did the plush rug at the foot of the bed. A wide wardrobe, vanity, and writing desk crowded the edges of the room, along with a patterned dressing screen separating one corner of the room from the rest.

Felicia could comfortably live in such a space. More than comfortably, in fact—it was fit for a princess. She was uncomfortably aware of every spec of dirt and dog hair on her dress.

"Are you certain this is meant for me? Perhaps a smaller room out of the way..."

If Lucy noticed Felicia's unease, she didn't address it. Instead, she airily waved her hand as she sat on the foot of the bed. "Nonsense. This is where we always put our guests."

Maybe, but her usual guests hailed from a different world than Felicia. They were accustomed to such luxury and demanded it as their due. If Felicia stayed here throughout the winter, she would feel as though she relived a fairy tale. A tight knot formed next to her sternum at the thought of returning to a life of poverty after growing accustomed to the grandeur of the Graylocke household.

She rubbed at that knot to loosen it. She didn't need luxury. She'd survived on her own for the last thirteen years—she would do it for the next thirteen, too.

Unconcerned, Lucy offered her hand to Chubs. He gave it a thorough lick.

Lightly, Charlie touched Felicia's shoulder. "If it makes you feel better, your room is smaller than mine. Mine has a marble fireplace *and* a dressing room."

Surprisingly, the young woman's sympathy did make Felicia feel better. Something in the set of her mouth led Felicia to believe that Charlie hadn't lived in such splendor all her life, either. She might know exactly how Felicia felt.

Like an imposter.

As she took a deep breath, she reminded herself that she'd never once led the Duke of Tenwick to believe that she needed to be treated like a queen throughout her stay. She was perfectly happy to have a roof over her head and be paid for her services. That was exactly what her stay was about.

The sky growled outside. Felicia pursed her lips. "I'd better fetch my trunk before the storm begins." She didn't relish the thought of dripping mud into this pristine home.

Lucy rose again. "Let's find one of the footmen. He'll do it for you."

Let a stranger into her wagon? No, thank you. "It's no trouble. I'll have it up in the twitch of a cat's whisker."

Snapping her fingers to call Chubs, she turned on her heel and hurried back through the house. Her mastiff bounded after her. She let him precede her down the stairs so she didn't go tumbling head over heels.

From the echo of footsteps, Lucy and Charlie followed her. Felicia pretended not to notice. If she hurried, she could reach her wagon and fetch her trunk before they had time to summon a footman. Along the hall she went, slowing her steps and keeping Chubs nearby so he didn't disturb the artwork. In the antechamber, she let him run free again, hurrying to follow.

The moment she opened the door, the wind whipped it from her grasp and it thunked heavily against the wall. She winced. Strands of her hair whipped back and forth across her vision. Chubs barked and whined. He backed up behind her skirts. "Stay here," she told him, not wanting to force him to brave the storm. Grabbing her skirts, she stepped out into the wind.

Scattered icy drops of rain pelted her as she bolted for her wagon. For all his fear, her mastiff accompanied her, his eyes rolling as he responded to the growl of the sky. She opened her wagon and dragged her lone chest out from beneath her cot. The cot sagged without its sturdy support, but as she wouldn't be sleeping on it, it didn't matter.

When she reached the door again, Chubs was dancing in place. He let out a plaintive whine. Huffing with effort, Felicia pulled the trunk down the steps and onto the ground. She locked the wagon door. That should prove enough of a deterrent against thieves until the weather cleared.

Her arms trembling with the effort, Felicia tried to heft the trunk herself. Although it was small, her muscles were no better than water in the face of its weight. She would have to drag it. Letting the trunk fall back to the ground, she straightened and gulped for air.

"Allow me, Miss." A trim footman in blue-and-silver livery with the ducal crest—a stag rampant—leaned down and easily hefted her trunk.

She gritted her teeth. *Braggart.*

With the four-foot-long trunk easily balanced in his arms, the footman peered over the top. "If you'll direct me to the rest of your luggage, I'll get that as well."

"I have no other luggage."

The footman didn't bat an eyelash. "Very well, Miss." He turned on his heel and sidestepped the two young ladies who had followed him out into the growing storm.

Lucy gaped. "That's all you have?"

Heat climbed up Felicia's neck. Without looking the young woman in the eye, she said, "It's all I need. Perhaps we should return indoors?"

"Oh. Of course."

Chubs sprinted for the safety of the abbey, arriving first in front of the now-closed doors. Felicia, second to arrive, opened them. She held the door open as the two young ladies scurried inside. Rain pelted from the sky in earnest. It slithered down the back of her neck as she chased the women inside. The antechamber rang with the sound of the door slamming.

"Come," Lucy said, twining her arm through Felicia's, "let's warm ourselves."

"I thought you meant to show me a tour," Felicia said.

"I will once we're warm again."

Felicia couldn't argue with that.

Lucy led her and Charlie to a parlor half again the size of Felicia's room. Plain patterned wallpaper interspersed the area between paintings of flowers and other still life. The furniture, primarily upholstered in green, looked plush and inviting. The best feature of the room, around which the furniture was positioned, was a chuckling fireplace. Felicia chose a seat close to the warmth as Lucy rang the bell pull and ordered a tea service. When Chubs tried to climb onto the settee next to her, she snapped her fingers and pointed to the floor. With a pathetic look, he slung his body across her feet and rested his head on his paws. Charlie cooed and knelt beside him to give his head a scratch.

The moment Lucy perched on the settee next to Felicia, she loosed a tide of questions that it must have taken a herculean effort to withhold until now. The tea service arrived as Felicia found herself recounting her afternoon, including her argument with Gideon.

"Oh, pish," Lucy said. She waved her hand so vigorously that tea sloshed over the edge of her cup and into her saucer. "As if Giddy knows anything about industry. Don't you listen to him."

Felicia smiled. "I didn't. I returned ahead of the storm."

After a sip, Lucy offered, "The next time you return to the village to sell your wares, I can accompany you and act as your assistant."

The daughter of a duke, an assistant to a woman who peddled perfumes? Felicia shook her head. She tucked loose strands of her hair behind her ears. "Thank you, but that won't be necessary. I can manage quite well on my own."

"Please?" Lucy's velvet-brown eyes turned as round as Chubs's at his most pathetic. "I'll never know what it's like if I don't try it."

Felicia pursed her lips. "I doubt you'll ever find yourself in a position where you'll need to sell a product in order to survive."

"Of course not, but I ought to know for my book."

No, even after retrospection, that comment made no sense. "I beg your pardon?"

"I write books. Didn't I say that?"

If she had, Felicia had been too consumed with travel and settling in to remember. She offered a slim smile. "You must have. Forgive me. Your characters are peddlers?"

"Well, not these characters. But perhaps I'll have one in my next book." She drummed her fingers on her knee. "In order to write it authentically, I'll need to experience it for myself."

Helpless, Felicia turned her gaze to Charlie in the chair across from her. The young woman shrugged. "It isn't the first thing she's researched."

Lucy added, "I promise not to get in your way."

Gideon would strangle Felicia if she let his sister accompany her on such a demeaning task as selling her perfumes. For that reason alone, Felicia almost said yes. Instead, she hedged, "I don't know when I'll next find the time, since your brother and I will soon be working together."

Lucy brightened. "Then, that's perfect! You can work with Giddy while I sell your perfumes for you. I'll be helping."

Oh, dear. That wouldn't work at all. "Do you know how to drive a wagon?"

"No. You can teach me to do that, as well."

Her forced smile wavered. "Perhaps when the weather is nicer."

Perhaps she would forget.

"Excellent! I'll tell Mother."

Then again, perhaps she wouldn't.

Felicia cleared her throat, desperate for a change of topic. "Is it too soon to ask for that tour? If you're too busy, perhaps you could point me toward the orangery, so I can learn where I'll be working."

Lucy set down her half-finished cup and bounded to her feet. Chubs, sensing an adventure, followed suit. "Nonsense, I'm never too busy to give a proper tour. Follow me!"

Charlie grinned as she got to her feet. "Lucy does know the history of the abbey the best. You won't be disappointed."

It was an enlightening tour that began with the ballroom and the neglected ancestor's room and ended with the library. As Lucy shut the door on the two-story, book-lined room, Felicia's mouth was still agape. How could one person have so many books? She couldn't wait for a free moment to scour them and discover if there were any on chemistry or botany. Given that Gideon was in residence, she was willing to wager there would be more than one volume to catch her fancy.

As Lucy led them around the corner from the library toward a hallway that she claimed led to the orangery, a figure stepped through a door that clearly led outside. A gust of cold wind and a splash of rain preceded the woman's drenched form. She peeled her cloak from her outfit, a blue dress with silver piping and the Tenwick stag on the breast.

A grin enveloped Lucy's face. "Rocky!"

With the friendly greeting, Chubs darted forward to investigate the new arrival. He reared on his hind legs and planted his front paws squarely on the shoulders of the curvy woman no taller than Felicia. He then proceeded to lick her face, including her rain-flecked spectacles. She pressed her lips together to avoid getting his tongue in her mouth.

"Chubs! Get down now." Felicia snapped her fingers to punctuate the command.

Flicking his ears back, the mastiff lowered onto all fours once more. His tail beat the air. Felicia stepped forward to lay a restraining hand between her dog's shoulder blades.

"Please forgive him. He isn't usually this rambunctious."

Chubs, his tongue lolling out the side of his mouth, twisted his head to meet her gaze, the picture of innocence.

The young woman, Rocky, blinked. As she removed her spectacles to clean them on her skirts, her eyes looked smaller. "It's no trouble."

Although she spoke the words in a light, airy tone of voice, Felicia didn't believe them to be genuine. Who looked kindly on a person whose pet jumped on them before being properly introduced? As the woman finished cleaning her spectacles, Chubs bumped her hand with his nose, leaving a wet smear on the lens once more. Rocky angled her body away in order to clean it.

With a broad smile, Lucy stepped forward to command Rocky's attention. "This is Chubs. He belongs to Felicia, Giddy's new business partner."

A frown turned down the corners of the young woman's mouth. "His business partner? He didn't mention having a new business partner."

"No?" Lucy's smile turned sly as she narrowed her eyes. She leaned closer. Although she lowered her voice, it still carried. "Have you spoken to him since he returned from London?"

"Of course." Rocky gestured absently over her shoulder to the wall and door she'd emerged from. "I saw him just now in the orangery."

Felicia's stomach flipped. Gideon was in the orangery? That was where she, Lucy, and Charlie were headed. Maybe if they pointed out the door, Felicia would be able to find her way there tomorrow without trouble.

She couldn't avoid him forever. However, ever since he'd alluded to the fact that he might respect her as a scientist, she hadn't been able to purge thoughts of him from her mind. His respect would negate the battle of wills between them once they got to work, but what would it mean for their kiss?

Nothing. It meant nothing. She'd been influenced by the perfume. By tomorrow, the effects would have dissipated entirely and she would have a clear head around him once more. All she needed was a night's respite.

Lucy lowered her hand to scratch Chubs between the ears. "I'm surprised Giddy didn't mention it to you. Felicia will be staying with us while she and Giddy work on a project together."

Rocky's gaze strayed toward Felicia for a moment before returning to Lucy. In the light spilling from the candle in Charlie's hands, Rocky's eyes were unreadable.

"You mean the way he and Catt work?"

Felicia frowned. What was she talking about?

Lucy leaned closer with a conspiratorial smirk. "Not quite. My brother and Felicia have a different sort of relationship."

Drawing herself up, Felicia added, "That we do. A business relationship. Not at all that of a man and his... cat."

Rocky and Lucy met each other's gazes and burst into laughter. Even Charlie joined in, her laughter light and musical to their raucous guffaws. If Felicia hadn't been at the mercy of the Graylockes' hospitality, she would have turned on her heel and stormed away. She was not a cat. The idea was ludicrous.

"No," Rocky said, wiping her eyes. "I mean Mr. Catterson, or Catt as we call him. He and Giddy are working on blooming an orchid together."

Ah. That bloody orchid. If it was the one Felicia suspected, they would have much better luck if only they listened to her.

Lucy said, "This is Rocky. She's Giddy's other botany-minded friend."

The young woman held out her hand and said, "Joy Rockwood. My friends call me Rocky. I'm the head gardener at the Tenwick estate."

A gardener? Rocky was not only a woman in a position typically filled by a man, but she was also much closer to Felicia's social class than Lucy. Even so, Felicia found it curious that Lucy introduced her first as Gideon's friend. Could Felicia not be the only person in their lives with whom they didn't stand on social class? Felicia didn't know how Lucy could forget the difference between them for a second. To Felicia, it yawned like a chasm.

Better she not try to decipher the Graylockes' minds. Soon enough, she would have finished her task and continued on to the next adventure in the nomadic life she'd chosen. She couldn't afford to get attached to them or her treatment here.

Clasping Rocky's hand, she gave it a firm shake and said, "Felicia Albright. I'm a chemist by trade."

"And you're working with Giddy?" the woman asked, cocking her head. "Has he developed a new interest I'm not aware of?"

"You'd have to ask him. It's his botanical expertise I seek. We're collaborating on a project. Until I know more about whether or not it will work as planned—" *It will.* "—it's best that I keep my lips sealed as to the details."

Fortunately, Rocky seemed to accept the lie easily enough. She dipped her knees and inclined her head in a shallow curtsey. Felicia's throat grew tight at the gesture, even though it seemed to be directed to the group rather than to her personally. *I'm not a lady like Lucy...*

Rocky said, "If you'll forgive me, I have to change out of these clothes. If you're going to see Gideon in the orangery, I recommend using the corridor rather than cutting through the garden. The rain is wicked outside."

She slipped past. The three women continued along the hall, Chubs once again padding at Lucy's heels. The light from the candle reflected off a glass window as Lucy and Charlie pulled ahead. Felicia paused, squinting as the light retreated and her vision adapted for her to overlook the grounds. The gray canopy of clouds, heavy with rain, shielded most of the daylight, making it seem a later hour than it was. Just enough light remained to discern the contours of a long, narrow covered and walled walkway marched from the abbey to a glass-walled hothouse lit by the yellow glow of a lamp. Rain pelted the space between, but Felicia discerned movement in the distant hothouse. A man—Gideon.

She swallowed and stepped away from the window. "Forgive me, but it's been a long day and a long journey. I think I can find the way to the orangery from here." After all, that walkway had to intersect the manor at some point along this corridor.

Ahead, Lucy and Charlie paused. They turned, the light from the candle spilling onto the ruby runner beneath their feet and reflecting on some metallic threads near the edges. Chubs whined, looking between them and Felicia.

"Are you certain?" Lucy asked. "It isn't far now."

"I'll be fine." Felicia forced a smile. "In fact, I hope it wouldn't be too much trouble to cry off from dinner tonight. I don't think I'm feeling quite the thing."

The two younger women exchanged a glance. "Are you ill?" Charlie asked. "You had a voracious appetite at breakfast."

Since the Graylockes had graciously offered to pay for meals during their travels, Felicia hadn't wanted to squander the opportunity. If she gained another stone while she was here, she might not feel the lean winter as much as she usually did.

Then again, given the amount the duke had agreed to pay her, she might not have to worry about a lean winter again for a long time.

"I'm tired, that's all. I didn't sleep well at the inn."

Lucy made a face. "Yes, their mattresses did leave something to be desired."

It hadn't been the mattress that had kept Felicia tossing and turning all night, but the man in the room adjoining hers. She pressed her lips together to keep from sprouting such a confession.

When she rustled her fingers, Chubs lifted his ears. He padded a step or two closer. "Come now, Chubs. Let's return to our room. I'm sure the storm won't last long and you can go back out to the wagon before long."

He cocked his head to the side with one of his pathetic looks, as if he knew what she was saying. When he glanced behind him, the other two women cooed.

"He doesn't want to be left alone, do you boy?" Charlie said. She balanced the candlestick in one hand while she reached out to try to coax him nearer.

Lucy added, "You can keep him inside. The wagon is safe here."

Felicia nodded, reluctant. "If you're sure your mother won't mind."

Lucy waved her hand. "She loves animals. I'm sure she'd be delighted."

Although Felicia was less sure, she hadn't slept without Chubs for years, barring last night. She didn't want to relegate him to the increasingly cold nights while she lounged in luxury.

When she turned, the two women hurried to catch up and direct her back to the guest chambers. Felicia had taken care to memorize the path, but they still had to correct her once. When she reached her door, she thanked them both and slipped inside. Lucy promised to send up a tray and a bowl of chopped meat for Chubs. Felicia couldn't turn away the prospect of food.

Inside, she found a candle burning low on the vanity. Her small trunk had been deposited at the foot of the bed. She unlocked it with a key from her reticule and neatly put away her dresses and underclothes into the wardrobe. Four dresses, two sets of underclothes, and two nightgowns. That was everything she owned. Lucy, no doubt, would be appalled. Even if Felicia longed for a larger wardrobe—which she did not, as hers served her well—she wouldn't have the space to cart around so many clothes.

The sort of people she usually cavorted with didn't mind if she wore the same dress twice in one week.

By the time she finished putting away her belongings, a knock at the door signaled the arrival of the promised tray. Felicia accepted it with thanks, doled out her pet's dish, and ate while sitting at the vanity, next to the sputtering candle. The patter of rain and Chubs' snorts were the only sounds to keep her company. As directed, she left her tray and the dog's bowl outside her door for removal.

The near silence closed in around her as she shut the door once more. Slowly, she undressed and washed using the basin hidden behind the dressing screen. She donned her nightgown. When she snuffed the flame, darkness pressed against her eyes. Evening blanketed the world beyond the abbey. Leaving the drapes wide, she climbed into bed, her eyes adjusting enough to see the contours of the furniture.

The ropes holding the mattress in place were firm. The mattress felt as soft as a cloud. As Felicia sank onto it, she couldn't believe that she was here, being treated like a queen. She curled her bare toes against the smooth bedsheets. Her pillow cradled her neck, lulling her to sleep. Although she shut her eyes, it didn't come.

The abbey was too quiet. She was used to the bustle and vigor of a city or marketplace. Even at night, the stamps and protests of animals filled the silence. Here, she had only her thoughts to keep her company.

Living like a queen was lonely.

Chubs whined somewhere in the vicinity of her feet. When she shifted, he stood and rested his chin on the bed, over her foot.

"Oh, very well. We won't tell." She patted the empty space next to her, big enough to fit two more people.

Chubs jumped up. He curled around and flopped onto the bed in a ball with his bottom in her face.

"Oh, no you don't." She shoved at his rump until he turned around. With a sigh, he curled up with his head on the pillow next to her. She draped her arm across his warm middle and rested her cheek on his shoulder.

She fell asleep to the strong sound of his heartbeat.

Chapter Twelve

Chubs snored. When he was stretched out, he took up half the bed, but that wasn't enough for him. He had to have the center half of the bed. Felicia woke quite early to find that she had no more than a foot of space on the end. With a colossal grunt, Chubs rolled over and braced his passive paws against her side. When he stretched out, he nearly thrust her off the bed.

Felicia tried to adjust her position, but the mastiff was as moveable as a boulder. With a sigh, she slid out of bed.

The storm had passed sometime during the night, leaving an almost deathly quiet on the abbey. The sun hadn't yet separated from the horizon, but the sky was a light gray. The ambient light streamed in through the glass window, outlining the silhouettes of the furniture. A brisk morning chill permeated the air, raising goose bumps over the exposed skin of her neck. She danced from foot to foot on the cold floorboards.

Trying to bare her skin for as small a time as possible, she exchanged her nightgown for a pair of woolen stockings and chemise. She covered it with the first dress she found in the wardrobe. By the time she was finished, Chubs continued to snore. She snapped her fingers.

"Chubs. Do you want to go outside?"

Usually the O-word perked him up immediately. This morning, he was dead to the world. She only intended to go to the orangery for an hour at most. She would return for her dog afterward.

Tenwick Abbey wasn't as silent as it seemed from the guest wing. As she meandered down to the ground floor, she started to encounter servants. They stepped aside, tugging on their forelocks or giving her a brief curtsey. After trying to correct the first two or three, she gave up the effort. Word had spread that she was a guest of the Graylockes. Nothing she said made an impact on the servants, even if she pretended otherwise.

She hurried through the abbey to the corridor where the tour had ended the day before. As she spied the orangery, a still silhouette against the grounds, she paused to test every doorway leading off the corridor. At last, she found the one leading to that long walkway.

Light glimmered along the horizon, filtering through the row of glassed-in arches along the east wall. The western wall and floor consisted of symmetrical marble bricks fitted tightly together. The light reflected off the smooth surfaces, creating a sheen. The sunrise created the illusion of walking along a diamond-crusted walkway. It was beautiful and forbidding all at once. The heels of her slippers clicked as she quickened her step, leaving behind the illusion.

At the end of the corridor was a foggy glass door. It opened easily and she slipped into the hot interior of the orangery. It smelled sweet, the perfume of flowers mixed with a hint of citrus. The thick moisture in the air made her hair start to curl. She brushed it away from her face as she surveyed the interior. The light of the sunrise barely peeked through the foggy glass walls. By the time it reached the ground, it was no more substantial than mist. She should have brought a candle.

Rows of dirt were interspersed by a narrow stone walkway leading to a work bench in the center of the room that was covered with potted plants. At the end of the long, narrow table, Felicia found a lantern. She used a tinderbox sitting next to it to light the wick. When the light flared to life, she lifted the lantern to study the orangery in more detail.

Plants spilled in every direction. Given Gideon's preoccupation with botany, it came as no great surprise. The variety inside the orangery stole her breath. Her knowledge of botany couldn't hope to match his, but her gaze fell on several specimens that must have come from the very edges of the earth, given that she didn't recognize the species. It was one more reminder that the Graylocke family had the money to buy the earth, if they so pleased—or, at the very least, to fund an expedition. What must it be like for Gideon to have everything he needed to pursue his passion at the tips of his fingers?

Pushing away the resentment that surged at the thought, Felicia shut her eyes. She breathed the soothing, floral scent. The trickle of water met her ears, but when she opened her eyes, she couldn't find the source.

On the other side of the work bench, after a row of neat pots that appeared to be newly tended, either with new seedlings or with fresh cuttings, was another long, narrow work bench identical to the first. It had been cleared of everything, but several unopened crates cluttered the foot. Felicia smiled. Gideon had made her a space in his abode, as promised.

Setting the lantern on the bench where she wouldn't accidentally knock it over, she got to work unpacking the chemicals. These were only the ones that had been shipped from London; she had others in her wagon to add to the bunch, not to mention the specimens of the plant they would be using to create the serum. She unpacked the bottles of liquids and powders one by one, mentally crossing off ingredients in her head, and was astounded to find that the Duke of Tenwick had procured every item on her list save for the *brugmansia* plant itself. Even the ingredients she'd added to the bottom, in case the theory she'd long ruminated about proved wrong and she needed to start from scratch. Did Britain have a secret chemistry laboratory she didn't know about? It wouldn't surprise her to learn that they did. She could think of no other way the duke could have filled the entire list of ingredients she'd requested.

Once she lined them up, she retrieved Chubs from her room and strolled with him to the wagon. After he did his morning business and she fed him a snack, she left him to guard the wagon—or in his case, lounge on his back in the dew and early morning sunshine with all four paws in the air—while she carried the rest of the supplies she would need for the project into the orangery.

She trekked across the open ground, cutting through the garden. This late in the year, precious little foliage remained to line the paths. Although the plants were neatly tended and pruned, with the frost over the past week, many plants had died. Others had already entered the dormant stage of their cycles. The gravel crunched beneath her shoes as she carried the crate containing her supplies to the glass-encased orangery.

The heat and humidity in the orangery chased away the autumn chill the moment she stepped inside. Since she entered by means of the glass door on the far wall of the hothouse, the source of the heat and trickling water was immediately apparent. In the wall next to the brick-enclosed walkway, she spotted a contraption that looked a bit like a kiln. A vent attached the kiln to the wall of the orangery, built into the brick side around the door. Once inside, her gaze flew to that portion of the wall to find the vent emitting the hot steam that filled the orangery.

Next to the door leading onto the grass, on the opposite side of the orangery from the vent, was a small man-made pond. The trickle of water was a combination of a small fountain circulating the water and the percolation of the moisture that gathered at the top of the orangery and trickled along a set of half-pipes down the wall. The pipes were intricately set like veins along the wall. When she set down the crate for a moment to dip her fingers into the pond, she found the liquid pleasantly lukewarm. Only aquatic flora populated the pond, no fauna.

Humming under her breath, Felicia carried her box to her workbench. She unloaded it with care, starting with the vials and containers encircling the pot housing one of two *brugmansia* plants she had in her possession. Both were relatively young specimens grown from cuttings. Without a hothouse like this one, her plants had difficulty surviving the winter, even when she tried to keep them indoors. Housing the angel's trumpets in ceramic pots rather than planting them in the ground stunted their growth as well, but she hoped—for the good of the nation—that it hadn't impacted the potency of the plant's side effects. Namely, the tendency to inebriate anyone who consumed it and cause memory loss. In combination with some of the ingredients she'd requested, she hoped the natural side effects could be amplified and directed to more specific purpose.

As she lifted the pot from the crate, a shadow in the garden caught her eye. She lifted her head, blinking in the direct sunlight spilling over the tree line. No one was there. She must have been mistaken. Returning to her task, she inspected and watered the plant. Would it thrive in the orangery? The atmosphere in here was much closer to the plant's natural habitat.

The door to the abbey opened. A figure stopped short. Felicia raised her gaze to meet Gideon's. A tingle swept through her, one she struggled to suppress. So he, like her, tended to rise early rather than lay abed. She shouldn't be surprised. It wasn't the only thing they had in common.

This early in the morning, he presented a tidy appearance. His hair was neatly combed, his shirt buttoned to his chin, and his cravat was on straight. He carried a dove gray jacket. As he beheld her, he lifted his arm, holding the garment between them like a shield.

Felicia smirked. Her amusement faded as she squashed the urge to flirt and make him uncomfortable. She knew she could invoke that sentiment in him, but ever since the revelation yesterday she didn't want to.

She gestured to the pot holding her plant. "This is the *brugmansia* specimen we'll be using for our project. I've distilled some oils from the plant and dried out the leaves, stem, and roots—" She pointed to each container in turn.

Gideon interrupted her. "It's dehydrated."

She scowled. He couldn't possibly know that from across the room.

His posture wasn't accusing, but hesitant as he stepped forward. He laid his jacket on his work bench. "May I?" He didn't take a single step closer. His eyes, shadowed in the mixed ambient light and glow from the lantern she had yet to douse, gave away none of his intentions.

Of the pair of them, he was the botanist. She had to work with him if she was to prove her theory. Inwardly, she sighed. She stepped away from the potted plant. "By all means."

He didn't wait for further invitation. The walkway between the bench and the nearest flora was narrow. Even when she stepped on the very edge of the stone, with the side of her shoe kissing the dirt, he still brushed against her when he slipped past. And again when he carried the plant to his side of the work benches. Her body reacted to his nearness, every one of her senses attuned to him. Could the perfume still be gripping her?

The shrewd air Gideon cultivated during conversation dissipated as he attended to the plant. He seemed lost in his own world as he examined it from the roots—sticking his bare fingers in the soil—to the buds forming at the top of the plant. He pinched off several, tossing them to the ground.

A lump formed in Felicia's throat. She dashed closer. "Hey!" That was her plant, one she'd painstakingly grown hoping it would form those exact buds.

"It isn't healthy," Gideon said, his voice absent. "If it expends energy on those buds, it will die and we'll get nowhere."

She glared at his back and crouched to pick up the discarded buds. "At the very least, you shouldn't throw them away. I can distill them for oil."

He shrugged. "Do what you want with them." He continued to examine, prune, and water the plant.

After she collected all the material he cut away, Felicia separated it into piles to either dry it or insert it into her portable distillery to extract the oils. Her distillery was in her wagon, so for now she carefully preserved the buds in one of her containers for easy transportation. When she moved to exit, Gideon raised his head, proving that he wasn't as deaf to the world as she'd assumed.

"Where are you going?" His voice was sharp.

She fought not to frown. "My distillery is in my wagon. I won't be able to extract the oils without it." Not to mention, she should probably bring the second of her plants into the orangery for him to tend.

"Must it be done immediately?"

It must if you want the other plant. She pressed her lips together. "No, but the more dry the buds become, the less I'll be able to extract."

He waved his hand to indicate the orangery. "This room is kept in constant humidity. Your buds will survive the morning."

"I beg your pardon?" What was he talking about?

He sighed. Running his fingers through his hair, he mussed it. "We don't have the time."

"That plant will survive the hour it will take me to distill these oils. I may be a crackpot, but I've managed to keep it alive this long." She planted her free hand on one hip, raising her eyebrows in silent challenge.

He winced and tugged his cravat out of place. "Forgive me. I shouldn't have allowed my temper to run wild yesterday. You are, of course, entitled to do or sell anything that you want."

That was nothing that she hadn't known already. Was she supposed to express her gratitude over earning his permission to do the very thing she would have done anyway? She pressed her lips together to keep from starting another argument.

He added, "This will be a long and arduous assignment if we don't come to some kind of truce. Can we agree to work together as best we can? Let's not prolong this mission any longer than it needs to be."

He delivered the offer in a terse manner, his jaw clenched. His expression left no doubt that, given the choice, he wouldn't work with her. Drawing herself up, Felicia matched his imperious expression. The sentiment was mutual. After all, why would she subject herself to the condemnation of an arrogant son of a duke if she didn't have to?

Lifting her chin to meet his gaze squarely, she held out her hand. "A truce. For the good of the nation."

His shrewd air returned as he fixed his measuring gaze on her. "Yes… for the nation." He gripped her hand. His long fingers were gritty with dirt, but he didn't seem to notice. His warm palm burned her as he gripped her hand firmly.

She retracted her hand and dropped it to her side.

Stepping back, he gestured toward the door. "Shall we? We won't have much time to eat as it is."

"What do you mean?"

He stared at her blankly. "It's Sunday."

That would make sense, following Saturday.

"Church?" His voice lilted at the end of the word, making it a question. "My mother will insist we attend."

Felicia's cheeks heated as she realized that she hadn't even thought of attending church. She'd been on her own, traveling from town to town for so long that she rarely attended a service anymore. It would be one more reason why her father would condemn her lifestyle.

Although she was out of the habit, she didn't go out of her way to avoid the institution, nor did she see reason to draw attention to her lapse. If the Graylocke family attended church every Sunday morning, she would as well, at least for the duration of her stay.

She nodded and slipped the container she held back onto her work bench. "Of course. Let's go to breakfast."

As she stepped past him, he dropped his hand to the small of her back to steer her through the orangery and out the door. The light, possessive contact burned her. It left an imprint long after he dropped his hand.

She gritted her teeth and tried not to show it.

***

The clergyman, a perfectly affable fellow outside of the church, droned on in a monotone best suited to lull a man to sleep. Giddy pinched the inside of his wrist as he fought back a yawn.

Sunlight glinted off the frost-crusted windows, slowly thawing them as the morning blossomed. A small, portable brazier with glowing coals gave off heat in the corner of the second floor box where Gideon and his family sat. The congregation, including Catt, Rocky, the Locksley villagers and the Tenwick servants, crammed into the pews below. The very front of the pews was reserved for a local squire, a baronet, and the clergyman's family.

Given the way Felicia squirmed beside him on the hard wooden bench, he suspected she would have been more at ease if she had been squashed next to the rest of the congregation. From time to time, a matron or gentleman glanced at the balcony where the Graylockes resided with their guest. Giddy maintained a stony expression, pretending not to notice. As the local landowners of the majority of the area—barring the smaller patches of land that belonged to the baronet, the squire, and the rare gentleman farmer—the Graylocke family was under constant scrutiny. If he reacted to the frequent stares of the villagers, the local gabble grinders would hone in on his weakness and bandy about the lewdest rumors, true or unfounded.

Unfortunately, Felicia didn't seem to realize this. With every less-than-surreptitious glance, she shifted in place. Flashes of alarm and unease, quickly hidden, crossed her face.

Giddy leaned closer, angling his face so her bonnet wouldn't poke him in the eye. She smelled like the orangery, divine. "You might want to shield your discomfort better. I suspect they've noticed."

He didn't have to elaborate as to whom he referred. By now, almost every member of the congregation had turned to peek at them at least once. The only people who didn't care to gape were the Tenwick servants. Given that Felicia now resided at the abbey, they would have plenty of opportunity to espy his intentions over the next couple of weeks.

On his other side, Lucy shifted her position again, widening her skirts and forcing him to slide closer to his rival. Since she, Charlie, and Mother had claimed the rest of the bench, that left only the corner for him and Felicia. The press of her thigh and arm against his was agonizing, all the more so every time she moved.

Frowning, she turned enough for him to glimpse her profile. The bonnet shadowed her eyes, but a frown played at the corner of her mouth. If she fought against showing the expression, she failed.

"I thought they were looking at you."

"They are," he assured. By this point in his life, he was used to it. "But, as you are sitting next to me, it is inevitable that some of their scrutiny is turned towards you."

She stiffened. If anything, the knowledge that they *were*, in fact, measuring her seemed to make her even more uncomfortable. Giddy clenched his jaw, afraid to say something else and make matters worse.

A stir turned away the stares of those beneath them as the clergyman faltered in his sermon. A woman dressed in a mint green dress with matching trim on her bonnet ducked her head as she claimed a seat in the back row. When she turned to look behind her—to look at the Graylocke family—he recognized her instantly.

Miss Merewether. Why was she late to the sermon? She was the most prompt, pious, proper young woman in Locksley. The only time she'd ever acted out of turn in his memory was when she'd purchased that horrid perfume from Felicia yesterday. Surely that perfume hadn't led to the kind of untoward behavior that would cause her to be late to church.

Who was he trying to fool? After only a moment's interaction with the serving maid at the inn, he'd found her half-dressed and in his bed! He imagined that the perfume Felicia had sold to Miss Merewether was every bit potent enough to lead her down the path to perdition. But who was the gentleman? No one entered behind the forgettable young woman and from his vantage, Giddy couldn't adequately judge who was missing from the congregation. He gritted his teeth, hoping that Miss Merewether hadn't thrown her good name away for a moment's temptation. It wasn't any of his business what she chose to do with her body, but he knew firsthand how the perfume befuddled common sense. Even his, as the wearer. He had kissed Felicia while under the influence, after all.

Not that she had made any indication that she hadn't enjoyed it.

Although he tilted his head to glare at the peddler in question, she didn't seem to notice. For the first time since they'd arrived, she held her hands clasped on her lap and her shoulders straight in a serene expression. She must have mastered her emotions for the moment.

If only he felt the same. With the perfume fresh on his thoughts, he couldn't help but recall the feel of Felicia's mouth against his, her curves pressed against his body. It was insanity.

And certainly not the sort of thoughts he should be having while in church. He slid closer to his sister despite her attempts to force him in the other direction.

The moment the sermon ended and the congregation rustled with movement, Gideon jumped to his feet. He strode to the opposite end of the bench to help his mother to stand. He then offered his assistance to the other two women in his family. When he reached Felicia, she had already stood on her own. Mother linked arms with her and drew her toward the staircase, casting an inscrutable gaze over her shoulder at Giddy.

His heart jumped into his throat. Surely she wasn't thinking of matchmaking? Ignoring the sly looks cast his way by Lucy and Charlie, he quickened his step and followed in his mother's wake.

"How did you sleep last night?" Mother asked.

"Splendidly, thank you for asking." If Felicia hadn't glanced over her shoulder at him briefly, he might have believed her. Despite the smile curving her lips, her eyes told a different tale. The slight crinkle in the corners was one of worry or fatigue.

"I'm glad. I was disappointed to learn that you were feeling unwell."

More likely, Mother had been disappointed to learn that she couldn't foist Felicia and Giddy together like Lucy seemed determined to do.

"I'm feeling much better today," Felicia answered.

As they reached the bottom of the steps, the flood of people forced a stop to the conversation. Giddy insinuated himself between Felicia and his mother. Mother moved to the side of the stairwell as she waited for people to pass. She always did, despite the fact that they stopped whenever they saw her and made room for her.

She claimed that remaining behind gave her the opportunity to greet her tenants and neighbors.

So she did, as did Giddy. He shook hands with the local farmers while his mother exchanged a few words with their wives. Miss Merewether lingered near the stairwell, likely trying to remain above the thoughts of those in the congregation by means of letting the Graylocke family take the spotlight away from her. Given that he noticed her dawdling, he doubted she achieved her goal. More than one man tipped his hat toward her.

As the last family drifted through the door, Miss Merewether saw fit to emerge from hiding. Mother greeted her with a warm smile and laid a hand on her arm. "Come, Miss Merewether, walk with us for a moment."

The young woman obliged with a nod. "Thank you, Evelyn."

Had Mother given her leave to address her by her given name? She must have, because she offered no rebuke at the familiarity, despite the fact that she hadn't returned it. Together, the family strolled toward the entrance.

"Have you met Miss Albright?" Mother asked.

Miss Merewether's mouth thinned as she looked toward Felicia, whose smile didn't dim despite the reception. Gideon realized that he'd neglected to offer anyone his arm, but now that they were almost at the threshold of the church, the notion seemed silly. He clasped his hands behind his back instead.

"Indeed I have," the young woman answered. "We met in front of the Golden Goose yesterday."

Mother said, "Miss Albright is working on a project with Gideon. She's staying with us at Tenwick Abbey."

"Oh?" Miss Merewether made a polite sound, but nothing in her manner indicated she was interested. "Are you a botanist as well, Miss Albright?"

"I'm afraid not," Felicia answered with a warm smile. "If I was, I wouldn't need Lord Gideon's help." She didn't look in his direction, for which he was grateful.

They entered the brisk autumn air. A chill raised goose bumps over his neck. He turned up the collar of his coat to keep the cold air at bay. Mother didn't appear to notice the bite in the air, nor Miss Merewether's frosty demeanor. Did she disapprove of Felicia staying at Tenwick Abbey because she sold perfumes and was reaching above her class? Or because she was a woman in a field of study typically dominated by a man? The Miss Merewether with whom Giddy was familiar disapproved of many things she didn't deem quite proper. Until yesterday, he would have added "love perfumes" to that list.

"Why don't you have some tea at the abbey with us?" Mother asked. It wasn't uncommon for her to ask a young lady or two to sit with her and Lucy on a Sunday afternoon.

Miss Merewether accepted with a smile. When she smiled, her prim attitude dissipated and she was actually quite pretty. Not as alluring as Felicia in her low-cut bodices that drew the eye to her figure, her black hair always managing to escape her coif and frame her cheeks. Whereas Felicia dominated a man's thoughts and filled his dreams, Miss Merewether was pretty in an understated, demure sort of way. The sort of pretty many a man looked for in a wife. Not Gideon, but other men of the *ton* who wanted sedate wives. Giddy had never given much sort to the kind of qualities he wanted in a wife, and he suspected if he thought of it now, the only image to spring to mind would be Felicia's.

Better he didn't think of it.

Since Miss Merewether was already on Mother's arm, he couldn't offer to escort her to the house. Gideon knew without asking what his sister or Charlie's answer would be to such a polite gesture. Surrendering to the inevitable, he offered Felicia his arm. "May I escort you to the abbey, Miss Albright?"

Her eyebrows twitched. In combination with the way she pursed her lips, they spoke volumes. *You don't think I'm capable of walking on my own?*

With his gaze, he willed her to understand that his offer was meant to be polite, not demeaning or diminishing. To his surprise, she opted not to start a row with him—at least, not while in polite company. She slid her hand onto his arm.

"Thank you."

The group turned toward the path that meandered through the trees and onto the lawn of the Tenwick estate. Mother asked, "Gideon, will you and Miss Albright be joining us for tea?"

He tried to catch Felicia's gaze, but she stubbornly averted her gaze. He answered for them both, hoping he didn't overstep. "I'm afraid we'll have to decline, Mother. As you know, Miss Albright and I have business to which we must attend. We'll join you for supper, of course."

Although he expected his mother to object to their working on a Sunday, she turned back to

Miss Merewether and struck up a conversation about the weather of late. Mother was congenial and friendly, showing the same amount of interest in Miss Merewether's opinions as she had in Felicia's.

Had he been mistaken? Didn't she want to encourage a romance between him and Felicia, after all? He should be grateful that his mother wasn't trying to play the matchmaker, but he couldn't suppress a twinge of disappointment.

What could Mother possibly hold against Felicia that would make her an unsuitable match for Giddy? It wasn't every day that beauty and brains were married in the same woman, especially not one with an interest and aptitude in science. Felicia was special. If one didn't peer too closely at the way their personalities clashed, she might even be considered an ideal match for him—in theory. The reality was far different.

It doesn't matter if Mother doesn't think her suitable. After all, Giddy wasn't going to marry Felicia. They were business partners, nothing more.

If Mother had discovered the truth of that statement sooner rather than later, all the better.

Chapter Thirteen

The warmth of the orangery was a welcome change from the frigid air outside. The chill still hadn't abated, despite the sun teasing in and out from behind the clouds. When Felicia retrieved the second *brugmansia* specimen from her wagon, she invited Chubs to join them in the hothouse. Once she assured Gideon that her pet wouldn't wander, he allowed the mastiff's presence. Drawn to the heat, the mastiff lay sprawled beneath the vent, along the warm brick wall.

As Felicia set the plant on Gideon's work bench, he tsked under his breath. She gritted her teeth, but didn't call him on his reaction. Instead, she waited as he devoted the same treatment to this specimen as he had to the first. He didn't say a word. Once she'd collected all the buds and other plant matter he pruned away, she called Chubs to her and returned to the wagon to distill oil from the plant. Her portable distiller used coal to heat water into steam, so she left Chubs inside the wagon with the heat while she returned to the orangery.

By the time she stepped inside, Gideon had finished with the second plant. He raised his gaze and she paused inside the threshold of the glass door. His green eyes were penetrating, but unreadable. The tension between them grew palpable. Felicia resisted the urge to cock her hip or bat her eyelashes at him. If he truly saw her as an equal she must treat him that way as well.

Gently, she pulled the door shut and returned to Gideon's side. She hesitated.

"Shall we get to work?" He gestured to his work bench, clear for the moment of any projects. Without gloves to hide them, the muscles in his hands rippled with the movement, drawing her attention to his long fingers.

She forced a smile as she met his gaze once more. "How much of my research on the subject have you read?" She knew, from arguing with him, that he had at least a cursory idea of what she hoped to create from the *brugmansia* plant. Before she went into detail, she wanted to know how much he recalled of her theory.

Running a hand through his hair, he admitted, "All of it. I refreshed my memory last night."

He'd kept the journal containing her hypothesis? That had been published years ago!

Trying to hide her surprise behind a smile, she quipped, "Well, that will make this simpler, then. The distilled oils themselves won't create the exact effect your brother wants."

A tick started in his jaw. Rolling his neck, he muttered, "At last, something we can agree on."

She balled her fists, resisting the urge to smack the smug expression off his face. In a cold tone, she added, "I believe if we combine the oils with ingredients that have the properties we need—much the way laudanum with a strong liquor base lowers inhibitions and increases the effect of sedation—we can essentially create a serum that, when ingested, will yield the desired results."

His expression twisted in distaste. "Surely you aren't suggesting that we combine the oils with laudanum? That could be deadly!"

"No, that isn't what I was saying at all. It was an example."

Her chest warmed with anger. Rather than spouting the words she wanted to say, she turned her back and stomped to her side of the work tables. Retrieving an empty beaker and a vial of the distilled oils, she returned to Gideon's side and laid both on the work bench. He made a grab for the oil and uncorked it.

"Be careful with that—" She recoiled at his glare.

"I'm not a child." He sniffed the oil. Did the fumes have some effect? It wasn't heated and therefore wasn't giving off steam, so she hoped not. "From which part of the plant did you distill the oils?"

"That vial is from the seeds. Given the potency of the seeds of most plants, I deduced that it would yield the highest concentration of the chemical we need."

After jamming the stopper into the vial once more, he thrust it onto the work bench. "And potentially prove toxic!"

She scowled. "It isn't intended to be consumed in its concentrated form. We'll dilute it."

"Very well." He snatched the beaker from the table and stormed to the pond on the far side of the orangery.

As he returned with a cup full of water, Felicia crossed her arms. "With *clean* water. I don't know what compounds your plants have secreted into that water. It might have undesired effects."

A muscle in his jaw ticked as he lowered the beaker to the table with an audible click. "We'll boil it."

"I have a small brazier in my wagon for just such a purpose. Allow me to fetch it."

She didn't wait but vacated the orangery in pursuit of her task. Despite the fact that she should return quickly, she lingered to give Chubs some attention and check on the distilling process. Using tongs, she liberated a hot coal from the distillery to start the brazier. By the time she reached the orangery with it, the others had started to glow. Hopefully it wouldn't take too long for the water to boil. Usually, she refused to rush the process out of the fear of creating an error, but with the hostility infusing the air between her and Gideon, the quicker they worked, the sooner they could part ways.

Felicia attached the stem of the beaker to an iron stand fixed to the brazier. Without looking at Gideon, she stepped back to let the heat of the brazier do its work. Even without turning her head, she felt his gaze on her. The hairs on the back of her neck stood on end. Pressing her lips together, she willed the water to boil.

Unfortunately, a watched beaker never boils. The water stubbornly took its sweet time to heat.

In a gruff voice, Gideon asked, "Did you have an idea of which ingredients you wanted to mix with the oils?"

Here came the tricky part. She hadn't been able to successfully create the serum with her attempts, using herself as a test subject—or, in one lonely case, a willing friend. Although the diluted oils made her woozy, when quizzed she felt no need to confess her sins. In some cases, she didn't even remember what she said come the morning, but those who had helped her test the serum informed that she had not divulged the correct answers when badgered. Meaning that, even while under the influence of the *brugmansia* oils, she still had the presence of mind to hold her tongue if she wanted to. The one time she had convinced a friend to try the serum instead, she had noticed a quick onset of sedation, dilated pupils, and slurring of speech. Unfortunately, the sedation had taken effect too quickly for her to press as hard as she would have liked for the answer to her questions. Once asleep, she hadn't been able to rouse him until morning, when the serum wore off and left him with a horrible headache.

In a polite tone, Felicia explained what she had already tried in an attempt to replicate the serum. "I have everything logged in a journal, if you'd like to read it."

"I would." He didn't look at her, his gaze fixed on the beaker. Small bubbles formed in the bottom, not yet rising to the top.

After a moment of terse silence, she said, "There's a tea from China that purportedly calms hysteria. If we can isolate the compound from the tea, we might be able to use that lowering of inhibitions in the serum to loosen the recipient's tongue."

"That sounds more like your area of expertise." He tucked his hands into his jacket pockets.

The silence stretched on. More bubbles formed, some slowly drifting to the top of the beaker.

"If you're looking for something that lowers anxiety, why not try valerian or passion flower?"

Felicia shook her head. "Both are sedatives, aren't they? I tried valerian once and the mixture rendered my test subject unconscious within minutes. He couldn't stay awake long enough to answer my questions."

The water boiled. Gideon removed his hands from his pockets. "Let's try the tea, then. It's a place to start." Given the dubious quality to his voice, he didn't believe that it would work.

Since the tea was out of her price range for the quantities she needed in order to experiment on it, she didn't know that it would work. It was only a theory.

"There's a bottle on my work table labelled *Wuliqing*. Did you want to try mixing it with the oils and seeing the outcome before I try to isolate the compound I spoke of?"

Gideon shrugged. "We might as well." Since he was closer to her work bench, he retreated to the neatly lined rows of bottles arranged by compound and perused the titles.

Meanwhile, she used tongs to remove the beaker from the heat. She uncorked the bottle with the oil and carefully added several drops into the water. Until they determined the effect of both ingredients, weaker was better. Besides, without the plants flowering again and producing seeds, she would be unable to replicate this particular batch of oils.

As she carefully returned the vial to the row among the others, she slipped past Gideon. When she turned, she found him about to pour out the contents of the bottle into the water. The collection of small grayish lumps in mineral oil was *not* the tea to which she had referred. Her heart jumped into her throat. She flung her hands into the air, though she was too far away to push him.

"Wait! Stop!"

He paused, his hand tilting over the beaker.

"Step back. Now."

He heeded the urgency in her voice and took a healthy step back, out of harm's way. Her pulse beat fervently in the base of her throat.

The moisture in the air. *Lawks.*

"Put the stopper back in the bottle. Don't let it touch the water." Or the air. Oh God, the humidity.

It was a miracle the bottle hadn't exploded. The mineral oil covered the lumps—for now.

"Have you lost your mind?"

"Have you?" Her voice was shrill. "That isn't tea—that's pure sodium! Sodium catches fire when exposed to water!"

He thrust the bottle into the air between them, a little too close to the beaker of hot water, in her opinion. She took it from him, ensuring that no licks of flame contaminated the inside. She couldn't be sure. She should dispose of it, just in case. Or, at the very least, store it somewhere other than the humid orangery.

"How was I supposed to know?"

She glared. "You're a botanist. You should know when something doesn't look organic."

"I thought you had already brewed it and isolated the compound you were talking about. Why do you even have it?"

"In case I need it."

His eyes were wild now, to match his hair. Given the look on his face, he wasn't pleased with the mix up.

Neither was she. She carried the bottle to the door and, for now, set it on the ground outside. With the clear windows, she would be able to see if anyone neared it. And it was cold outside, bitter and far from humid.

She clenched her teeth as she shut the door. "I know you aren't stupid. Does the word 'sodium' look like 'wuliqing' to you?"

He pulled a face. "It was labelled as Wuliqing." To be on the safe side, he spelled the word—correctly.

Felicia opened the door and checked the label on the bottle of sodium. It was wrong.

"Impossible." Her fingers were numb. "I arranged these bottles this morning. They were labelled correctly."

"You must have misread."

When she glared at him, he ran a hand through his hair and amended, "Maybe the humidity caused the label to peel off and fall and when a servant replaced it, they accidentally returned the label to the wrong bottle."

The wax that adhered the label to the bottle was still soft, though that could partially be due to the heat of the orangery. Felicia gritted her teeth. "Maybe someone switched the labels on purpose."

"You're mad."

After carefully peeling off the label and soft wax, she stomped to the row of bottles to return it to its rightful place. The sodium wasn't the only thing mislabeled. "Am I?" She shook her head. "Nothing here is correct." An exaggeration maybe, but it was more than coincidence. She set the label down on the table before she crumpled it in her fist. After several deep breaths, she steadied her hand enough to work on rearranging the labels to their rightful places. She pressed the wax onto the bottle with more vigor than necessary, as if by doing so, she could meld the label onto the glass.

Gideon loomed over her right shoulder, silent. Her skin prickled with awareness from his stare.

When she glanced at him, he spread his hands and said in a calm voice, "You're overreacting. Take a moment to breathe and we'll approach this rationally."

"Rationally?" She set down the bottle in her hand with a clink before she turned to face him fully. She crossed her arms. "Let's review the facts: not one, not two, but *eight* of my ingredients have the wrong label. Earlier this morning, they did not. Because of the mix up, you might have ruined our sample of the serum along with the two plants that we have—" She gestured to the potted plants, lined to one side of Gideon's work bench. "—and you could have burned yourself badly in the process."

He ran his fingers through his hair. "Even assuming that someone would purposefully switch the labels—which is ludicrous—they had no means of knowing that I would choose that precise bottle. Not to mention if you had been the person to choose it, you would have known instantly that it wasn't the right bottle. In terms of sabotage, the culprit would have done better to steal our plant. This was an accident, nothing more."

He was wrong. Felicia knew it in the pit of her stomach. Call it instinct, but no one fiddled around with her projects. Most who glimpsed the bottles had enough sense not to touch what they didn't understand; those who recognized the contents were aware of their hazards.

Stepping closer to him, she canted her chin up to meet his gaze. Beneath the citrus-and-floral scent of the orangery, he smelled of cedar. She lowered her voice.

"What we are doing is vital to the nation, yes?"

His eyes turned guarded. "Yes."

"Then, is it such a stretch to believe that our enemies might have caught wind of our assignment?"

A muscle in the hinge of his jaw twitched. "Yes." He sounded less convinced this time.

"Don't be stubborn, Gideon."

Look who she was talking to!

She shook her head. "Consider, for a moment, that the French learned of our assignment. Wouldn't they want to stop it at all costs?"

"Perhaps..." His voice trailed off. He lifted his arm, likely to run his hand through his hair or fiddle with his collar, but she stood too close. He brushed against her instead. They both sucked in a breath as he stepped back.

He dropped his hand to his side again, balling it. "Even if a French spy learned of our assignment—and considering that only you, I, Morgan, Phil, and Strickland know about it, I think that is unlikely to say the least—they would never be able to infiltrate this estate. Zeus, half the servants here are British spies, either on leave, between assignments, or in training. How would they have evaded the prying eyes of over fifty servants?"

Felicia dropped her hands. She fought the urge to mirror his hostile stance and make a fist. "Tenwick Abbey is huge. It isn't inconceivable."

"Yes, it is." His voice cut off, strained. He finger-combed his hair and glanced toward the glass ceiling. When he released a breath, the tension in his shoulders visibly deflated. His gaze still glittered with hostility when he lowered it to hers. "I am trained in field work. I could walk this estate with my eyes closed, and *I* wouldn't have been able to slip in or out of the premises without detection. You are overreacting."

"And you are underreacting." She stormed around him to pluck one of the two *brugmansia* plants off his work bench.

"What are you doing?" He sounded exasperated.

"I'm taking this back to the wagon."

"You can't do—"

When she turned on her heel and strode away, ignoring his protests, the clip of his boots against the stone walkway trumpeted the fact that he followed her.

"That plant isn't healthy. It needs to stay here."

At the glass door leading to the lawn, she rounded on him. "It is my plant and I will do whatever I want with it." Namely, she would keep it safe. If Gideon refused to acknowledge that there was a threat, she would take precautions herself.

"Fine," he spat. "Take your bloody plant. It's not as though this serum is going to work, anyway."

The words—and sentiment behind them—sliced her deeply. Far deeper than she expected, from a man as infuriating as Gideon. He didn't respect her, after all. Not her life's work, in any case. She didn't trust herself to speak.

Without a word, she exited the orangery and stopped only to scoop up the sodium on the way.

She didn't need Gideon's help, not beyond ensuring that the plant remained alive and bloomed should they need more seeds. But if someone wanted to stop her from completing her task, it would make a difficult task impossible.

She couldn't let that happen.

Chapter Fourteen

Felicia fumed as she reached her wagon. She opened the door one-handed, raising her knee to fend off her overexcited dog as he barreled down the steps to sniff her skirts. Given his level of excitement, one might think she'd been gone for days rather than less than an hour. As she climbed into the wagon, he squeezed in next to her.

She carefully set the plant down on the counter she used as her work table. After she tucked the sodium into a special section of her cabinets, she checked the distilling process. Satisfied that it was complete, she gathered the oils, spread the coals, and disposed of the excess water.

As she turned the corner around her wagon, basin still in hand, she came face to face with a black beak and a beady eye.

"Giddy!"

Chubs barked. He was also giddy to see the visitors.

Squawking, Antonia flapped her wings and hopped from Lucy's arm to her shoulder. She flipped her tail at Chubs, who danced around the young woman as if looking for the right angle to jump. Felicia shifted the heavy basin into one hand as she lunged for the mastiff's collar. She missed. He balanced on his hind legs and stretched to deliver a single lick to Antonia's beak. She snapped at him as Lucy stumbled for balance. Chubs, pleased with himself, sat and thumped his tail on the ground. Felicia wrapped her hand around his collar.

Charlie, who had dawdled a step behind Lucy, leaped forward to offer her assistance. She got a wing to the ear for her troubles, but Lucy remained on her feet.

The moment the young women turned, Felicia burst, "Forgive me. I didn't know you were there or I would have restrained Chubs."

"It's fine." Lucy's voice was strained as she battled to calm her parrot. After several minutes of soft words and strokes to her ruffled feathers, Antonia perched quietly on Lucy's shoulder. Her feathers were puffed out to twice their usual size, making her resemble a fluffy ball. When the parrot glared at Chubs, he thumped his tail with more vigor.

Felicia tightened her hold on his collar, just in case.

"We thought you might be hungry," Lucy said. She angled her body to put more space between her pet and Felicia's. Her mouth was tight—the parrot's grip must be painful.

Charlie chimed in. "Would you like to take tea with us inside?"

Inside sounded like a better option than trying to keep Chubs in line. Nodding, Felicia stood and herded the mastiff toward the wagon. "Tea sounds lovely." After all, it would give her and Gideon some time apart to cool off.

Her chest tightened at the thought that someone was trying to sabotage their project. The fact that he refused to believe her... She loosened her hold on her dog's collar before she choked him by accident.

"Come along, Chubs," she said, forcing a smile. She guided the mastiff into the wagon and told him, "Guard."

He cast a forlorn glance at Antonia, but sat in front of the distillery. With the coals banked, the warmth would slowly recede but it would remain at a comfortable enough temperature for the dog while they ate. After she slid the distillery basin back into its rightful place, she shut the wagon door and left Chubs on watch. No one would harm that *brugmansia* plant, that she could guarantee.

As for the other... she didn't want to liberate it from Gideon's hold while he was still in a foul mood. She had to trust that it would be safe for the time being.

When she strolled toward the abbey doors, Charlie and Lucy linked arms with her—Antonia on Lucy's outside shoulder. They chattered away, Charlie enthusiastically discussing embroidery and asking after Felicia's favorite stitches.

As they reached the abbey doors, Charlie added, "If you come down to supper tonight, I'll show you my latest project in the drawing room. We always sit there after supper and I do my embroidery while Lucy and Evelyn chat."

Lucy's hand tightened on Felicia's arm. She sensed that, even if she'd wanted to, she would not have been allowed to cry off for a second night.

Felicia smiled. "That sounds delightful."

Lucy's hold lightened. Felicia flexed her fingers as they tingled.

"What happened to Miss Merewether?" she asked. "Did she go home?"

Charlie made a face. Lucy's expression was serene and polite, undoubtedly learned from her mother. "She's still sitting with Mother. She's a nice enough woman, but..."

"Stiff?" Charlie suggested.

They exchanged a glance around Felicia.

"Grasping," Lucy corrected. "Haven't you noticed the way she addresses Mama and me with such familiarity?"

"I assumed you invited the intimacy," Felicia put in, even though the question had seemed rhetorical. "You did with me, after all."

"You're different," Lucy said, shrugging her parrot-free shoulder. Even a one-armed movement jostled Antonia into an indignant squawk. The tie linking Antonia's leg to Lucy's wrist went taut.

After a scuffle with the parrot that ended with Antonia perched on Lucy's leather glove once more instead of her shoulder, Lucy resumed the conversation. The trio entered the abbey through the main entrance.

"You're Giddy's friend, so you're our friend, too."

Felicia bit the inside of her cheek to keep from laughing. "I don't know if you would call your brother and I friends."

"No?" Lucy's eyes narrowed as she cast a coy sideways glance at Felicia. "Would you say more than friends?"

"Certainly not."

Felicia must have sounded appropriately decisive over the notion, because Lucy's face fell. Charlie sent her friend a sheepish look and a shrug. Felicia pretended she hadn't seen the exchange.

Her heels clicked on the marble floor as she took the lead. At the corridor, she paused to let her two companions draw nearer. She didn't know in which parlor they intended to take tea.

Lucy hailed a footman as she entered the corridor. The young man tugged on his forelock as he stepped nearer. She handed her parrot to him with instructions to bring her to Evelyn, then linked arms with Felicia.

"She isn't allowed in the kitchen. Our cook barred her from entering after she stole a baked apple."

"And defecated in the soup," Charlie added. "Don't forget that."

Felicia made a face. "I understand why she was banished."

She fell silent as they arrived at the kitchen. The room, small when compared to others in the house, was in chaos. Aromatic steam thick with the savory scents of meat and spices collected from pots on the stove and wafted from the oven when opened. Men and women shouted to one another as they attended to various tasks. They wove in and out of each other like a swarm of bees. Their general, a short man with wide shoulders, a barrel chest, and a bit of a paunch, shouted encouragement, criticism, and orders all in the same breath as he paced the room.

When he noticed the trio of women in the doorway, he wiped one hand on his apron and jabbed the finger of his other hand toward Lucy. "You'd best not have brought that blasted bird, my lady."

"I left her with Mother." Lucy had to raise her voice in order to be heard above the cacophony. The kitchen staff offered her an inclined head or curtsey as they passed, but otherwise ignored her.

"Good. We have enough to handle in here as it is. Did you know that the dowager ordered a four course meal tonight on account of your guest?"

Felicia winced. She shrank back behind Lucy and Charlie's forms, hoping not to be noticed. Surely Evelyn wouldn't have gone to such trouble for Felicia. Perhaps Miss Merewether had been asked to join or the Graylockes expected someone else.

Fortunately, Lucy didn't draw attention to Felicia. She ignored the cook's remark—given his flippant and harried tone of voice, it had sounded rhetorical.

Instead, Lucy informed, "Giddy missed lunch."

The cook rolled his eyes heavenward. "Of course he did. I'll make up a plate. I assume he's in the orangery?"

"No need to trouble yourself. We'll take it to him."

"Is his friend in there with him today?"

"Yes."

Felicia frowned as the cook expertly navigated the staff and began to put together a large tray of cold vittles. She leaned closer to the two women. "I thought you said you wanted to take tea."

"We've already eaten," Lucy said smoothly, "but we know you and Giddy haven't. You'll have to take his plate to him, of course."

Felicia rubbed her forehead. "It might be best if I didn't see him for a while."

"Oh?" Lucy turned, a glint in her eye as she pinned Felicia beneath her gaze. "Are you having *difficulties?*" She dropped her voice to the barest whisper on the last word, infusing it with suggestion.

Felicia clenched her teeth and silently counted to five before she answered. "Gideon and I had a disagreement involving our joint project. I think it's best if I give him some time to come to his senses."

Lucy and Charlie exchanged twin smirks. They didn't believe Felicia's explanation at all. Never mind that it was the truth.

"You could always try to sweeten him up," Lucy suggested.

Charlie giggled.

Felicia sighed. She had already tried to inform these ladies that she had no romantic designs on Gideon, to no avail. Her protests would fall on deaf ears. Better she remove herself from their company and prove to them through action that she and Gideon were nothing more than partners for this one assignment.

Besides, he was too stubborn to see what was in front of his eyes. By this point, she would be lucky to survive another day with him without getting into a row, let alone the duration of their assignment.

When the Tenwick cook presented the completed tray, Felicia snatched it from his hands. "I'll deliver this to Gideon. We have to continue work in any case."

Lucy and Charlie didn't protest, like Felicia thought.

Her peace and quiet lasted the mere minutes it took to traverse the manor. Once she reached the orangery and crossed the long corridor to the glass door, she paused. Gideon stood inside, his stiff shoulders raised almost around his ears. He tended to his plants with jerky movements. He still fumed.

Perhaps her design to elude his sister's matchmaking attempts hadn't been well thought out at all. She took a small step back, intending to leave, but he turned, catching sight of her.

For a moment, their eyes locked. His hostile posture relaxed. He crossed to the door, opening it for her, but didn't say a word. The humidity radiating from the orangery caressed her skin.

Sheepishly, Felicia lifted the tray and said, "Peace offering?"

He stepped aside to let her in.

***

Giddy wanted to accept Felicia's peace offering and continue with their work, but four hours later, he found himself in the middle of another argument.

Darkness had fallen. The only light emerged from the glow of the lantern poised on the edge of the nearest work table. The humidity fogging the glass obscured everything outside, making it seem as though they were alone in the world. He wished they weren't.

He ran his hands through his hair. "If you'd just let me look at the distillery, maybe I could devise a better way to extract the compound that we need."

"No."

The infuriating woman crossed her arms, drawing his attention to her breasts. She probably did so for just that result, to weaken him.

"Chemistry is my domain. Yours is botany."

His forehead throbbed. "Yes, I know that, and engineering is not one of my strong points either, but we've been working at this for hours. In half a day, we've used up half the oil you collected and we've gotten nowhere. It's worth taking a look. If the distilling process is weakening the potency of the plant—"

"It isn't," she snapped. "I've done this before a time or two, using these exact oils harvested from the very same specimen. If they worked then, there's no earthly reason they shouldn't work now."

"Perhaps they've lost their potency over time," he said between gritted teeth. He turned, pacing the length of the work bench to keep from doing something he would regret, like throttling her.

Or kissing her. When he turned back, her lips were pursed. The lamplight reflected off her eyes, making them glitter with promise.

"The vial was sealed. No contaminants could have gotten in to weaken the potency."

Kissing was an infinitely more appealing use for that shapely mouth than arguing. He turned away, balling his fists as he paced the length of the table again. It wasn't enough. When he turned back, she remained in exactly the same place, one eyebrow arched as if she believed that she was winning the argument.

He took a deep breath to keep from shouting. When he spoke again, his voice was stiff, but even. "If you won't involve me in the distilling process, will you at least let me try something different with the plant you removed?" The plant she was likely killing. Although Giddy had tended specimens in worse shape before, he didn't think the chill of October was doing the plant any favors, even housed inside a wagon away from the elements. The humid orangery was much closer to its natural habitat.

"No."

Stubborn woman.

"We have one here. We can't demolish either plant in pursuit of—"

"Of what?" He stepped closer, looming over her. "In pursuit of science? Of our project? This is what you want, isn't it, Felicia?"

His breath caught as her name escaped his lips. He'd been very careful thus far not to utter it aloud while they were alone. The intimacy reminded him that there was no one around to see what he did and didn't do.

No one but her, that was. If he kissed her again, she would never let him live it down.

She isn't attracted to you.

He gritted his teeth as that unfortunate truth flashed through his mind. As flirtatious as she had been at first, the moment they were alone together, that playful demeanor dropped away, replaced with hostility. Why couldn't she just work *with* him instead of trying to prove that her way was better? They'd tried her way—it hadn't worked.

Her chin jutted out, mulish, as she countered, "We only have two plants. I'm not letting you chop one up when we have a perfectly good sample of the oils right there, and more from other parts of the plant. If you'd only check your ego for a moment, you'd see that we're far from out of options."

Yes, because his ego was the problem here.

"We have to work together on this project."

"I'm *trying*—"

He grabbed her by the shoulders, startling her into silence. Startling himself, as well. He had to bend down to reach her, and that brought their mouths closer. Every inch of him was aware of her body heat and the curve of her figure, especially when her chest heaved with her quick breaths.

He gentled his touch, not wanting to hurt her. *Release her.* His common sense battled with the awareness of her proximity. "Try harder."

Her eyebrows snapped down over her eyes. If he hadn't been holding her shoulders, he might not have noticed the bunch of her muscles beneath his palms. He stepped back before she slapped him.

Rage simmered in her eyes. "You don't respect me—"

He glanced toward the ceiling, hoping for a stroke of guidance. Nothing.

"*I* don't respect *you?* I'm the botanist here, or have you forgotten?"

She grumbled something under her breath as she crossed her arms once more. He decided that he didn't want to know what she'd said.

"The plant you removed is more mature than the one we have here. If you'll consent to return it—"

"No."

Sometimes, he wondered if she knew any other words.

He battled the urge to rub his throbbing temple. "By Jove, Felicia, I'm not going to murder your bloody plant. I know I'm young, but believe it or not I actually know a thing or two about botany!"

Her lips thinned. "This is not about your age. I've read your essays. I know you're brilliant, if pigheaded."

He threw his hands in the air, exasperated.

Louder, she added, "This is about having only these two plants. When we finish with the oils I have on hand, these are the only plants that will yield more. If we squander what they have to offer prematurely, we'll have to wait months for another plant to arrive from South America."

She acted as though he was planning on pulverizing the poor plant. All he wanted was a few clippings from various parts. Once he determined whether it was only the seeds—as she seemed to think—that yielded the results they needed, they could formulate a more targeted approach. It could be the roots or the buds that held a greater concentration of the compound they wanted. But would she trust him for two minutes to take what he needed?

No, of course not. That would be rational.

Taking a deep breath, he chased away the frustration seizing his body. "What if I took a clipping? If I can manage to coax it to take root, we'll have three plants."

And he would have one all his own to experiment on. Of course, it would take weeks at the least for the plant to mature to such a point, but he didn't mind thinking ahead—against the eventuality that the plant in her wagon died from the cold.

Her thick eyelashes fluttered across her eyes as she narrowed them. After a moment, she nodded. "A clipping could prove useful."

At least she acknowledged that much. It was a start.

"Were you thinking of putting it in a water solution or in the ground?"

Hesitantly, he approached the bench and found his pruning shears. "I've had better luck with a water solution in the past." He'd experimented with the solution over the years and had devised one that worked to encourage root growth within a week, among most plants.

She said, "I have an unguent that you can apply to the cut edge to encourage growth."

Although he had his own remedy, he wasn't above hearing of something else that might speed along the endeavor. He nodded and followed her around to her side of the work space. She found a small jar from her neatly arranged compounds.

As he took it from her, their hands brushed. He swallowed, trying to hide the tingle that swept up his arm from that innocent touch. "What did you use to make it?"

As she began to explain her brewing process and results, the atmosphere between them relaxed. The ache in his shoulders eased as he turned his attention to finding the best clipping. Plants, now that he could understand.

Felicia, he couldn't even pretend to.

Maybe, with luck, their partnership would take root at the same time as this little plant.

Chapter Fifteen

The chill of the autumn air woke Felicia. Her breath fogged in front of her face as she opened her eyes, staring up at the comforting view of her wagon. On the floor next to her cot, Chubs twitched his legs and whuffed in his sleep. When she reached to press her palm against his rump, he settled but didn't wake. He shivered.

Pulling the blanket tighter around her shoulders, Felicia rolled off her cot. The moment her stocking-clad feet kissed the wooden floor, the chill permeated them. She darted to the brazier she'd stoked before falling asleep. Last night, she and Gideon had worked so late with such single-minded focus that they'd missed supper. She'd filched a plate of food for herself and Chubs before retiring, but with the mix up in the orangery earlier that day, she hadn't trusted her wagon to be unattended. Hence why she'd slept here instead of inside on the plush mattress.

Once the brazier started to give off heat again, Felicia checked on the *brugmansia* plant. She released a breath as she ran her fingers lightly over the plant and dipped them into the soil. No frost. The brazier must not have been out for long.

Although she knew the plant would be better off with Gideon in the orangery, she didn't trust that it would be safe there. For all his assurances that no one would be able to sneak past the spies in the household, she still didn't believe they were beyond their enemies' reach. Better to leave the plant in the wagon, a small space that Chubs could guard with ease.

As she chased her dog outside to do his morning business, Felicia wrapped her arms around herself. The sun was separating from the horizon, the looming tree line blocking out most of the light. A dusting of white coated the ground, frost that would evaporate as the sun rose higher and warmed the day.

She surveyed the estate. The trees didn't come directly onto the grounds. A vast, sweeping yard of grass ringed Tenwick Abbey, with copses of trees springing up around it. Anyone who entered the premises on foot would have to cross one hundred yards of lawn at the narrowest section. Any servant to glance through one of the many windows of the abbey would see the approach. It was a vast estate, so wide that Felicia couldn't see how the servants could possibly be monitoring all areas of access. As she already spotted a few faces pass across the windows of the silent mansion, doubt uncurled in Felicia's stomach. *Could* Gideon be right? Was it impossible for an enemy to infiltrate the estate?

If so, that left only one other option: the enemy was already inside.

A chill washed down Felicia's spine as she herded Chubs back into the wagon. Once she ordered him to guard, she banked the coals in the brazier and shut the door.

If the French had infiltrated the Tenwick household, she couldn't tell Gideon. He wouldn't believe her. She had to find proof on her own. Now, before the house awoke.

On the guided tour that Lucy had given her when she'd arrived on Saturday, Lucy had bypassed an entire wing of the house that she claimed held, "Morgan and his assistant, Mr. Keeling's, offices." Although that wing of the house had held no interest to Lucy, Felicia suspected that it was the hub where the spies of the household convened. The Duke of Tenwick, after all, was entrenched in the spy effort.

Still wearing the dress she'd slept in, the one she'd worn to church the day before, Felicia slipped through the quiet manor. It was like walking through a graveyard. Although she spotted the scattered servant from the corner of her eye, they were like shadows. By the time she turned her head, they had already moved into another room. This early in the morning, they trudged about their duties without the cheerful chatter they engaged in during the day. The only sound Felicia heard were her muffled footsteps on the runner.

When she reached the wing of the house containing the duke's office, she turned the corner and nearly collided with a pair of maids deep in conversation. The pair, one old and one young, stopped their conversation immediately. They parted, forming an empty path between them as they pressed against the walls of the corridor. When they curtsied, Felicia reflexively did the same.

Idiot! She bit the inside of her cheek and continued on as if she knew where she was going. She counted three steps before she glanced behind her. Although the maids hadn't resumed their conversation when she'd passed, they hadn't lingered. They might have gone anywhere.

At least they aren't watching me. She laid her ear against the door, ensuring no sound escaped the room within, before she slipped inside.

The room was dark and unoccupied. Only a thin sliver of light snaked between drapes that hadn't been properly shut all the way. The crack of light illuminated a sideboard crowded with decanters. It stretched a long finger of daylight across a vivacious painting that featured a man on horseback on the heels of his hounds as they chased a wily fox.

What was she doing? She didn't know the first thing about spy work, nor about the spies that riddled the Tenwick estate. How was she supposed to find a traitor in their midst?

Her head throbbed. She meandered to the chair in front of the desk and sat, lowering her forehead into her hand. Scant inches in front of her nose was a piece of correspondence addressed to Morgan Graylocke, the Duke of Tenwick. She must have bumbled her way into his office.

She straightened. "This is as good a place to begin as any." After all, she couldn't conceive of giving up. This traitor had crossed not only her country, but he had tampered with her work. That was unforgivable. She would see him to justice if it was the last thing she did.

Gritting her teeth, she rounded the desk. She tugged open the drapes to give her greater light as she began to rummage through the duke's desk. She searched for one specific thing—a roster of Tenwick spies, or at the very least Tenwick servants. It was a start. From there she would have to find a reason to find herself in their company in order to observe them properly. She worked as quickly as possible, systematically going through the desk from corner to corner. She found nothing approaching the list she sought. In fact, she found multiple pieces of correspondence that didn't even appear to be in English.

When she reached the far edge, she put everything back in its place and sighed. "I should have known that would be too easy." Although she'd never searched for a hidden compartment before, she hadn't found anything in the duke's desk that might have led to a hiding spot.

Dejected, she slinked toward the door. Did she still have time to search another room? As she opened the door and slipped into the hall, she came face to face with Gideon and her question was answered. The shock and confusion on his face soon darkened into something more sinister.

He did not look happy to see her. In fact, he looked as though he loathed her now more than ever.

***

Even as Gideon searched his mind for a viable reason for Felicia to be here, stepping out of his brother's office, he found nothing. *She's the enemy.* The words swirled round and round his head, growing stronger with every revolution.

No. She couldn't be. Why would she agree to create a truth serum for the Crown only to sabotage her own project and draw his attention to it?

What she was, was an untrained spy under his command. He was tasked with keeping her in line. At the moment, she was so far from in line, she might as well have been on a different continent.

Besides which, there was no saboteur. She had been overreacting—and, most likely, still was.

Glancing over his shoulder to ensure that they weren't being watched, he crowded her, herding her back into Morgan's office. Once there, he shut the door, leaning his full weight against it.

"Are you going to tell me why you're in this wing of the house?"

She crossed her arms. She wore the same dress as yesterday, a little tight across her chest. It emphasized her every curve. Biting the inside of his cheek, he forced his gaze to hers once more. If she was worried, she didn't show it.

"I'll tell you after you tell me why *you're* here."

Surely she wasn't about to accuse him of wrongdoing. He *lived* here. He raised his eyebrows. "I have a report to give to Keeling as to our progress, since my brother is not here."

She opened her mouth and shut it once more.

He frowned as he took in her rumpled clothes. She hadn't even combed her hair yet this morning, judging by the way it fell around her shoulders in disarray. "Did you sleep in your clothes?"

Her mouth tightened, mulish. "I did."

Even so, she would have changed into fresh clothing when she'd awoken, unless... "In your wagon?"

When she dropped her arms to her sides, simultaneously balling them into fists, his instinct was to step back. Unfortunately, the door at his back prevented him from retreating.

"Yes, in my wagon."

She answered his next question—why—before he fully opened his mouth.

"Someone had to guard our project."

"This again," he groaned. When he leaned his head back, his scalp cracked against the wooden door. Pain splintered across his skull. He fought not to wince.

"Yes, this again." Her eyes took on a pugnacious glint. She stepped closer, not that there had been more than two feet of space between them before.

Now there was less than one and she had to stand on her tiptoes in an attempt to even her height with his. His neck ached as he craned it all the way down, still stiff from sleeping wrong last night.

"Someone switched those labels, whether or not you want to believe it."

He didn't contest that the labels had been switched—if she said they were correct earlier in the day, he believed her. He contested the fact that someone had done so with malicious intent.

"It might have killed us."

That, he couldn't protest. If he believed her claims as to the volatile nature of the raw sodium—and he did—they had been on the brink of disaster.

He hunched his shoulders, trying to make himself smaller to match her. It was in vain, but he hoped to avoid a shouting match in the middle of his brother's office. Even he shouldn't be in here.

"I've already mentioned that over half of the servants here are spies or former spies."

Her mouth tightened but she didn't contradict him.

"What I didn't mention is that spies retired due to injury or ones between assignment get bored easily. They have games between one another to see who can be the most observant, who can slip in and out of such a part of the mansion without detection, who can best whom. Consider every inch of these grounds watched at all times. To be honest, I'm not even certain that my bedchamber is private." Though, given that he dressed in there, he hoped no one was spying on him. By now he had washed the damnable perfume off his skin, or he sensed that he might have walked in on a spy in his bed.

At the moment, he would rather sleep alone.

He clasped his hands behind his back to stifle the urge to run them through his hair. If he lifted them, he would brush against her, and he didn't want the temptation.

"Trust me when I tell you that the only people on the grounds are those who have a right to be here or who have been invited by the family. The household spies would know otherwise."

A triumphant smile crossed her face. The sight of it pinched him in the gut. Her eyes sparkled with a smug kind of allure.

"Exactly."

She prodded him in the chest. Awareness spread through him like ripples, born of her touch.

"It's one of your spies. They've switched sides."

He'd never heard anything more ludicrous in his life. "My brother trained these spies himself. I trust his judgment."

She still hadn't removed her hand. Her touch muddled his thoughts, as if *she* was the one to wear the perfume this time. When he breathed deep, he didn't smell a hint of musk, only her. And she smelled incredible.

He straightened his shoulders and forced himself to think about the matter at hand. "They're loyal. In fact, I'd stake my life on it."

Her hand curled in his lapel for a moment before she dropped her hand. She didn't step back. The heat of her body imprinted on his. He could have imagined the her shape with his eyes closed.

Her words were a far cry from the lustful bent of his thoughts.

"Still the stubborn prat, I see."

Her lip curled. He wanted to draw it into his mouth, to kiss the expression away.

"You refuse to see what is in front of your face simply because you didn't think of it first."

That wasn't it at all…

"Well, if it takes a woman to show you the truth, that is exactly what I'll do."

He didn't answer. Anything he said would only rile her further. From the set of her jaw and the glint in her eye, she refused to back down. And she called him stubborn.

Raising his hand, he drew away a strand of her hair that had fallen onto her cheek. *Kiss her.*

Don't.

He didn't know what he wanted anymore.

He stepped to the side and opened the door for her to leave. From the saucy way she swung her hips as she strode past him, she thought she'd won the argument. At that moment, he didn't feel as though he'd lost. His gaze dropped down to her rear as she strutted down the corridor to the main section of the house.

No, he felt as though he was on the cusp of winning, if only he'd reach out and grab his prize. Turning, he strode in the opposite direction.

Whatever he did, he refused to contribute to the madness between them. Felicia was too confusing as it was.

Chapter Sixteen

After the high stress and frustration of the day, the quiet evening in front of the fireplace melted away the tension in Felicia's shoulders. The steady *tick, tick, tick* of a grandfather clock reminded her of every moment that passed without her and Gideon making a breakthrough.

Not that they would have screamed, "Eureka!" had they been working at that moment, if the lack of luck that day was any indication. However, Felicia wasn't accustomed to leisure time. She stabbed her needle into the handkerchief, thinking of the problems with the serum at the back of her mind. Her theory was sound. Why was the application turning so awry?

No, awry was the wrong word. *Awry* implied spectacular failures and mishaps. She had none of those. It simply wasn't working. Though, to be honest, since Gideon had barred her from tasting her own work and refused to sample it himself, a lot of time was wasted tracking down an appropriate subject for the test each time. Felicia had even tried recreating one of her old attempts, the one that had come the closest to the desired effect, but hadn't been able to replicate her results. Perhaps Gideon was right and the oils had weakened with time.

If so, it would be a long time before they were able to complete their assignment. The plants weren't in the right point of their life cycle to harvest the most potent oils.

Felicia sucked in a breath as she accidentally stabbed herself in the finger. She stuck the digit in her mouth to soothe the sting and examined the handkerchief for blood. It was unmarred.

At the small, square table set between two armchairs, Gideon glanced up. His eyebrows lifted quizzically. Averting her gaze, Felicia reapplied herself to her embroidery.

Gideon moved a chess piece. He set it down with a decisive *click*. "Checkmate."

"What? Impossible!" Lucy tried to find a place to move her king, to no avail. With a disgusted sigh, she reset the board.

Leaning back in the armchair, Gideon nursed his brandy and waited. His posture and expression were neutral. He didn't say a word to brag about his victory. Likely, he feared losing another partner. His mother had already played him and lost, retiring with a book to the settee between Felicia and Charlie.

Lucy glowered as she moved a pawn into the center of the board. "I *will* beat you this time."

Gideon grinned. "With what, the chess board?"

He raised his arms to shield himself as she tried to smack him.

"Bare-handed, I see."

Lucy made a noise reminiscent of Chubs when he didn't want to move. The mastiff stirred from his lazy position on the rug in front of the fire.

Kicking her brother beneath the table, Lucy said, "Make your move before I die of old age, please."

Felicia smiled as they exchanged banter. Although she didn't know much about chess, she could tell that Gideon wasn't playing to his strengths. Several times, he let his sister place him in check, only to turn the advantage around and pin her in a couple uncomfortable situations.

Evelyn glanced up from her book, marking her place with one finger as she witnessed the match devolve into a childish fight. The dowager wore a fond smile. "He's the closest to her age, you know."

Given the way Gideon spoke about his brothers, she had suspected he was the youngest of them. She nodded, but didn't know what to contribute.

Fortunately, Evelyn carried the conversation. "When they were small, Lucy used to follow him everywhere. They got into more scrapes than I can name."

As Gideon glanced up, his hair flopped into his eyes. He brushed the ebony locks away. "If I did, they were all of Lucy's doing. I was an angel." He deftly evaded her kick, moved his bishop, and in an absent tone of voice said, "Checkmate."

"Not again! You distracted me." With a disgruntled huff, Lucy stood. She batted a lock of her hair out of her face. "I'm going to check on Antonia."

At the parrot's name, Chubs perked up his ears. He lumbered to a stand.

Lucy glared and jabbed a finger at him. "You can't come. You're the reason she doesn't want to be in here with us."

Chubs parted his lips and his pink tongue fell out as he picked his way across the room to her. Felicia whistled. He paused near the door, glancing over his shoulder at her. When she pointed to the rug near the hearth, his ears pinned flat against his skull and he gave a plaintive whine.

"None of that. Antonia doesn't want to see you. Go lay down."

With slow, hulking steps, he crept across the parlor like he was a dog three times his age. He curled up on the rug, settling his head on his paws. He wore a pathetic look.

Knowing this was all a part of his plan to terrorize the bird, Felicia ignored him.

Linking his fingers together, Gideon stretched his arms over his head and cracked his knuckles. "Who's next? Mother? Charlie?"

Charlie snorted. "I'd rather read Lucy's book."

Given the level of enthusiasm she showed for the prospect, it was a good thing that Lucy was no longer in the room to hear.

"Felicia, why don't you play?" Evelyn suggested.

She glanced up from her embroidery—one more stitch and she would have the finishing touch. Everyone's eyes rested on her. She made the stitch and tied off the thread.

"I've never played."

Gideon shrugged. "I'll teach you. If you're interested," he added belatedly.

He didn't seem to hold it against her that she'd never played. If he'd looked smug or superior, she would have declined. However, he seemed genuinely interested in teaching her, so she soon found herself ensconced in Lucy's place.

Gideon patiently explained the rules as he set up the board. He then explained them again as they enacted the first game. When they came to a stalemate, he flipped his king on its side and they began in earnest.

Chess was surprisingly fun. It was like a formula. She could predict some of his moves and reactions from having watched him play other people, but not all of them. Before she knew it, she found herself engrossed in the game. She lost twice and was in the process of possibly winning this time when the grandfather clock chimed the hour. It was after midnight.

She glanced up. The fire had died down, giving off only enough light to see the outline of the pieces. No wonder her eyes ached. She rubbed at them as she surveyed the room, empty except for where Chubs snored and twitched by the fire.

"When did the others leave?"

Gideon smiled sheepishly. "I don't recall. I suppose we'd better call it a night."

She hid a yawn behind her hand as she stood. "You're only saying that because you're afraid I'll trounce you."

His eyebrow twitched as he accepted her hand to stand. Once he straightened, stretching his shoulders, he surrounded her.

"I've already beaten you twice. What makes you think I wouldn't be able to do it again?" His eyes glinted with the promise of the challenge.

His smile faded into something more serious as the air charged between them. She dropped her hand, her skin tingling from contact with his. They stood close. If she stood on her tiptoes and leaned forward, he would probably take the hint and kiss her. Shifting on his feet, he narrowed the space between them.

Her heart hammered against her ribs. She shouldn't do this. Gideon had his entire life ahead of him and she...

She had already turned her back on the chance for a lifelong romance. She didn't need it; she could take care of herself. And, with the conflict between them over their shared project, neither of them needed a temporary fling.

Stepping back, she snapped her fingers to call her dog to her. "Goodnight," she said to Gideon, her voice soft.

"Goodnight."

Was that disappointment in his eyes? No, it was a trick of the shadows. She scooped up a candle, lit it from the fire in the hearth, and left with Chubs padding on her heels.

You made the right decision.

Her stomach somersaulted, urging her to change her mind and turn around. She steeled herself and hurried to the guest wing of the house.

Lucky she'd cracked her window open earlier in the day—she might need some cold night air tonight.

At the top of the stairs, Chubs balked. He whined, bunching the runner as he scrambled backward. Felicia frowned. "Chubs, what's wrong?" She grabbed him by the collar and tried to pull him forward, but he wouldn't budge.

When she took a deep breath to steady herself, an acrid bite to the air scratched at the back of her throat. She coughed. Was that smoke?

Releasing Chubs, she approached her room. The stench tainted the air. She touched the doorknob. It scalded her. There was a fire on the other side of her door.

And Charlie and her mother slept in the rooms next to her.

Chapter Seventeen

For a brief, blissful moment, Giddy had lost all notion of common sense. If Felicia hadn't stepped away, he would have kissed her. By night, he'd been tormented by dreams of her taste and the feel of her mouth beneath his. By day, he was reminded what an infuriating, stubborn, hot-tempered woman she was. While they attempted to work, he was constantly incensed with her and it showed in their lackluster results. But, in a fickle instant, he would have forgotten all the ways she irked him for the pleasure of her kiss.

Given another second, he would have thrown caution to the wind and given in to temptation. She would have slapped him. He would have deserved it.

It would have been worth it.

Zeus, he needed a walk in the bitter cold evening. If that couldn't douse the part of him that insisted kissing her was a good idea, he didn't know what would.

He exited into the gardens, the glass-encased walkway and the orangery beyond shimmering in the light of the moon. His breath fogged in front of his face, the chill immediately seeping through his thin jacket and into his bones. As he waited for common sense to return, he tucked his hands in his pockets. Felicia dominated his thoughts. He strode away from the abbey door, watching the shifting play of moonlight on the glass of the orangery.

Wait. There was no moon out tonight. What...?

He turned. A bright light gushed from the second story, too bright to be a candle. Was that a fire?

Giddy bolted for the abbey door. The lump in his throat made it hard to breathe. That fire was near the guest quarters. Could Felicia...

His mind blanked, refusing to consider the question.

He raced through the manor. As he approached, more and more servants—half-dressed in their shirtsleeves and in some cases night shirts untucked over breeches—convened on the spot. Giddy's heart pounded painfully in the base of his throat as he clambered up the stairs.

It was true. The guest wing was on fire. Smoke poured from one of the nearer rooms, thick and gray. After yanking his cravat loose and stuffing it in his pocket, Giddy hauled his shirt up to over his nose and mouth. He ducked his shoulders, squinting to see through the stinging smoke. Bodies swarmed, some clustered around the apparent source of the blaze, contained to one room, and the others forming a line down the stairs and handing off a bucket from person to person to meet the flames. As the first reached the front of the line and was thrown into the room, steam hissed. More buckets came.

"Charlie!"

Giddy stiffened as he heard his sister's voice. He turned as his mother and sister, each with their nightgowns hauled above their ankles, dashed up the stairs to the top. To the left, away from the blaze and out of the servants' paths, Mrs. Vale and her daughter huddled. Charlie had her hand wrapped around Chubs's collar as he whined and strained toward the source of the fire. His eyes were wild, his ears flat against his head. Lucy helped to restrain him as she reached the pair.

Mother, her voice sharper than usual with alarm, said, "The servants woke us to alert us about the fire. Is anyone hurt?"

"No." Charlie swallowed and shook her head, her blond curls limp against her ashen cheeks. "Felicia woke us and got us out of the room."

"Where is she now?" Lud, did that panicked tone belong to him? He needed to calm himself.

The moment Charlie untangled one of her hands to point at the fire, he turned on his heel.

No. Nothing could have happened to her. He'd just bloody well seen her.

He dashed into the fray, keeping well away from the heat radiating from the open doorway. He tried not to get in the way of the lineup as he squinted. The smoke stung his eyes, making them water.

There. A woman *in the room*, coughing as she tried to beat out the flames with—was that a rug or a blanket? He lunged inside, grabbing her by the arm and pulling her out of the way of the servants. She wasn't helping the efforts, only hampering the spread of the water from the buckets.

She stumbled through the doorway before she balked, struggling to get free. "Let me go. Don't you see there's a fire?"

Definitely Felicia. Her voice was hoarse, but she'd lost none of her spirit. His knees weakened at the confirmation that she was unharmed.

When she started to cough—violently, doubling over—he had to amend that statement. The smoke from the fire.

"You've breathed in too much smoke." He urged her away from the door. Weak as she was and battling for air, she didn't have the strength to fight him.

Several others in the line also coughed. If he didn't do something, their health would be in jeopardy, too.

"There are windows in the other rooms. We can open them, dissipate some of this smoke."

"No, don't." She battled to stand. "It will draw the flames and bring them beyond control. They shouldn't even have opened the door. We have to snuff the flames before we introduce more air."

When she tried to return to the room, he caught her around the middle and pinned her to his body. He backed up, holding her there, keeping her out of harm's way.

She thrashed against him. For all that she could barely move without coughing, she'd lost none of her strength. He grunted as her elbow jabbed him in the side.

"Let me go. I can help."

"No, you can't. The servants have it well in hand." She was going to hate him once she calmed down, but he couldn't let her put herself in harm's way. In fact, he had to get her into fresher air posthaste or the smoke might kill her.

When she continued to fight him, he adjusted his hold and tossed her over his shoulder. He wasn't as strong as his brothers, but she weighed less than he expected. Didn't she eat enough? He loped away from the fire.

Felicia continued to fight him. As they approached the others, her dog went mad, lunging and snapping as he tried to escape Charlie and Lucy's joint hold. Giddy ducked down the stairs inside before the two young women lost control of the dog and he attacked.

He found Mr. Keeling, in charge of the household spies in Morgan's absence, at the bottom of the stairs.

"Relieve those who have been near the fire the longest. The smoke will kill them."

"We have a system in place. You and your family should stay clear." Keeling passed a full bucket along the line. The thin man barely glanced at Giddy, which suited Gideon just fine.

Without another word, he dashed for the nearest exit. The air on the first floor cleared enough for him to breathe easy, but it was still stuffy. Felicia needed clean outdoor air.

She stopped fighting him as he reached the door. A clamor from behind and vicious barks alerted him that the women had lost control of the mastiff. He bolted outside and dropped Felicia to the ground, taking several healthy steps away from her.

As the door started to swing closed of its own accord, Chubs burst through. He bounded to Felicia and stood over her as she gulped for air. His hackles rose as he growled at Gideon.

Giddy tried to be as non-threatening as possible. What did one do to calm a dog? He knew running wouldn't be a bright decision, not to mention it would leave Felicia to her own devices.

Lying flat on her back and taking deep, even breaths, Felicia laid her hand on the mastiff's haunches. "I'm fine, Chubs." Given her voice, she was not fine. She sounded like she was on death's door.

The dog must have heard the raspy, pained quality of her voice because he whined as he turned to look at her. The moment Giddy relaxed his stance, the mastiff whipped his head around and bared his teeth.

Felicia fought into a sitting position. "Chubs, no. Giddy is a friend. A *friend*."

Something intangible and warm unfurled in Giddy's chest. She might only be emphasizing his relationship with her to her dog, but it was the first time she'd called him by his nickname.

Don't be ridiculous. Your nickname has two syllables, whereas your full name has three. Her throat is sore.

She beckoned Giddy closer. "Come here. Hold my hand."

And get it bitten off? "You have to be joking."

"I'm not." She leaned over, coughing, and he took an involuntary step forward. Chubs didn't seem to like it. Although he placed himself squarely between Gideon and his owner, he didn't growl. Her hand remained on his haunches.

"Sit. I'll come to you."

"That doesn't seem wise, either." At least while standing, it was unlikely that the mastiff could rip off his face.

Felicia glared, but it was weak and watery.

Slowly, with much coaxing on both parts, Gideon was reintroduced to Chubs as a friend. The mastiff didn't harm him, though Giddy couldn't quite shake the feeling that he wanted to. The moment the dog let Giddy scratch him behind the ears, Felicia leaned heavily against his chest, as if her strength was failing.

He wrapped his arms around her, as an excuse to surreptitiously check her pulse. Rapid, but strong. He didn't like the shallow, slightly ragged quality to her breaths.

"So, what's the diagnosis?"

She'd noticed him checking her pulse, it seemed. He rested his cheek on her head. "You're a lunatic."

She jabbed him in the stomach with her elbow, but didn't otherwise deign to answer.

"We should get you to a physician. He might be able to do something for your lungs. Unless you have a tincture on hand...?"

"I don't."

Perhaps it had been too much to hope that, as a chemist, she might have created medicines as well as perfumes and truth serums that didn't work.

The door to the abbey opened, admitting a stream of people. Lucy was first, supporting Charlie next to her.

"There you are!" She glanced at Felicia and dropped to her knees. "Are you all right?"

When Felicia nodded, it prompted another coughing fit. *Liar.* He adjusted his arms around her so he didn't suffocate her. Her dog tried to crawl into her lap.

"Send the physician," Lucy hollered.

A figure turned away from the group to comply.

"I'm fine," Felicia said weakly.

She struggled to move. Giddy rubbed her arms to calm her. Some of the tension pinching his gut faded when she relaxed against him.

"You didn't have to call the physician on my account."

"I didn't," Mother informed. "There were a lot more people exposed to that fire. You're all going to be assessed."

Felicia curled her fingers into Giddy's sleeve. "We should get to the orangery."

"Why?" Had the lack of oxygen gone to her head?

"We can make a tincture to help with the smoke—"

She dissolved into hacking coughs. Giddy helped her lean over, rubbing her back. When she spit onto the ground, dread crawled up his spine. Her saliva was not supposed to be black.

Resisting the urge to sweep her in his arms again, he urged her to stand and supported the bulk of her weight. "I thought you said you didn't have any medicine to help."

"I don't, but I know how to make it. With everything I asked your brother to supply us with, we must have the ingredients on hand."

That, he didn't doubt for a second.

"Very well, but I'll prepare the tincture. You can direct me."

She rested her head somewhere in the vicinity of his heart. "I'm not an invalid." Her words were muffled against his jacket.

"No, but you are ill. I won't let you overexert yourself. We can do this together."

Tilting her face up to meet his gaze, she studied him for a moment before she nodded. "Very well. Let's do this together."

A knot of tension he hadn't realized he'd been carrying loosened between his shoulder blades at her verbal agreement. They were finally on the same page.

Chapter Eighteen

Felicia and Gideon were *not* on the same page. She glared at him, struggling to breathe properly in the humid air of the orangery. Despite sleeping the night and into the morning, her lungs still ached and her throat still scratched from the smoke of the fire. She and the Vales had been allotted rooms in the family wing while the servants aired out the smoky guest wing and prepared new rooms. Felicia didn't want to know the state of her belongings. She'd worn the same dress today as she'd worn last night, despite the fact that it reeked of smoke. Every inhale only reminded her of the raw state of her throat. Although she and Gideon had successfully prepared a tincture last night, its effects weren't instant. She would need to take it for the next several days, perhaps even weeks, as she healed. It tasted horrible and put her in a foul mood.

Though her mood, at the moment, was entirely Gideon's doing. She crossed her arms. "You can't be serious."

His eyebrows climbed toward the lock of hair dripping onto his forehead. "I could say the same for you. Why would someone have deliberately set fire to your room?"

To stop our project. From the stubborn set of Gideon's stubble-lined jaw, he wasn't willing to hear the truth. His eyes were steely. He mirrored her posture.

"I didn't leave a candle burning in my room." She lived in a flammable wagon, for goodness sake. She'd long since gotten into the habit of never leaving an open flame where it might fall over, especially not upon leaving the room for hours.

A tic started in the hinge of his jaw. "One of the servants, then. It was an accident, Felicia. No one is deliberately trying to hurt you."

First, their experiment might have been compromised and one or both of them seriously injured because of a switched label. Then her room was set aflame? It was not a coincidence. Someone in the Tenwick household wanted her out of commission.

Did they know that she suspected the truth? The servants were already awake, despite the late night and several being treated for smoke inhalation. She wouldn't be able to sneak into the business wing of the house and search for the culprit.

But she couldn't just stand here and face Gideon's disbelief, either.

She turned away. "Very well. I won't trouble you with it any further."

A sigh echoed from behind her as she walked toward the exit. She was physically drained, her legs weak, a byproduct of not being able to get enough air no matter how hard she tried. She should be abed, like the other servants in the same condition. However, she refused to wait for the next attack. If Gideon wouldn't believe her, she would search for the culprit on her own.

"Felicia, wait—"

Had he changed his mind?

When she turned, he looked resigned and maybe a bit worried. It wasn't the expression of a man who intended to help her.

"Don't leave. You're ill. You need to rest."

She infused her spine with iron will. "I can take care of myself, thank you." She snapped her fingers to Chubs, who attached himself to her shadow. Ever since her close call with the fire yesterday, he refused to leave her side. He disobeyed her when she told him to guard the wagon. She'd locked it, and hoped that it would be safe enough while she healed. Her dog was clearly unwilling to allow anything to happen to her under his watch and, to be honest, she was grateful to have him nearby to look out for her. Despite her bravado, she was in no shape to look out for herself.

The journey through Tenwick Abbey to the guest wing was agonizingly slow. Every few minutes, Felicia needed to find a spot to sit. She waved away offers of assistance from the harried servants going about their tasks. She didn't know who to trust. Besides, she could take care of herself. She always had before.

Eventually, she reached the chilly second floor. The air still reeked of smoke. The stench, in combination with the biting air, stung her throat as she breathed. Her head spun, woozy. She bit the inside of her cheek and hobbled to the charred door that had once led to her room.

It was a disaster. Everything was partially burned. Felicia didn't even trust the floor. She jammed her hip against the doorframe to bar Chubs from stepping inside. The bedding and mattress had been stripped, but the wardrobe along the far side of the wall looked intact. Black streaks rippled up the doors and the claw feet nearest the fire had broken, making the contraption lean precariously against the wall. Could any of her clothes have survived the catastrophe? The blackened floorboards didn't look likely to hold her weight.

This, Gideon thought had been caused by a mere fallen candle? Impossible. The wind whistled through the broken shards of the window. Shards of glass glistened on the floor. A candle wouldn't have broken the window, certainly not toward the inside. Someone had thrown something in. Some of the shards on the ground looked a different color than those from the window. Could she make it across the room to investigate further?

Her knees trembled. She had to sit. Whistling weakly to Chubs, she backtracked until she entered the room next to hers. This was where Charlie had slept, if she remembered right.

The room was almost intact. The fire had started to eat through the adjoining wall, a scorching hole leading into her former room. The floor was untouched, but she still used the walls away from the damaged area to navigate the perimeter until she reached the bed. Her head swam as she lowered herself onto the edge.

When her head cleared, she found the mastiff's wet nose in her face as he sniffed her. She offered him a weak smile and kissed him on the nose, pulling away before he could reciprocate. She buried her hand in the fur between his shoulder blades.

"I'm fine, boy. Give me a second."

She had to stand. She couldn't stay here. The crisp, bitter air hurt worse than the humidity of the orangery. If she wanted to regain her breathing, she had to leave.

Questions swirled in her head. What had someone thrown in her room? Was she the intended target? She hadn't been in the room—but Charlie and her mother had been in theirs. If the attacker had miscalculated, he could have gotten the wrong room.

They slept on the second floor of the house. How had someone thrown into the room with such accuracy?

He's a spy. He's had practice.

She had to know for certain. Gathering her strength, she stood and rounded the bed toward the window. This one was intact. The glass was foggy from smoke, but it was unbroken. She unlatched the window and opened it, leaning out into the cold, howling wind.

Was that a scorch mark on the stone wall of the abbey? Yes—and there was another. Felicia counted four such marks. The arsonist hadn't lobbed the catalyst to the fire directly into Felicia's window on the first try. But, given the grouping of marks, she had definitely been the target.

How could the Tenwick spies not have seen the person hurling dangerous objects at the manor?

Wait. She didn't know for certain that no one had seen anything. After all, she hadn't asked them.

She rested once more on the bed before she slowly made her way down to the kitchen. She managed to arrive during a lull. Everything was chopped in neat piles and arranged for cooking, but the pots and pans were not yet being used. The only people in the kitchen were a pair of scullery maids scrubbing away as they cleaned the dishes from breakfast, a young man in an apron who pulled a tray of buns from the oven, and a straight-backed, thin woman of middling age. The kitchen's general, it seemed, was one of those laid abed by smoke inhalation.

As his stand-in, the hawkish woman, turned to Felicia, she offered a smile. "Might I beg a cup of tea and a place to sit for a moment? I fear I've overexerted myself."

She wasn't lying. Her voice was hoarse from her raw throat and her head felt thin and watery. The woman nodded toward a table set in the corner of the room with three stools around it.

Felicia hobbled to the nearest stool and sat, grateful for the respite.

The woman clucked her tongue. "That beast cannot come in here."

Chubs slinked along in Felicia's shadow, his head down and his ears flat against his head as if he was trying to be invisible. Felicia snapped her fingers and pointed to the corridor. "Door. Guard."

Chubs whined, but complied. His steps were heavy, slowing the farther he got from Felicia. Eventually, he reached the door and dropped his rump to the floor.

Giving the cook a thin smile, Felicia said, "I haven't had the chance to feed him all day. Could I beg you for a bowl of water and a bit of food?"

The woman eyed Felicia critically. "You look like you could use the same."

Coming from a woman who might be bonier than Felicia, that was rich. The glimmer of a smile crossed her face before she tamped it down.

"Thank you, but I don't know that I could stomach anything." She raised her hand to her throat as she spoke.

A gentler expression eased the predatory look on the woman's face. "One of those affected by the fire, are you?"

Felicia nodded.

The woman, no longer reluctant, poked around the kitchen and soon set down a bowl of water and one of chopped meat that had been stashed separate from the chunks in piles next to the vegetables. Chubs wagged his tail at the offering and dug in. By the time the woman had finished serving him, a kettle on the stove whistled and she used a cloth to pour out the water into a teapot to steep.

"You should be abed, Miss," she admonished.

Felicia smiled sheepishly. "I'm afraid that won't be possible for me. I have to brew more of the tincture for the household, or we'll run dry."

That wasn't strictly true. In fact, Gideon had barred her from helping at all. He had an impeccable memory and recalled her every instruction. Now that day had dawned, he'd enlisted the help of his friends Catt and Rocky to prepare more tincture in order to keep a ready supply for those who would need it in the coming week. Despite the fact that they were, all three of them, botanists by trade, Catt and Rocky had warmed to the task once Gideon had issued a challenge. They were currently embroiled in a battle to brew and bottle the most tinctures in the shortest amount of time.

Admittedly, their competitiveness only added to the hostile air in the orangery.

As she set a cup and saucer in front of Felicia, the cook's eyebrows climbed up her forehead. "You are the woman who created the medicine for everyone?"

"I am indeed. Do you know how it has been received?"

"Most everyone affected is sleeping—far more peacefully than I would have imagined, given the coughing."

Felicia nodded. "That is to be expected. The tincture contains a healthy dose of laudanum. It is best for the body if they sleep as much as they can while they heal."

When she took a sip of the hot tea to ease the pain in her throat, she winced. It burned on the way down. Better to let it cool a moment more before she took another sip.

"You'll give advice but not take it, I see."

Felicia mustered a wan smile. "I don't have the luxury. It was my room that was hit the worst through the fire."

Pouring herself a cup of tea, the woman took a seat on the stool opposite Felicia. For some reason, that made her smile. This woman, if not most of the staff, wasn't daunted by her. Felicia much preferred to be treated like an equal.

"I don't suppose anyone saw who set the fire?"

The woman leaned closer. "You don't believe it an accident."

Felicia cocked her eyebrow. "I didn't leave an open flame in the room, and I won't insult the staff by suggesting they did such a thing."

The woman made a face that looked as though she sucked on a lemon. Her expression made it perfectly clear what she thought of such a notion. Triumph burned in Felicia's chest, a little like the tea, but she savored the sensation. She was right, and Gideon was wrong. It couldn't have been an accident.

"This is such a large estate, but I imagine someone setting fire to it must be noticed. A stranger doesn't belong here."

For now, she kept her theory that it had been a rogue member of the staff to herself.

The cook stiffened and slipped off of the stool, clasping her hands in front of her. She peered at something—or someone—over Felicia's shoulder.

When Felicia turned, she stopped short. She had never seen Gideon look so cold or forbidding. He clasped his hands behind his back. "Miss Albright, a word?"

It was not a request.

Struggling to hide the pain in her throat and lungs, Felicia crossed the kitchen with a clipped gait. Chubs followed her into the hall, done with his meal.

The moment they stepped out of sight of the doorway, Gideon rounded on her. She leaned against the wall, weaker than she cared to admit. Especially to him.

"It is not your place to question the servants."

Gideon's gaze snapped with the rebuke.

She gritted her teeth. "Even if you don't care to consider the fact that we may have an enemy—"

He stepped closer, as if trying to shield her with his body and thereby contain her words. After glancing over his shoulder he said sharply, "Stop right there."

There was an edge to his voice. She closed her mouth. Anger simmered inside her and she used it as fuel to stand. Between the wall and Gideon, she was well enough supported not to be in danger of sinking to the floor.

His expression was stony as he returned his gaze to her. "*If* the fire in your chambers was deliberately set, Keeling will learn of it. He does not need your help on that account."

Felicia lifted her chin, but Gideon wasn't finished talking.

"Not every servant here is a spy. One wrong word in the wrong ear could send twitters throughout the staff that might reach back to my mother."

He planted his hand next to her shoulder, hemming her against the wall as he caught her gaze and held it. He lowered his mouth to her ear. The intimacy sent shivers over her skin.

"You weren't here when my father died. Mother retreated from us all. At first, we weren't certain she would survive. Even though she rallied, she hadn't truly returned to her happy self until Tristan met his wife earlier this year. I *will* not jeopardize that by having her learn that her sons are spies and amplify the worry that she already feels for us and Anthony. Do you understand?"

He drew away just far enough to meet her gaze. His eyes were just as intense as his voice.

She nodded. "Forgive me. I didn't mean to cause your family pain."

She hadn't. All she wanted was for him to believe her so they could tackle this problem together...

Forcing the thought from her head, she straightened her shoulders and met his gaze. "Mr. Keeling will look into it?"

Gideon nodded. "Whether deliberate or accidental, he'll look into the fire and its cause either way. It might have killed someone if you hadn't gotten there when you had."

Yes—it might have killed me. She still didn't know what the attacker had used to set the fire, but given that it had grown to such a strength without being noticed and doused, she assumed that it would have harmed her had she been in the room at the time.

The tension in the air between Gideon and Felicia intensified. "Will you leave Keeling to his job and trust that he'll be able to get to the bottom of the situation?"

What if Mr. Keeling were the French spy? Perhaps it was best if she didn't consider such a thing. Given that Mr. Keeling was presumably the Duke of Tenwick's second in command—at Tenwick Abbey, if nowhere else—it wouldn't bode well if his loyalties had been twisted.

If the spy were someone else... She had to presume that Keeling would be able to discover who. Before she passed judgment, she could wait to hear what he had to say about the fire. Would he take Gideon's side?

He'd have to be a fool.

Then again, Gideon was no fool, and he refused to believe what was in front of his eyes.

"I won't ask again," Felicia said. *For now,* she added silently. If there was another mishap...

She had to remain vigilant. Another mishap could result in the end of someone's life.

The hostility in Gideon's face and stance melted away. "Thank you."

She changed the subject. "How are Catt and Rocky faring with the tincture?"

Taking a step back, Gideon clasped his hands behind his back as he answered. "Quite well. I'm afraid the orangery won't be free for our work for several hours, at the least. They've each claimed one of the work benches."

That was a shame, but given that she could barely breathe while in the orangery, perhaps it was for the best.

Softly, he suggested, "Why don't you take the opportunity to rest? And maybe bathe."

Felicia pressed her lips together to keep from laughing. Was he trying to tell her that she stank? Given that she wore the same dress as yesterday, one which seemed to have infused the smoke in every fiber, she knew exactly how bad she smelled.

Still, it was fun to look at him blankly and say, "I beg your pardon?"

His cheeks turned pink. He averted his gaze. "Not that you don't look beautiful even when you smell like a cheap cigar—"

She pressed her hand over her mouth, shaking.

Now frantic, Gideon held up his hands in surrender. "I'm sure many men find that alluring. It's just... um... forget I said anything. Carry on."

The cherry-red stain of embarrassment colored Gideon's cheeks, ears, and dipped beneath his collar. Turning on his heel, he retreated into the kitchen. Felicia slumped against the wall and struggled to breathe while she battled laughter. She stifled it against her sleeve.

My, she did reek. If she was going to find a bath, she would need fresh clothes. Did the ones in the wardrobe smell as bad as the one she wore? Most likely, but perhaps she could find something salvageable. It was worth a look.

***

Felicia had almost made it to the top of the stairs when she ran out of breath and had to sit again. She hated the weakness that came from her illness. Why hadn't she tied a handkerchief over her mouth and nose last night? She knew why—she hadn't been thinking. Once she'd seen the fire, she'd panicked and done everything she could to try to smother it.

Her heart beat uncomfortably fast in the base of her throat as she caught her breath. She hunched over her knees, waiting for the weakness to pass. Praying for it to pass. She wouldn't always be like this, would she? She smothered the irrational fear. This was a temporary illness.

"Felicia, dear."

She glanced up as someone called her name. Evelyn breezed up the stairs toward her.

"Whatever are you doing up here?"

Felicia mustered the brightest smile she could manage. "I was just going to see about salvaging a few of my dresses, if I'm able."

"Nonsense."

When Evelyn offered her hand, Felicia resignedly took it. It appeared that her rest had ended. She accepted the dowager's help to stand.

"Your dresses will be a mess. They'll need washing and pressing at the very least. Let the servants handle it. You may borrow something from me in the meantime."

"That isn't necessary—"

Evelyn raised her eyebrows. "Please don't tell me you mean to wear that dowdy thing forever."

She had a point. Admitting defeat, Felicia inclined her head. "Very well. One dress. Something you don't commonly wear, perhaps."

The older woman's expression brightened. "We'll try a few on and see which fits best."

If Felicia could manage to remain standing for that long. She gripped the banister hard.

Evelyn must have noticed because a worried furrow formed between her eyebrows. "Do you need some help walking down the stairs?"

No. The word was on the tip of her tongue, but she squelched it as she remembered what Gideon had said. It was difficult to think that this caring, composed woman might have been on the brink of death through grief. But Felicia could all too easily imagine it. After all, she'd only been acquainted with her a handful of days, and yet the dowager looked as though she genuinely worried after Felicia's health.

She smiled. "Please. I get winded easily."

The trip to the family wing was long, but not as arduous as traversing it herself. Evelyn proved a skillful conversationalist, guiding Felicia through a myriad of topics from her love of chemistry to her love of dogs. The one topic she thankfully steered clear of was that of Felicia's relationship with Gideon. Although Felicia had feared that Evelyn might prove as tenacious on the subject as Lucy, her fears were soon put to rest.

In fact, Evelyn spoke of none of her children. The focus was solely on Felicia. Perhaps because of the gentle interrogation, Felicia was grateful to sit in a padded armchair upon reaching Evelyn's room. Unlike some of the rooms in the house, hers was decorated simply, in neutral colors with a splash of pink or yellow here or there. The one fixture to the room was the massive portrait of the family. Lucy, only two or three years old. Gideon, not quite ten. Three other boys in their teenage years. The oldest, certainly the current Duke of Tenwick, stood in front of an older man who had a hand on his son's shoulder. The entire family beamed.

Evelyn peeked over her shoulder, her eyes softening. Her eyelashes fluttered as she fought against the moisture shining in her eyes. "That was commissioned almost four years to the day before my husband's accident. My family." She fished out her handkerchief and dabbed at her eyes.

"Gideon looks like quite the rascal there. I can picture him about to pull his sister's hair."

The older woman laughed. "Actually, I believe he'd done something to Anthony's trousers. He's the boy standing next to him. Throughout the entire sitting, Anthony couldn't keep still."

Felicia didn't know what to say to that, so she stroked Chub's ears instead.

Turning, Evelyn opened the doors to her wardrobe and ran her hands over the dresses inside. "Do you have any brothers or sisters, Felicia?"

"Not to my knowledge."

With a frown, the dowager turned. "What can you mean?"

"My father might have remarried. I haven't been home in—" *Thirteen years.* "—a long time."

"How dreadful! Don't you and your father get along?"

Felicia grimaced. She adjusted her position on the seat. "We used to, Papa and I. I haven't spoken to him in a long time."

For years, she'd thought about writing home. Asking how he fared, if he missed her. To what end? She'd railed at him as she tried to convince him that a marriage was not what she wanted or needed. He hadn't believed her then—she highly doubted he would believe her now.

Abandoning her task at the wardrobe, Evelyn perched on an ottoman in front of Felicia. She gathered one of Felicia's hands in both of hers. "I'm sorry. And your mother?"

I don't remember her. Felicia choked back the tears that formed a lump in her throat. That wasn't strictly true, she did remember some things—a musical laugh, the way she would stroke Felicia's hair, her soft voice. But the recollections were muted, as if seen from a far distance.

"She died when I was very young. It was just me and Papa, growing up."

It's why I am who I am today. If her father had remarried, she might have been taught all the frivolous skills a lady learned instead of the thorough education she'd received from her father.

"May I ask what happened between you? If I'm prying, please say so."

Of course she was prying. But Felicia felt indebted to her for opening her home and welcoming Felicia with such graciousness. Not to mention, this was the closest Felicia had felt with a maternal woman in years. Perhaps ever. If she closed her eyes, she could pretend that Evelyn was her mother, asking a seventeen-year-old Felicia what troubled her.

"I wanted to study science. My father arranged a marriage to a man who would never have allowed it. It became clear to me that if I wanted to pursue my independence, I couldn't do it while under the charge of any man, not even my father."

Evelyn's hand tightened on Felicia's. "You ran away?"

The eve before the wedding. "I had to."

Although she expected Evelyn to show some form of condemnation, the expression on the dowager's face was kind. Sympathetic, even. "How old were you?"

"Lucy's age."

"And you've been on your own ever since?"

Felicia straightened her shoulders. She didn't need pity or sympathy. She'd made a spectacular life for herself. Yes, it was hard at times, but it was on her terms.

"I have. I like traveling," she lied.

She hated traveling. The same places, different faces. Always having to be her best, most brilliant self to attract customers. Calculating how much to flirt with the men so she wasn't chased out of town or didn't invite too much attention once her stall closed. Her favorite time was when she wintered among friends and could simply be herself.

Evelyn patted her hand. "Then I'm sorry my son is keeping you from doing so." She had a knowing gleam in her eye, as if she suspected that Felicia didn't mind as much as she pretended.

Felicia shrugged. "Winter is almost upon us. I would have had to stop soon, in any case."

"Well, then I hope you'll stay the winter here with us, regardless if you conclude your business with my son by then."

Felicia smiled thinly. She didn't think Gideon would be happy if she accepted such an arrangement without first speaking with him. A week ago, she would have said he was vehemently against her presence, seeing as they were rivals. But now their relationship was often volatile, but there was something akin to camaraderie at its core. She was afraid to name it.

Instead, she said, "I believe I've recovered my breath. Which dress do you think I might wear?"

A broad smile capped Evelyn's face as she scurried toward the wardrobe again. "Let me see. Hmm... it's a shame I don't have many bright colors anymore. All my colorful dresses predate my husband's death."

Felicia had noticed that the dowager remained in half-mourning, wearing shades of gray, lavender, and black. "I don't mind wearing an older dress." Especially if it would be one that Evelyn wouldn't miss because she didn't wear it.

The dowager shook her head. "Oh, those old rags? They wouldn't do. Here, try this one on." It was a muted yellow so light, it almost appeared to be an off-white color.

Any dress would be better than the one Felicia currently wore. "Thank you, that seems perfect."

"Try it on first," Evelyn admonished. "I'm not terribly taller than you, but you are thinner and I'm afraid it will look like a sack on you. Come here and I'll help you undress."

Without much of a choice, Felicia obeyed the command. As Evelyn undid her buttons, she said, "Perhaps once we've found you a dress, I can fashion your hair. I used to do Lucy's all the time, before we hired her a lady's maid for her come out."

She sounded wistful. Felicia couldn't deny her. In fact, she didn't want to. Spending time alone with a woman as loving and maternal as Evelyn was... nice.

Too nice, perhaps. The raw feeling in her chest didn't entirely have to do with her injury. Spending time with Evelyn made her wish for things she couldn't have.

Like the mother that she'd never known.

Like the promise of a husband and children that she had turned her back on when she'd run away from home so long ago.

Chapter Nineteen

Catt caught Giddy admiring Felicia's figure as she leaned across the work bench to reach for a jar. With a smirk, Catt leaned his hip on the corner of the work table and crossed his arms.

"Having trouble concentrating, Giddy?"

Gideon glared at his friend. *Why would you say that?* Catt had witnessed the hostility between Giddy and Felicia firsthand; he knew how rare a moment's peace was while they were working. Now was not the time to insinuate that Gideon found his partner attractive.

Even if it was true.

He plucked at the cravat that was uncomfortably tight around his throat as he struggled to think of a witty reply. Unfortunately, with Felicia near enough for him to smell the clean scent of her soap, he could barely remember his own name, let alone formulate words. As difficult as it was to maintain his distance while they were at odds, after hours alone together working peacefully, he couldn't remember why she'd frustrated him to begin with.

Or nearly alone. Catt, after all, had made himself at home in the orangery despite Giddy's speaking looks. Felicia didn't seem to mind.

In fact, she took his friend's teasing comment in stride and feathered her hand over Catt's arm. "Who wouldn't have trouble concentrating with you batting your eyelashes over there? That is why you removed your jacket when you came in, wasn't it—to draw the eye?"

Giddy clenched his hands as a surge of emotion raked his chest. Felicia delivered the quip with a touch, a flirtatious smile that brought color to Catt's cheeks, and a musical tone of voice. For one small moment, Catt was the center of her world.

Then, in the next breath, she turned away to add one more ingredient to the serum and adjust the beaker over the brazier, for all the world like she'd never flirted at all. Catt adjusted his position on the edge of the bench, looking uncomfortable as he divided his gaze between Giddy and Felicia.

The hot, jealous feeling in Gideon's chest persisted as Felicia ignored him. A week ago, she'd teased him just as mercilessly as Catt. Now... he didn't even get a smile. Had something changed? When she interacted with him, she was professional, serious, sometimes even cold. He shouldn't be craving the flirtatious glances and remarks that had irritated him at first.

But, at the same time *her smiles should be for me, not Catt.*

He ran his fingers through his hair. *You, sir, are an idiot.* Fortunately, Felicia had her back turned to him as she hunched over the work bench. In fact, she had a death grip on the edge. Alarm spiked through him and he straightened his spine. Was she having trouble breathing again?

"Perhaps you should sit."

She didn't argue, which spoke volumes in itself. He pulled the stool closer to her so she didn't have to walk as far. Her lips were parted. She looked unnaturally pale, her skin a contrast to her dark hair. Her chest, her bodice a periwinkle blue lined with delicate lace not suited to the task at hand, rose and fell with steady breaths.

"You're over-exerting yourself." He should have guessed. Although the servants had returned to work, Felicia had been exposed to the smoke for longer than anyone else. Not to mention, even his mother hadn't been able to convince her to take a few days of rest. She had been up, keeping herself busy even when working in the orangery had been impossible.

She cast him an irritated glare. "I'm fine."

"Perhaps I should leave. You two seem busy."

They'd been busy with the project, refusing to disclose its purpose, for the last hour, not that that had mattered to Catt then.

Giddy didn't bother answering his friend. He was more concerned with Felicia. It was getting late, but he knew better than to suggest they retire for the evening just yet. "Some water, then."

He blindly reached for the handful of flasks they had lined up on the edge of the work bench. His hand bumbled against the lot, knocking them over. The cap of one, not shut tightly enough, sprung open and the contents drenched the tan tailcoat hung over the edge of the bench.

"My jacket," Catt exclaimed.

"It's only clothing." He found the water flask and held it out to Felicia.

Catt, unfortunately, didn't consider the matter settled. "Easy for you to say! You don't have to walk back to the village in nothing but your shirtsleeves."

"Take my spare coat." Giddy gestured at the neatly folded bit of fabric tucked between two pots. It was one of his formal coats done up in the ducal colors, that he'd worn into the orangery months ago and forgotten here ever since. He didn't particularly like it, for all that it represented the family. Matchmaking mamas and debutantes who didn't know him by face but who recognized the ducal seal tended to latch onto him when he wore it. Hence why he'd conveniently lost it.

"I can see I'd best take my leave before I have to return home naked."

Giddy rolled his eyes. "I'll have your blasted coat washed and returned to you. It probably won't even stain."

In a huff, Catt shoved his arms into the jacket and left by means of the garden door. The orangery, so humid in relation to the crisp outdoor air that wafted in, was encased with glass windows that were completely befogged. He couldn't even discern the light of the setting sun or moon—depending on how late the hour had grown.

Felicia finished with the flask and leaned forward to thrust it onto the work bench. "He gets cranky when he's tired."

The observation startled a laugh out of Gideon. "You could say that."

After releasing a deep, audible breath, she slipped off the stool to resume work. Her complexion didn't look as wan. In fact, spots of color had returned to her cheeks. Her gaze twinkled with good humor. He moved the stool out of her way and set in to help her.

Their hands brushed, the burn of bare skin searing him. He wasn't the only one who noticed. Before she teased him again, he grabbed an empty flask and fetched more water to boil for their experiment. Although he'd taken to keeping two full buckets on hand from the well, she still insisted on purifying any water before using it in their experiment.

When he straightened from filling the flask, he caught her gaze on him. She averted it instantly. The air charged with something he dare not name.

She coughed into her fist as he returned to her. Not the rough, ragged cough that had plagued her immediately following the fire, but a lighter one as if she had a persistent tickle in her throat. He set the flask on the work bench next to the others as she reached for the beaker to remove it from the heat.

He frowned. Was it supposed to be frothing like that? None of the others they'd tried had done so. Perhaps he ought to try harvesting some oils from the new roots of the cutting he'd taken. He'd noticed the beginning only this morning through the clear glass and water solution. Every time he checked back, even if only an hour had passed, more of the roots had come through. In a couple days he would feel confident transplanting the clipping.

With a disgusted sigh that led into another little cough, Felicia poured the mixture into a jar, corked it with perhaps more vigor than was necessary, and started to move away from the bench.

He stepped in her path. "What do you need? I'll get it."

She had more color—in fact, the flush over her skin now reached to her chin and forehead—but he didn't like that persistent cough. Better she didn't strain herself yet again.

Fortunately, she didn't fight his help. "The pen and ink, please."

He fetched it from her side of the work table. He held the vial as she scrawled on the label in large, easily decipherable letters: DO NOT DRINK.

Ah. So the frothing hadn't been desirable, after all.

Once she finished and capped the ink once more, she used a handkerchief to clean the nub of the pen. She set them both down on the work table, which was where Giddy added the useless serum. He didn't quite understand why she wanted to keep their failures, but they already had a wide array lined up on her half of the work bench. She insisted.

Looking weary, she rubbed her head. "I don't understand how it was contaminated. It shouldn't have done that."

Since he didn't have any insight to offer, he didn't say anything at all. Instead, he reached past her for the beaker. "I'll rinse it outside. Maybe that will help."

As his hand closed around the warm neck of the beaker, his body brushed against Felicia's. She wasn't the only person to have trouble breathing—but in his case, the lack of breath was due to her proximity. His head clouded. Reason fled as her lips parted. He couldn't think of a single reason not to kiss her at that moment. He lowered his head.

This is a bad idea. He squashed that thought as he pressed his mouth to hers. As he abandoned the beaker and wrapped his arms around her, he realized that she'd risen on tiptoe to meet him.

***

Gideon's mouth was warm. Hot, even. It scorched her. Felicia wrapped her arms around his neck, pinning him in place against her. Not that he seemed willing to part ways any time soon. He kissed her with an intensity that stole her breath. His hands roved over her back and hips, fitting her against him. She ignited at his touch.

Her throat burned as she inhaled through her nose and she broke the kiss. She turned her face to the side in order to cough. As apt as the analogy was, she shouldn't actually smell smoke right now, should she? Had they knocked into the brazier?

Her eyes watered as she opened them. The orangery was humid but it hadn't been this foggy when they'd started kissing... had it?

Gideon plucked at his cravat as he started to cough, too. The uncomfortable sting in her throat wasn't just a byproduct of her injury. She spread the coals in the brazier to encourage it to cool.

"I need some air." The fog in the orangery was so thick, she could barely choke out the words. Gideon's face had become indistinct, never mind that it was only a foot away from her.

"Agreed." His voice was strained. He took her by the hand and led her to the nearest door, into the marble corridor leading to the abbey. Her head spun due to the sharp stench of smoke, but his hand in hers anchored her. For a brief moment, she felt safe.

The door wouldn't budge. Gideon dropped her hand in order to try with his dominant hand. "It's stuck," he said, his voice sharpened with surprise and disbelief. He turned away. "Let's go out the other door."

That one wouldn't open, either. Felicia's heart throbbed painfully in the base of her throat as she used the sleeve of her borrowed dress to wipe away some of the moisture fogging the glass. A long stick had been shoved through the handle, barring the doorway. Someone had shut them in here.

If so, the smoke was not a byproduct of the brazier. It was something else entirely. And it didn't bode well.

Gideon shoved at the door with his full weight, though what he hoped to accomplish, she didn't know. She backed away, struggling to think. It was as though the fog had clouded her brain as well. She coughed into her fist.

Giddy took her by the shoulders. "It's going to be all right. I'll get us out."

He didn't sound as though he thought it would be all right. He maneuvered her, still coughing, back to the work bench. Here, the smoke was thicker. It stung her eyes. She pulled her bodice up over her nose and mouth as she squinted.

Gideon disappeared into the smoke. His form became no more than a silhouette. Before long, even that was hard to discern. A sickly sizzling sound caught her attention. She peered around for the source. There—by the vent. The air was too foggy around the sound to discern color, but it looked like a pool of liquid slowly spreading across the ground. The smoke wafted from the areas where the liquid touched plant matter, devouring it. Felicia stared as it slowly inched closer. What chemical had that reaction? An acid?

Thank God she'd left Chubs with the women tonight as they entertained a couple of the ladies from the nearby village. That hazardous liquid pooled exactly where her dog usually chose to lay. Was someone trying to kill her dog?

Or her.

A shattering crash rang through the air, startling her from her slow thoughts.

Chapter Twenty

The smoke clouded Giddy's mind. He tried not to breathe in it, but that only made his lungs throb and his head spin. Someone had shut them in the orangery. He had to get Felicia out before she suffered more lung damage. She'd come so close last time...

The thought of her granted him clarity. The moment he turned away from her, he found himself enclosed by fog, unable to escape due to the glass walls. If he broke them, his plants would die upon being exposed to the elements. If he didn't, Felicia would die.

He groped for the stool, took a step forward, and hurled it at the nearest wall. The glass shattered with an almost musical lilt. He stepped sideways and turned his back, hoping to shield Felicia from the spray. When he opened his eyes, he couldn't spot her silhouette.

"Felicia?"

"Here."

She'd moved away from the work table. He reached out, fumbling until he found her hand. The moment he did, he drew her to him and lifted her into his arms. Her shoulders shook as she battled a cough.

"I can walk—"

Like hell she could. "Don't struggle. There's broken glass. I don't want you to get cut."

Using his body to shield hers, he stepped sideways through the opening he'd made. Jagged edges of glass sliced through his jacket and into his shoulder. A scratch. He ignored the sting.

The fresh, clean outdoor air was like Heaven. But they still remained too close to the smoke now wafting from the opening. His knees weakened, but he walked as far as he could and set Felicia on her feet before he lowered himself onto the crisp, dry grass.

The cold air burned his throat as he rolled onto his back. Felicia collapsed next to him, coughing hard. He battled a tickle in his throat as he sat up and rubbed her back.

The moment her wheezing eased for a moment, he glanced back at the orangery. The lantern inside only provided an indistinct glow against the dissipating fog. The night air, at the very least, tore the mist to shreds without mercy. It didn't reach Felicia and Giddy.

"What was that?" His throat was raw from the sting of the smoke. He still tasted the bitter undertone.

Felicia slumped against him, gulping for air. "I think... someone poured something... into the vent." She swallowed and took several breaths before she added, "It's corrosive. I saw the way it was eating through your plants, creating the smoke. We have to stop it."

When she started to stand, he wrapped his arm around her waist and pinned her next to him. It took an astoundingly small amount of strength to hold her. She was still weak from the smoke and her injury.

"Don't. Let the smoke dissipate first. It isn't safe."

"But your plants—"

"Who cares about the bloody plants?" He rested his forehead against the top of her head.

I do. Or, at least, he used to. But he cared about Felicia more. When had that happened?

When he stretched out against the grass, Felicia followed. The chill of the air, granting clarity at first, soon penetrated his jacket to seep into his bones. Felicia wore even less, only a borrowed dress better suited to summer than fall. If he didn't rouse himself and get them indoors, they might catch their death. His limbs trembled with weakness. *One moment more*, he promised himself. Then he would stand.

As his body recovered, his mind whirled a mile a minute. The crisp air sharpened his thoughts.

"This was no accident."

Felicia shifted next to him to look him in the eye. "That's what I've been trying to tell you all along."

***

Finally. How long had Felicia been trying to convince Giddy of the truth? She hadn't wanted it to take the destruction of the orangery to convince him, but now at least they were on the same page. They could handle this situation together. Strength flooded her at the thought that she wouldn't have to face such a daunting task alone.

But first, she had to move them from the lawn. Night surrounded them, the temperature plummeting from earlier in the day. They had to go inside before they caught a chill.

She hadn't quite caught her breath—but, ever since the fire, she hadn't been able to, anyway. Steeling herself, she rolled onto her hands and knees and started to stand. Giddy tried to pin her down with his arm, but she used it to haul him into a sitting position.

"Where are you going?" His voice was still gravelly from the smoke.

The inside of her throat still burned, too, a prickling sensation like she'd swallowed a cactus.

"We can't stay here. We have to get inside."

He groaned, but otherwise didn't protest. As he tried to tuck his long legs underneath him to stand, his shoulders slumped in defeat. "I don't know if I can walk."

She didn't want to push him. She didn't know what that corrosive liquid was, and therefore didn't know the effects of the smoke it had produced. Getting his blood pumping could aggravate the toxic effect.

Then again, both their hearts were beating fast from their narrow escape from the orangery.

Firming her chin, she said, "The alternative is freezing. My wagon isn't far, just around the corner of the manor. We'll go there." Maybe, with luck, she would have something inside to counteract the effects of the smoke. At the very least, they should both take a dose of the tincture they had created to treat smoke inhalation.

With difficulty, she and Gideon managed to stand. They leaned heavily against each other as they slowly traversed the gravel walks of the garden. His heat next to her was like a furnace. It brought the chill on her other side into stark relief. She tucked herself closer beneath his arm.

Giddy leaned on her far more than he would have usually, a testament to the effect of the smoke. Truthfully, Felicia didn't know how she continued standing throughout the distance. Her lungs burned but she refused to show it. She focused on walking, one foot in front of the other. When her wagon came into view, an indistinct shadow against the larger backdrop of the stable, she focused on that. All her energy poured into reaching her safe haven.

Once she reached the wagon, she unlocked the door and helped Gideon inside. He winced as he hunched his shoulders to get through the door. She heard the hitch in his breath.

"Are you hurt?" Of course he was, they both were, but that noise hadn't sounded healthy.

"Just a scratch."

He'd been cut? When? The glass. It must be.

By memory, she guided him through the wagon to sit on her cot. It was less firm without the trunk underneath, but it held his weight. Once she lit an oil lamp affixed to her counter, she ran out of breath and had to sit as well. The only other place was the crate in the corner. She lowered herself onto it and leaned heavily against the wall.

The light reflected off of Giddy's eyes as he looked her over. He didn't say a word. His expression was pinched. Lines formed between his eyebrows and around his mouth.

To distract him, she asked, "Where are you hurt?"

"My shoulder, mostly. The glass caught me. I'll be fine."

Another moment and she was renewed enough to pluck a bottle of the tincture out of her cupboard and drag the crate into the narrow aisle between bed and counter. "Exactly right. You will be fine. Drink this. A mouthful will do for now."

He didn't argue. His hand trembled as he lifted the bottle to his mouth. He took a swig, then passed it to her. She did the same. The mixture burned against her raw throat, but the sensation soon subsided, taking away the raw pain with it as her throat numbed. She took a deep breath, relieved at the lack of ache.

"Take off your jacket."

Uncertainty crossed his features. "I'm not certain this is the place..."

She fought a smirk. "I'm not going to ravish you."

"I meant because it's bloody cold in here." Did he look disappointed? She tried not to think of their kiss. It had happened in the heat of the moment, and they had more important matters to which to attend. Like his wounds. What if some of the smoke got into the cut and infected him?

"I'll light a brazier." Mustering her strength, she did exactly as she said. She found a flask of water and another of pure alcohol to clean the wound, as well as one of her handkerchiefs. When she returned to the crate in front of him, he still hadn't budged. "Your jacket. Or do I have to take it off for you?"

She doubted that she would have the energy or strength to wrestle with him, but her threat did the trick. He grimaced as he peeled his jacket from his injured shoulder. The cut was a lot deeper than a scratch, given the look on his face.

"Your waistcoat, too. And probably your shirt, as well."

He fiddled with his cravat. "Perhaps we ought to fetch the physician."

"For a scratch?" She raised her eyebrows. Her hands were full or she would have crossed her arms, too. "If you'd like to fetch him, go right ahead. I'll stay here."

With a few flicks of his fingers, he unknotted his cravat and tossed the cloth onto his coat, next to him. The space was crowded, his knees rising nearly to his chest when he planted his feet on the floor. He hesitated as he traced the top button of his waistcoat.

"I'm sure I'll be able to handle cleaning the cut myself."

She glowered at him. "Take off your shirt, Giddy. I've seen you bare-chested before, or have you forgotten?"

Color poured into his cheeks. He glanced away. "I haven't." His voice was so soft, she barely heard.

Within seconds, he unbuttoned and removed his waistcoat. His shirt proved more troublesome. Even after undoing the fastenings so the collar gaped open, he had to lift his arms in order to pull it over his head. When he hissed in pain, Felicia set the flasks at her feet in order to help him. Blood from his shirt wet her hand. His wound was much deeper than he'd thought. Would she need her sewing kit? She hoped not; her eyes were starting to blur from fatigue.

The cut on his shoulder wasn't the only place where the glass had caught him, but it was the deepest. She started there, and told him to bite down on his cravat if he needed to. "This might hurt."

He grunted when she poured water onto the wound to wash away the blood. She shifted, moving onto the cot with him in order to examine how deep it was. She should stitch it, to be safe. Fortunately, she usually kept her sewing supplies near her bed, where she did most of her mending and embroidery. The needle was within easy reach. She sterilized it with the alcohol. She used undyed thread.

"I'm going to clean it with alcohol now." As she splashed from the flask onto the wound, he made a strangled sound through gritted teeth. She dabbed at the wound with her handkerchief and made two neat stitches. She rubbed his uninjured forearm. "That's the worst of it. I'm just going to clean the smaller cuts. I don't recommend you put your smoky clothes back on, though. We'll have to find something else."

"Thank you," he said as she moved on to the other shallow cuts along his biceps and shoulders. They'd already stopped bleeding. No doubt they stung a bit when she washed them, but he gave no indication that he was in further pain.

His voice was bland as he said, "Our research is likely ruined."

"I would say so." She gently removed the crust of blood from a small nick. "Even if the plants survived, we don't know for certain what the gas did to them."

He stared at the specimen she'd tucked into the corner, the last *brugmansia* plant they had. "I guess you were right to keep one of the plants in reserve."

She said nothing. This didn't feel like the right time to say, *'I told you so.'*

"If you'll let me tend to it, I'll take the plant to my room."

"We should keep it here."

"It's cold in here," he pointed out.

She wrinkled her nose. "Maybe, but we shouldn't leave it unattended somewhere else. We don't have the orangery to use as our laboratory anymore. The wagon is the closest thing we have to a controlled environment."

He tensed beneath her hands, but the only word he uttered was, "Agreed."

And what of the person who did this? Although the inquiry was on the tip of her tongue, she stifled it for now. She tended to the rest of his cuts in silence.

Even that small amount of exertion exhausted her. She leaned her forehead against Gideon's arm as she caught her breath. He shifted his arm to envelop her in his embrace. Her mind buzzed with questions and doubts but for now, she was too weary to think of them. She settled her weight against him as she recovered her strength.

Another sip of the tincture soothed the rising sting in her throat again. Knowing that it would make her even more tired, she took only the tiniest of sips. Giddy took a larger one. She removed the lamp to take with them and stripped the blanket off the bed for him to wrap around his shoulders as they returned to the abbey.

When she deviated from the path to the front door, he stopped her. "What are you doing?"

She rubbed her eyes. "I can't leave the spill in the orangery. It's dangerous. I have to clean it up."

He followed her. "I'm going with you."

Stopping him with a hand on his chest, she told him, "You aren't dressed. Go inside and find yourself a new shirt, at least."

"No." His voice was mulish. "What if the air makes you woozy and you pass out? If you won't leave this for someone else to clean up..." He trailed off, his voice rising in a question.

"I won't." She crossed her arms. "I am the most qualified person to safely dispose of chemicals. I don't want anyone else getting hurt."

"Then I'll stay to make certain you don't get hurt."

She sighed, even though inwardly she was glad of his presence. She felt guilty that he stood in the cold with no more protection than the blanket she'd provided, but knowing that he was there in case weakness overcame her made her feel safer.

Slowly, they meandered to the orangery. The lantern inside had guttered out. The only light came from the dim glow of the lamp she carried. She held up her hand and begged Gideon to remain at the door. "There's no sense in both of us being weakened if the air inside is still toxic." She pulled her dress up over her nose and mouth just in case.

First, she surveyed the damage. The plants had slowed the progress of the liquid. The bulk of the damage had already been done, but given the look of the plants, Felicia didn't trust stepping on the affected areas. She needed a base to neutralize the acid and render it harmless. Soap would work in a pinch, but she didn't have any on hand. The nearest place she kept some was the wagon. She locked her knees against the wave of weakness at the thought of venturing all the way around the side of the manor again.

Fortunately, the catastrophe in the orangery had drawn the attention of the household spies. Mr. Keeling was the first to arrive, and was quizzing Gideon when Felicia emerged from the orangery. He was more than happy to bring Felicia the supplies she needed.

The down side to the servants knowing about the event was that soon the entire house knew—including the Graylockes.

"This is abominable," Lucy exclaimed as she stomped up to the scene.

Felicia, having just finished sprinkling a base over the acid to neutralize it, was now seated on the ground waiting for it to take effect before she allowed the servants to clean up what they could. Most of the plants could not be salvaged.

"First the fire in your room, now this? Who would do such a thing?"

Felicia exchanged a panicked glance with Gideon, who had a fresh shirt and greatcoat, also brought by Mr. Keeling. They couldn't allow the family to think that the accidents had been deliberately arranged. It would raise too many questions—ones that led back to the spy business.

Felicia cleared her throat. "It was my fault. I knocked over the wrong chemicals and caused the spill."

"Really?" Lucy frowned. "That doesn't seem like you."

With a sidelong glance, Felicia leaned forward to brush her fingers against Giddy's arm. "I was distracted."

He frowned at her.

Play along. Or do you want them to guess the truth?

Fortunately, Lucy and her mother were too busy exchanging sly glances to notice the silent exchange between Felicia and Gideon.

Linking her arm through her daughter's, Evelyn said, "Perhaps it's best to stop working for the evening. I'm sure the servants will be able to handle cleaning this up without your supervision. Come, join us for the evening entertainment."

Felicia didn't know whether she could remain upright throughout the walk to the manor, let alone keep awake throughout whatever entertainment Evelyn had planned. The energy seeped from her like wisps of warmth driven out by the chill. She leaned against Gideon.

"It's been a long night," he said. "Perhaps we can sit with you tomorrow evening instead."

"Certainly," Lucy chirped. "You both should run off to bed. Don't worry about Chubs tonight, Felicia. I'll take care of him."

As she flashed them a wicked smile and turned away, Gideon groaned under his breath. He shifted position so they faced each other. By now, with all the servants carrying lanterns, the lawn was almost as bright as day. Gideon looked weary, uncertain, and maybe even a little annoyed.

"Why did you do that?" he whispered. "They're trying to force a marriage as it is."

Felicia's stomach flipped at the word *marriage.* A torrent of emotions overwhelmed her—fear, hope, and regret among them—but she was too weary to dwell on it. She shoved them aside, striving for equilibrium.

Fatigue edged her voice as she answered, "I didn't want them to ask too many questions about the nature of the accident or our work, otherwise your mother might become suspicious. This distracts them, doesn't it?"

The disapproval in his expression faded. He sighed and ran a hand through his hair. "They will make this very uncomfortable for us."

She leaned closer, lowering her voice. "Let them. We need to focus on uncovering who in the household has turned against the crowd."

His mouth flattened into a grim line. "We're exhausted. Neither of us is operating at the height of our faculties. Let's regroup in the morning."

Felicia nodded in agreement. The lure of bed was too strong. But tomorrow they had a mission to complete and a traitor to find.

Chapter Twenty-One

The morning was so young that the warmth from the kitchens hadn't yet seeped into the floorboards. Felicia danced from foot to foot as she rapped on Gideon's door. Since she and the Vales were still residing in the family wing of the house, she hadn't had far to walk.

No answer. Felicia knocked again.

This time she heard a faint, muffled, "Come in."

She did, stopping short on the threshold as the dim morning light peeking between the curtains lit on Gideon's naked torso. The bedsheets pooled around his waist as he sat up, rubbing his eyes. The moment he locked eyes on her, he yanked the sheets up to his chest.

"What are you doing in here?"

"You told me to come in."

He glared. "I thought you were a servant."

By will alone, Felicia kept her gaze fixed to his instead of admiring his form. If she shut the door...

But she wouldn't. They had business. A traitor in their midst. There wasn't time for her to recall the scorching kiss he'd delivered last night.

"Very well, I'll leave. Will you join me in the library?"

"Posthaste."

Gideon was true to his word. Felicia scarcely had to wait ten minutes in the large, book-encased room. When he joined her in the empty room, she reluctantly stopped her perusal of the bookshelves and met him in the chairs in front of the hearth.

"We have a problem," Felicia said.

That, he already knew, but perhaps the reminder would spur him to help her solve it.

With a sigh, Giddy dropped into the armchair opposite her. He rubbed the back of his neck as he leaned forward. "I know. Ferreting out an enemy spy will be difficult, impossible maybe. Morgan trained me, so I know exactly how he would have trained the rest of the household. They'll be on alert for any deviations from our normal behavior, any hint that we might have guessed at the culprit. We'll be watched."

Felicia formed a steeple with her fingers as she thought. "I considered that. I'm new here, so my behavior is watched already. I don't fit in with the staff and can't ask the right questions without being noticed."

"We need help."

Gideon's expression was serious, his green eyes gleaming as he read her reaction.

She made a face. "We can't afford to ask for any. The spy might even be Mr. Keeling, for all we know."

His jaw tightened, but he didn't contradict her. He must have seen the prudence in her warning.

"We can't do it ourselves. We've lost our work until now, and you must admit, that serum would prove vital in discovering who is truly responsible."

"It would. I can start with our remaining plant while you—"

Gideon cut her off. "We work better together and you know it. That plant needs my care right now, if we have any hope of getting it to bloom."

Felicia sighed. She rubbed her head. "Did the cutting survive?"

"The smoke contaminated the water. I can work with it, but I don't like the color permeating the roots. It might have an untoward effect if we try it."

"You're right."

He leaned forward, capturing her hand. His skin was warm. "We need help, Felicia. We can't do this on our own."

She gritted her teeth as she admitted he was right. They did need help, desperately. But who could they trust?

Gideon. She trusted Gideon. Squeezing his hand, she asked, "What do you suggest?"

***

Less than an hour later, Felicia found herself ensconced in a room with two people who hated each other more than she and Gideon ever had. Catt and Rocky sat on opposite ends of the sofa, but that didn't stop her from shooting him dirty looks every time he shifted his position. Which, due to his obvious discomfort and the way he continually wiped his palms on his thighs, was often. Felicia exchanged a look of trepidation with Giddy. Was he certain this was for the best?

But he must have been. With all of the staff under suspicion, Gideon had assured her his two closest friends were the only other people of the household that could be trusted. And despite their initial surprise at finding out about the spy network inside Tenwick Abby, the pair had seemed more than eager to take part.

He ignored her doubt. Leaning forward, he braced his elbows on his knees. "So, will you help? We're counting on you to go unnoticed where we can't. If this wasn't a matter of national importance..."

Rocky crossed her arms. Today she wore a replica of the frock she'd worn when she and Felicia had met, in the same colors as the footmen. "Me, I understand, but how do you expect *him* to help?"

She glared at Catt. This time, he met her gaze. Their eyes caught and held. The hostility in Rocky's expression slipped. Adjusting her glasses, she looked away.

Quietly, Catt said, "I can help."

Whether or not Giddy noticed the tension between them—or if, perhaps, by that time he was inured to it—he answered, "Catt is treated like family here. He's given free rein of the house and therefore it won't be unusual to find him anywhere you might be."

"Plus," Catt added, his smirk growing, "We wouldn't want you to shirk your duties while you do this favor."

"Actually, I couldn't care less. Forget your duties," Giddy said. "If you'll do it, this task takes precedence. But it will be difficult. I can provide you with a list of those in the household who are spies, but that doesn't mean that someone else hasn't infiltrated the house. I recommend looking at everyone and seeing who among the staff have changed their routine or joined the household recently."

Rocky shot a smug look at Catt. "*Among the staff.* It looks as though I have the advantage there, doesn't it? You can't even remember their names."

"I'm not a duke's son. I don't walk around utterly ignoring everyone around me."

"Don't you?"

As the argument veered toward juvenile, Felicia shot a glance toward Gideon to see how he was handling the insult. He looked resigned. Did he know the names of everyone on his staff? Given the amount of people he claimed worked at Tenwick Abbey for a time before returning to active spy duty elsewhere, Felicia wouldn't have thought so. However, he'd offered the list of spies too readily. Unless he planned to extract such a list from Mr. Keeling—a dangerous avenue, considering that even the duke's assistant was a suspect—he must be familiar with the staff.

Raising his hand to stall the fight, he asked, "Will you help us?"

"We will," Rocky snapped, her eyes glinting from behind her spectacles. Her expression took on a competitive edge. "I will find the person responsible."

'I.' Not *'we.'*

Although he'd undoubtedly heard the slip, Gideon pretended not to. He helped Felicia to her feet with a hand beneath her elbow. "Thank you. We appreciate it. We'll be in Felicia's wagon, should you discover anything. Shall we meet here this afternoon to discuss your progress? I'm sure I don't need to tell you that secrecy is paramount."

Catt and Rocky instantly assured him that they would be discreet. Felicia only hoped they wouldn't be engaged in a public row while they attempted to complete their task. When they stood, however, they shook hands cordially. Catt dropped his hand quickly and turned away.

Before she could see whether or not they would form a truce, Giddy steered Felicia out of the library. "We have work to do," he reminded her with a pointed look.

She squared her shoulders. "You're right."

At this point, they needed to complete the serum as soon as possible. It might be

instrumental in unearthing the French spy in
their midst.

Chapter Twenty-Two

"I don't understand how this is contributing to the plan."

Giddy smirked as he glanced up from his beef stew to pay attention to the alluring woman seated across from him at their table in the Golden Goose. Felicia flicked a stray strand of her inky black hair out of her eyes, not for the first time tonight. Her tresses fought to escape the hasty coiffure she'd secured them into before they left Tenwick Abbey.

"This was your plan," he reminded her.

When Rocky and Catt had returned from their search empty-handed, Felicia had suggested they switch tactics to draw out the culprit instead by leaving her wagon unguarded for the night. Mother and Lucy were looking after Chubs, who'd seemed content enough to lounge on the rug in front of the fireplace while Felicia and Giddy left the abbey to signal to the traitor that their work was ripe for sabotage.

In reality, Rocky and Catt were hanging around nearby to catch whoever infiltrated the wagon. The plan wasn't without its risks, but

Felicia had argued for it with such adamancy that Giddy had instantly suggested they try that same night. To his surprise, Catt and Rocky had agreed, for once not contradicting each other. The common denominator was Felicia. When she spoke, she delivered her opinions with confidence and authority. Others listened. He admired that about her.

It was one of many things. The way she held her lower lip between her teeth as she worked, as if she was afraid even a stray breath would impact their experiment. Her laugh. The way he'd caught her looking at him once or twice before—she made him feel invincible.

Then, of course, there was the way she kissed. Thinking of it was madness. They hadn't spoken or acknowledged their kiss in the orangery since the accident. Now wasn't the time, with someone out to prevent their mission from nearing completion. But he couldn't help but relive it during quiet moments.

She hadn't pushed him away. In fact, she'd returned his kiss with just as much fervor and heat as he felt for her. If he found a moment and kissed her, without a life or death situation driving a wedge between them, what would happen?

Felicia wrinkled her nose. "We've been away quite long enough, wouldn't you say? I thought we would circle back to keep watch with Catt and Rocky."

"And what if we were followed? It's better that we're seen, in public, to give the culprit time to realize that now might be their chance."

She grimaced and coughed into her fist. That ragged cough was better than it was, but she still had healing to do. Thankfully, the smoke from the day before hadn't had much of a permanent effect on him aside from a scratchy throat. "How much time?" Her face falling, Felicia pushed a chunk of meat around her bowl with the tip of her spoon.

She hated to be inactive. He understood and shared that feeling. Most of his life was in pursuit of knowledge, either by keeping up to date with the research of his peers or else by conducting research of his own. A pang struck him at the reminder that the orchid he and Catt had been attempting to bloom was one of the casualties of the acid. It would be months before they could begin anew with a fresh specimen. If, indeed, Catt still wanted to work with him given the strains on Giddy's time. As much as Gideon would love for the war to be over within a year, he didn't hold out much hope, due to their recent defeat.

We need that serum. Thankfully, he and Felicia had managed to work more in sync today than they ever had. They'd taken stock of the ingredients they had on hand and worked closely to revise the theory behind the serum. Which compounds would work best in conjunction with one another to bring out the full potency of the *brugmansia* oils? That was the question they had considered all day.

They had to ration what little oil they had left, or else wait weeks before he was able to get the plant they had remaining to the correct maturity to harvest more oils. He had spent some time experimenting with the roots and other parts of the plant they had in order to discover if it might be worthwhile to try pressing oil from targeted areas now.

Since they no longer trusted the staff, he'd ingested the raw plant himself. A risky move, but Felicia had monitored him closely. Although he thought he'd felt a bit woozy after chewing on the roots—a horrid, bitter taste—the feeling had quickly passed and yielded nothing worth following up on.

The whine of a fiddle being tuned returned him to the present. Given the agitated look on

Felicia's face, she badly needed a distraction. He stood and held out his hand.

"Come, let's dance."

Her gaze turned guarded. "Why? I don't often dance, Giddy."

"Make an exception. We have to be seen, don't we?"

Uncertainty crossed her face, but he waited patiently.

"We aren't the only people dancing. No one will notice if you miss a step." It was true. Men and women from the village paired up in the space left free in the center of the room. Even Miss Merewether seemed to have drawn the notorious flirt, James Brickleburr's attention.

A smirk teased her mouth, drawing his attention back to her soft lips. "What makes you think I'll miss a step?"

"An extrapolation of your last statement that you don't often dance."

She shot to her feet. Her chin lifted in challenge. "I'll have to prove you wrong then, won't I?"

If it convinced her to stand up with him, he didn't mind if she saw the dance as a competition. He wasn't the best dancer, in any case. He rarely took the time to practice. In fact, he avoided the pastime whenever possible.

As they joined the group on the dance floor, he amended that intention. The brush of Felicia's hand against his, the flick of her skirts as she kicked up her heels, her broad smile that made the room brighter. He'd sacrifice as much time in the orangery as she wanted, if only he got to keep her exactly the way she was now. His head spun as fast as his body as they kept time to the music. A heady, potent sensation akin to flying. He never wanted the night to end.

If it did, he suspected he might fall.

***

"Enough." Felicia held up a hand as she braced the other on her knee and bent over to catch her breath. "I need a break."

"I knew you couldn't keep up with me," he teased, even as worry gripped him. She still hadn't healed from her injury. Had he pushed her too hard? The fiddler played a lively tune that demanded the dancers' full enthusiasm, not like the stately music of the balls to which Giddy was accustomed.

He started to offer Felicia his arm to escort her away from the dance floor and laughing couples, but she had already turned away. He dropped his arm and quickened his step to keep pace beside her instead as she headed toward the table where they'd sat.

When he reached it, he realized that she wasn't with him. He turned, scanning the crowd until he found her. Her cheeks were rosy. Her hair had given up all pretense of behaving and framed her cheeks and chin. Her eyes sparkled as she nodded at something the serving maid said. Gideon straightened, expecting Felicia to turn to him at that moment.

Instead, she turned toward the door. Where was she going? Her pelisse lay on the back of her chair. He grabbed it and his greatcoat and used his long legs to advantage to catch her near the door leading out back.

When he touched her shoulder, she jumped and turned to face him. Her posture instantly relaxed when she saw him.

At least until he said, "Where are you going?"

Her eyebrows climbed higher, as if she couldn't fathom why he was asking her such a thing. "I need to use the privy."

"I'll come with you."

She took a step back, closer to the door. "I don't think so. I'll find it on my own."

"Have you forgotten that someone nearly killed you twice—no, three times?" He resisted the urge to run his hands through his hair. How could she have forgotten that they were the targets of a traitor? Even if the primary concern was their research. "We should go nowhere alone, just to be safe."

She snatched the pelisse from his hand and flung it around her shoulders. "For Heaven's sake, I'm only relieving myself. It won't take a moment."

Turning, she opened the door and took a step into the frigid October air. Her head crossed the threshold, but Gideon lunged for her arm and drew her back inside. "Give me a mo—" —*ment to put on my coat.*

He never finished the sentence. A heavy brick landed in the frozen dirt of the entrance with a thud. Chips of brick broke off, tinkling as they struck the door and side of the tavern. The brick was huge, easily five pounds of hard rock. If he hadn't pulled Felicia into the tavern and she'd been struck on the head, she would have died.

It was too soon to be a coincidence. Someone wasn't only trying to disturb their research, he was trying to kill the only scientist capable of reproducing it. And if Gideon hadn't been there, he would have succeeded.

Chapter Twenty-Three

Felicia would have died. If Gideon hadn't pulled her inside at that exact moment, it wouldn't only be chips of brick littering the walk. Her blood and brains would decorate it as well. She shivered, and not only from the cold seeping through the open door.

"My God." The words gushed from his mouth, as icy as the outdoor air. He herded her against the wall, pinning her there with his body as he craned his neck for signs of danger. His heat and body enveloped her.

Was he trembling? She was the one who had nearly died—she should be afraid, not him!

"I knew it. I knew it wasn't safe for you to go out alone."

She barely heard him. Her teeth chattered. She felt the vibration along her jaw, but was helpless to stop it. She stared at the open doorway, completely numb.

Think. You can't stand here.

"We should return to Tenwick Abbey."

Yes, that was a good idea. She should do that.

However, the moment she stepped toward the door to comply, Gideon stopped her. "I'll go first." He positioned her against the wall as he shrugged into his greatcoat. He flipped the collar up to shield his neck, but didn't fasten the buttons.

Raising his arms over his head to shield himself, he darted through the opening and away from the building. What did he think that would have done, had the assaulter thrown another brick? He would have broken his arms, at the very least.

She approached the doorway, but he held up his hand. "Stay there."

The sharp tone of his voice stopped her in his tracks. He craned his neck, squinting as he tried to see the upper stories of the tavern. He must not have spotted anything suspicious, because a moment later, he beckoned to her.

"Quickly."

She adjusted the pelisse around her shoulders and hurried to him. When she came abreast of him, she realized that they had forgotten something pivotal to their journey home. "I'll have the driver bring the carriage around."

The skin on the back of her neck crawled with her back facing the tavern, as if someone watched with sinister intent. When she turned, the upper stories appeared too dark compared to the bright light of the lantern next to the door.

"No. I'll go. You stay here. Exactly here." He positioned her in the middle of an open area. No overhangs, no trees, she was completely exposed. Her breath frosted in front of her face as she danced from foot to foot. The moment he disappeared, her full bladder made itself known once again. A tall, narrow outhouse resided in the corner of the open area, out of the way. She hurried to do her business.

As she finished, Gideon left the stables with his hands shoved into his pockets. The moment he scanned the courtyard and found her striding away from the outhouse, his face darkened. He met her in the middle.

"I told you not to move."

I don't do your bidding. She bit her tongue to squelch the sarcastic retort. It wouldn't help matters. Steeling herself, she answered in an even tone. "I had to relieve myself. I didn't go far." She couldn't believe that she was having an argument about the matter.

More than that, she couldn't believe that he was being so stubborn! The lantern near the tavern door cast fingers of orange light over his face, but his skin looked a bit ashen.

"You should have waited. I would have kept watch."

That sounded incredibly awkward. "I was fine."

"What if the spy had followed you to the outhouse?"

She crossed her arms. "And done what? Set it on fire?" That would not have been fun. She turned on her heel. "Whatever the case, our plan to use the wagon as bait did not work. I'm returning to the abbey."

"Wait." He lengthened his stride and caught up to her. He pulled the hood of her pelisse up over her hair. "It's cold out. You'll catch a chill or worse. Wait for the carriage."

Snowflakes sparkled in the air like stars slowly drifting to earth. Few and far between, but gusts of wind blew them into her face. Her ears burned from cold, only a touch warmer beneath the fur lining of her borrowed pelisse hood. Even so, she yanked it down again.

"I am a grown woman. I can choose for myself what to wear."

He made a face. "Far be it from me to attend to your welfare!"

When she stormed off down the street, he was on her heels, his boots making clipped steps in the frozen dirt. She couldn't believe he was treating her this way. She'd thought they were equals, but one little scare... very well, one big scare, on the heels of several others. But he had no right to treat her as if she was made of glass! Hadn't she proven to him that she was every bit as capable as he was?

How foolish for her to believe for a second that he had considered her to be his equal. The only reason he'd taken her suggestion in any matter had been in order for him to steal a kiss. And she'd liked it—she'd relived the kiss more than once despite the urgency of their situation. A day in close quarters with him had been torturous. At every brush of their arms, the memory of his kiss surged. The desire to repeat it had been overwhelming.

It was a desire she squashed now. Whatever madness had overcome her, it was done. They were done. They were colleagues, working together for the good of the nation, nothing more. Once they unearthed the traitor at Tenwick Abbey and completed the serum, she would part ways with him and her life could return to normal.

Never mind that she'd already accepted the invitation to stay the winter with the Graylockes. Surely Evelyn and Lucy would understand that she couldn't possibly stay near Gideon any longer. He was forming an attachment to her, one she couldn't return. They were from different worlds, and she'd long ago vowed not to diminish her worth for the sake of a man. She was a scientist, not a wife.

Giddy waited for the carriage in silence. When the driver pulled up alongside them, Gideon handed her into the coach. He seated himself next to her, not across from her, as though he hoped to guard her.

She didn't need or want his help. The anger burned hot in her chest, searing away her numbness and fear from her near-death experience. In fact, the longer she thought of it, the more a doubt niggled in her brain that it had been due to the traitor at all. Perhaps it had only been an accident, a loose brick falling at that unfortunate moment. Neither she nor Gideon had seen anything to suggest otherwise.

And yet, rather than lessening after the adrenaline of the moment wore off, Giddy's protectiveness only increased. When he tried to carry her out of the coach, her patience snapped. She pushed him away and jumped out herself.

The moment he followed her into the open air, she rounded on him. "Stop it! I am capable of walking up a flight of steps on my own."

He shoved his free hand into the pocket of his greatcoat as he scowled. "Forgive me for trying to be a gentleman."

When they'd first met, he'd tried the same thing. His manners were bred into him due to his status as the son of a duke. Alone, she could forget that, but every now and again something happened to remind her that she was a penniless peddler to his peer. He was growing too attached to her. Worse, a traitorous part of her wanted him to. She basked in the attention, even when he maddened her by trying to protect her.

But she couldn't get used to it. She couldn't rely on him.

She gathered her skirts in her fists. "I already told you that I'm not a bacon-brained debutante to be coddled. Get it through your thick skull."

The hurt that flashed across his face cut her to the core. She turned on her heel, searching for the burn of anger in her chest once more but it had died to the barest wisp. The emotion that remained was raw and hollow.

Yanking the door open, she left him and the lantern affixed to the coach. Her heels slapped against the marble floor of the antechamber. A slightly bobbing light led her toward the hallway. Without pausing, she turned the corner and nearly ran into Mr. Catterson.

His eyes widened. He held the candle and tray of biscuits in his hands higher, to avoid jostling her with them. "Felicia? I didn't expect you to return so soon. Is Giddy with you?"

"No," she snapped, then softened upon seeing the startled look on his face.

"But I thought you and he—"

"Never mind about that." Felicia didn't what to hear what Catty thought about her and Gideon. She didn't need or want Gideon Gralocke and the sooner she made that crystal clear to everyone, the better. Best to stick to business. She stepped closer and lowered her voice. "How is the trap progressing?"

"Not very well."

She noticed for the first time that Catt was a handsome man. His complexion and hair a lighter color than Gideon's, his shoulders not quite as broad, and although he towered over Felicia he wasn't quite the giant Giddy was. But even in close quarters with a handsome man, her thoughts were only of Gideon. Even though she stood a hairs breadth away from Catt, there was no flutter in her stomach, no coiling of desire.

Gideon stepped around the corner his brow furrowing at finding Felicia and Catt practically nose to nose. The narrowing of his eyes and the way they flicked from Felicia to Catt told her he'd misread the situation.

The air in the room turned tight with hostility and tension. Catt gave his friend a helpless look, sliding away from Felicia.

All hints of his concern for her had fled, replaced by a hard expression that made her stomach shrivel to the size of a raisin. "Forgive me for mistaking you for a gentlewoman," he said, his voice so soft that she barely caught the words.

Then he turned on his heel, Catt following and leaving Felicia doused in darkness. She clenched her fists to ward away the tremble in her limbs. The words had stung, but she didn't make an attempt to correct his assumption. This was the perfect thing to ward off Gideon's affections and that was exactly what she wanted, wasn't it?

Better to let Gideon think he'd stumbled upon something he hadn't. There was no way Gideon could have tender feelings for her after this.

Chapter Twenty-Four

Giddy couldn't do it. He couldn't spend another second trapped inside this cramped wagon with Felicia. He could see her, smell her, brush against her without recalling in vivid detail the scene he'd interrupted in the corridor. Damn it all, he'd thought he and Felicia had something special.

Clearly, he'd been wrong.

When she brushed against him yet again—inevitable in the meager space—he shoved away from the counter and the *brugmansia* plant he was trying to carefully prune. With his help and the use of the distillery boiler, the wagon had warmed to the proper heat and humidity to sustain the plant and coax it to thrive. He lunged for his jacket strewn across the cot. With his shirtsleeves pushed up to his elbows, the bare skin of his forearm brushed against Felicia's rump. The contact burned. A shiver rippled through him, desire hot on its heels. Even that died quickly when he recalled that he wasn't the man she wanted.

His best friend was. Lud, how had he been so stupid? She'd been flirting with Catt in the orangery in front of his eyes. He should have known. He should never have kissed her. Heaven help him, but he should never have fallen in love with her.

He shrugged on his coat as he crossed the two steps to the wagon door. Never mind that they still had no idea who the traitor was. Never mind that the fact that said traitor was trying to sabotage their work made it even more urgent that they perfect the serum as soon as possible. He needed to get out. To get away from Felicia. Now.

"Where are you going?"

He answered Felicia with a terse word, like he had all day. "Out."

Chubs whined, lifting his head off his paws from where he curled up in the corner. As Giddy opened the door, the mastiff shot to his feet. Not wanting to have any excuse to stay near Felicia, Gideon squeezed through the door and shut it. Finally, he could stretch to his full height again. His shoulders ached.

No more than his chest, for an entirely different reason.

Shoving his hands into the pockets of his jacket, he strode for the manor. "You don't need her."

He didn't want to begin to examine the veracity of that statement.

He'd been unlucky in love before, albeit not often. Most of the time, women chased him because he was the son of a duke. Not Felicia, of course. He couldn't imagine her chasing any man. She didn't have to—they all came to her.

Don't think of her. Easier said than done.

Reaching the door of the abbey, he yanked it open and strode inside. The door clanged shut behind him, encouraged by the wind. It was marginally warmer inside the antechamber. The wind no longer cut through his jacket and into his bones. But the chill lingered. He marched toward the hall in search of a room with a lit hearth.

The problem with women setting their cap for him due to his parentage was that they were easy to walk away from. They didn't truly see him. Even those who appreciated his intelligence and wit never truly knew *him*. Nor did he get close enough to know them. But working with Felicia, it had been unavoidable. He knew her every psychological tic—what it meant when she bit her lip or how to decipher

her myriad smiles. And, given the way they worked together, she read him the same way.

And she'd chosen someone else. Not just anyone, his *best friend.* How was he supposed to stand aside and offer his blessing? He couldn't. It would kill him to watch another man bring her happiness.

He gritted his teeth as he stepped into one of the parlors, empty for the moment. He dropped into the chair closest to the fire and stared into the flame, hoping that it would devour his thoughts and leave him without the sick feeling twisting him.

He didn't know how long he sat there, alone.

"Giddy? What's going on between you and Felicia? Did you have a row again?"

He jolted upright at the sound of his mother's voice. Before he got his feet under him to stand, she sat in the settee next to him and laid her had on his knee. Her touch was light and her gray eyes dark with concern.

If anything, her pity made him feel worse. He averted his gaze. "There is nothing going on between Felicia and I. I don't know why she ever led you to believe there was." His voice was thick with bitterness, but he couldn't hold it back. Why had she, for a second, pretended to be interested in him when she nurtured feelings for another man? Or did she have feelings at all? Perhaps she only craved the passion and excitement of a man's touch.

I could have given that to her.

He hated the small voice in his head today advocating for her. He was a gentleman, whether or not she appreciated it. He would offer her nothing less than marriage.

He'd never considered proposing to a woman before now.

"Giddy, a blind man could see there is something between you. She is such a sweet young woman, and she obviously likes you."

He let out a hollow, mirthless laugh. "I don't think that's true, Mother."

His mother retracted her arm. When he turned to look at her, he found her with her Duchess face on, stiff-backed and regal. "Then she fooled me."

"She fooled us both," he whispered under his breath. He didn't think she heard.

"What did you do to anger her this time? Perhaps we can still fix it."

He heaved a sigh. "I wish I knew, Mother."

When she opened her mouth, he reached out to clasp her hand. He knew she meant well, but he couldn't stomach this line of inquiry. If he and Felicia had ever had potential, it was gone now. The only course of action was to complete their mission so they could part ways.

"Please, Mother. There's nothing to be done. I have to get back to work." As painful as it would be to remain near her. He had to put his feelings aside, for the greater good.

At least, once she was gone, he could begin to heal.

***

Chubs whined, scratching on the door to be let outside. Felicia's heart pummeled her rib cage. She rubbed the ache in her chest.

In the wake of Giddy's departure, the air churned with the ghost of hostility between them. Felicia tried to tell herself that it was what she'd set out to accomplish, but it didn't make her feel better. She'd made a mistake.

With a sigh, she trudged toward the door and let Chubs out into the frigid open air. It helped to douse her self-pity, at least. Chubs shot off like a racehorse to find a good spot on the lawn to void his bladder.

Unfortunately, Felicia didn't have the luxury to wander far. She had to monitor the distillery to ensure that the wagon remained at the correct temperature. The weather had plummeted over the past couple days, leaving a distinct winter-like chill in the air despite the fact that it was only October. No matter what, she couldn't allow their one remaining plant to succumb to the elements. If she did, she would be stuck here with Gideon for months.

Dropping down on the steps of the wagon, she leaned her head into her hands.

She was a strong woman, capable of taking care of herself. She didn't need any man.

Unfortunately, it wasn't 'any' man that she was thinking about. It was Gideon. Giddy was... different.

Lucy's sharp tone pierced the air. "You're making a mistake."

A watery feeling swept through Felicia. She battled it down as she lifted her head. *Be calm. Be neutral.* She managed it time and again while facing difficult customers. Why couldn't she maintain equilibrium now?

Propping her hands on her hips, Lucy said, "Gideon is the best man you'll ever meet, and you know it."

What did she know? Felicia was afraid to ask and find out. Had Gideon and Catt bandied her deplorable actions around Tenwick Abbey? She wrapped her arms around her middle, suddenly sick to her stomach.

"Apologize," Lucy demanded.

Felicia shook her head. "It wouldn't help." Why had driving him away seemed like such a good idea in the moment? In the cold light of day, she wanted to take it back. She wanted their camaraderie, the sheepish smile he sent her when she caught him reciting passages from botany texts under his breath in order to keep his concentration. She craved the look in his eye when their hands brushed, full of desire and curiosity, as if he wanted to do it again just to see if it would feel the same. She wanted him, but she knew she could never have him, even if she hadn't driven a wedge between them.

She was poor and he was rich. She'd denounced her family and he cherished his. She was jaded from the life she'd led, but there was still an innocent kind of optimism to him. He didn't deserve the way she'd treated him. He didn't deserve her.

Felicia blinked against the sting in her eye. Chubs returned, cocking his head as he thrust his nose beneath her palm to be scratched.

Tentatively, Lucy crouched on her heels next to Felicia. She reached out to rub the dog's back. "Don't you like him anymore?"

Could she lie? No. Not to Lucy, and certainly not to herself. "Your brother is the best of men."

"Then what has happened between you? He's been staring into the fire for over an hour. He didn't even respond when Antonia called his name."

Frankly, Felicia was surprised to see Lucy without her bird, but considering they were outdoors and Chubs was nearby, she understood why the young woman had left her pet indoors.

"Did you have a fight?"

Clearly, Gideon hadn't told anyone what had truly happened. Felicia hadn't seen Catt, either, though perhaps he was avoiding her. Frankly, Felicia didn't blame him. She'd put him in the middle of this thing between her and Gideon, and likely caused a rift in their friendships as well.

"We didn't fight," Felicia admitted, her voice dull. At least, not about the way he'd found her flirting with Catt.

"Then what happened?" Lucy's mouth flattened into a thin, stubborn line. "Why won't you give him a chance?"

"Sometimes two people aren't meant for each other."

Felicia started to stand, ready to fall back on the excuse of her work, but Lucy stopped her.

"Bollocks."

Felicia fought not to laugh at the expression on the younger woman's face. A mix of determination and irritation.

"What makes you unsuitable? Because your father wasn't a duke and his was?" Lucy crossed her arms. Chubs, sad at having lost her attention, pawed at her skirts. "By this point, we're connected to so many families that marrying any normal woman of the *ton* would be inbreeding."

At that, Felicia did laugh. She pressed her hand to her mouth.

Lucy wasn't finished speaking. "Did you ever think that maybe Giddy doesn't *want* a woman like that? He could have his pick of debutantes."

"Maybe he hasn't met the right one," Felicia said diplomatically.

"He's met them all by now. And their penniless cousins from the country. I don't blame him for not forming an attachment to one of those shrews."

Did Lucy realize that she was in the same class as the women she insulted?

"It isn't our heritage." *Liar.*

Lucy narrowed her eyes. "Then what?" From her tone, she expected to be able to fix whatever problem had arisen between Felicia and Gideon.

How wrong she was.

Carefully, Felicia chose her words and delivered them in a soft tone. "I turned my back on marriage a long time ago. He'll find someone else."

Why did her chest tighten at the thought? She forced a deep breath.

Rocking her weight back to sit on her heels, Lucy crossed her arms. "So? You're still young."

"Not as young as Gideon."

"Oh, please." Lucy snorted. "You're not dead. You aren't even as old as Morgan."

"I'm almost thirty."

"And he's already been thirty for *months*." Given her belligerent tone of voice, Felicia half-expected Lucy to stick out her tongue in a juvenile attempt to win the argument.

"I believe that makes me more suited to Morgan in terms of age."

"He's married."

Thank Zeus.

"But Giddy doesn't care."

Felicia forced a joking smile, even though she felt all shred of mirth shrivel inside her. "Do you have many conversations with your brother about the age of his future bride?"

Why was she even speaking of marriage? With another man, she would have entered into a consensual, short-term affair and shared the comfort of taking a lover. Though she suspected Gideon would never have agreed to such a thing, even before she'd ruined his good opinion of her.

Lucy glared. She idly rubbed the mastiff's nose when he whined. "Giddy's always been older than his years. I suspect he would find someone his age to be too juvenile."

With a shake of her head, Felicia said, "It doesn't matter. I had a chance at marriage. I chose to be my own woman instead."

As she stood, Lucy did as well. "The two aren't mutually exclusive. Just look at my sisters-in-law. They are the same women they were when they married."

Although Felicia opened her mouth, she couldn't think of a single word to say.

Fortunately, Lucy had plenty for the both of them. Lifting her chin, she added in a decisive voice, "Perhaps you ought to re-evaluate. Are you the same woman you were when you turned down marriage the last time?"

She strode away, leaving Felicia in the shadow of the wagon, her breath frosting in front of her face.

She wasn't the same woman. She was stronger now, self-sufficient. She knew how to take care of herself—but she'd also learned about the cost of such a life. The loneliness.

Regardless, she didn't need or want a man to take care of her. Yes, Gideon had saved her life the night before. But that didn't mean she needed him to coddle and protect her. She could protect herself.

Maybe Lucy was right and she was a different woman, because a part of her craved to belong to Gideon. It was the same part of her that wouldn't stop thinking about him, even when he maddened her.

Could she have fallen in love with him? No. It was a concept more frightening than marriage. Because she'd already ensured that he would never share those tender feelings.

They weren't meant to be.

Chapter Twenty-Five

Felicia held her breath as she added the last ingredient to the beaker and spread the coals to encourage cooling. Was this it? From theory work, she and Gideon had entered an uneasy truce in order to put it into practice. He'd even pressed new oils for her from the plant they had. Not as potent as the seeds, but she diluted it less with water in order to gain the same potency.

However sound their theory, the last three attempts had ended poorly, with the oils separating from the rest of the ingredients and floating on top. The result hadn't even been worthy of testing, not if they couldn't properly blend the ingredients. That had led them to experiment with methods of combining the contents, as well as tweaking the ratio of plant oil to other ingredients. Would this attempt separate like the last ones, and leave them needing to start over—again?

She and Gideon had, for the time being, entered into a shaky sort of truce that involved speaking of nothing personal. There had been no further attempts to sabotage their work. Was the traitor biding his time? Watching and waiting for the perfect moment? For the time being they'd decided the best course of action was to keep a watchful eye and do whatever they could to complete the serum as quickly as possible

They focused only on work, Gideon tending to the plant more than anything else. For a time, Felicia had allowed herself to fall into her work, but now, with the potion nearing completion, her thoughts returned to the man keeping her company.

With his height and his broad shoulders, Gideon dominated the space inside the wagon. Even without turning to him, Felicia could feel the heat of his body bracketing her. It was inescapable.

The back of his hand brushed over her hip, sending a rush of awareness. Desire mixed with shame and regret as she recalled the reason why he wouldn't be kissing her again.

"Breathe," he said, his voice low.

She did, releasing her breath and drawing in another. She didn't dare turn to look at him. Instead, she swirled the contents of the beaker and waited for it to cool and settle again.

The liquid swirled, gradually slowing.

"Why Catt?" Gideon's voice was soft. She scarcely heard his words above the sound of her own breath.

Swallowing around the sudden lump in her throat, she looked down. She didn't have an answer for him, not a satisfactory one.

He raised his voice. "Why did you choose Catt over—" His voice broke. He didn't complete the sentence, but his meaning was clear enough.

"I didn't." She hadn't chosen Catt over him. She'd... she didn't know what she'd done. She'd driven him away—gotten exactly what she wanted, only to realize that she didn't want it anymore.

What she wanted was to be the kind of woman who could pursue Gideon. Ever since her conversation with Lucy, the idea had turned around and around her head. Fermenting when she was thinking about it directly. She always returned to it.

If her age and social status was no barrier, what was stopping her? Their past, and the wedge she'd driven between them. She was the only thing standing in the way of her own happiness. But she didn't know how to change that.

His hand brushed across her dress again, this time the small of her back. "Felicia—"

The grit had settled, leaving the beaker a solid color. Felicia used a thick cloth to grab the mouth of the beaker without scalding herself on the hot glass. She pulled it away from the brazier.

"I think we did it."

The words rippled through the silence. When she breathed them in, the implication filled her with warmth. The oil wasn't separated from the rest of the serum.

"We did it!"

She turned to Giddy, her face breaking into a grin. He looked stunned, a little overwhelmed maybe, but she only glimpsed his expression for a moment. She returned her attention to the serum.

"We have to test it." After all, before they tried it, they wouldn't know whether or not it worked. Just because the science was sound—the theory that they had combined their considerable intellect to puzzle out—didn't mean that the result would be as they predicted.

When she lifted the beaker to pour it into an empty bottle, Gideon slid his hand over hers, stalling her. The warmth of his hand seeped into her skin.

"Don't drink it."

He'd long ago made it clear his thoughts about sampling their own work. However, it was late; regardless of whether or not they succumbed to the effects of the serum, they wouldn't brew another tonight. Chubs snored in his corner of the wagon, oblivious to them and the world.

Felicia twisted to lift her gaze to Gideon's. Like always, the lamp clipped to the side of the counter cast a bright yellow glow. It shadowed his eyes. After a beat, he removed his hand from hers and dropped it to his side. He still stood near enough for her body to prickle with awareness of his proximity.

"We won't know if it works unless we test it." He knew that, of course, but perhaps if she repeated herself, he would change his opinion of the test. "This will work, I can feel it. The science is solid, and the ingredients didn't separate this time."

Hesitation crossed his face. "Are you certain?"

"I can't be, not without testing it. If not me, then we need to find someone willing."

One side of his mouth pulled up in a devilish smile. "Why not my sister? It would prove entertaining."

The warmth in his voice infused the air. A constriction around her chest loosened a little more. It was the first joke he'd made since he'd found her in Catt's arms. Had he forgiven her? Why would he? She craved the camaraderie they'd shared too much to question it.

Instead, she turned to face him fully. His shoulders were hunched in order for him to fit in the wagon without banging his head on the ceiling. The posture lowered his mouth closer to hers. His breath batted stray strands of her hair.

Matching his smile, she raised an eyebrow. "Do you really want to know your sister's secrets?"

He laughed. "Touché."

His smile was infectious. If she raised herself on tiptoe, she could capture his mouth and relive their kiss in the orangery. But did she deserve it? What if he pushed her away? Even though she expected it, she didn't know whether her battered hopes could handle his rejection.

She turned her back. "I'll bottle the serum before it spoils."

"Good idea. We'll go to Keeling in the morning with it."

Her hands shook a bit, but she managed to pour the liquid out of the beaker without spilling a drop. She shoved the cork into place with the heel of her palm.

"Do we trust Mr. Keeling? What if he is the traitor?"

Gideon sighed. The rustle of clothing behind her signaled that he was likely fiddling with his hair or cravat. "I'd like to think that if he wanted to kill us, he would do it in a more efficient manner. Besides, if you're right, we completed our mission. We have to tell someone."

As Felicia heated wax to seal the bottle of serum so no contaminants entered the vial, she answered, "Very well. We'll take a risk and tell Keeling."

"He'll scrounge up someone willing to test it, and then we'll know for certain whether or not we've done it."

Felicia danced from foot to foot as she waited for the wax to be malleable enough to mold around the cork. "Even if we haven't, this is the closest we've come. We should document our progress."

"I'll do that."

They completed their respective tasks within minutes. Once Felicia set the serum in a safe place, she retrieved a bottle of whiskey she had on hand for cold winter nights. "Let's celebrate." She found two tumblers and splashed a liberal amount of the amber liquid into two glasses. Giddy sat on the bed while she dragged over a crate for her to sit on.

Once they were nestled close together, their knees brushing, they clinked glasses. "To our completed mission."

Giddy raised his glass with a grin. "I didn't think it was possible."

Felicia narrowed her eyes, wondering if she should be offended. However, his posture was so casual as he sipped from his tumbler that she didn't rile over the statement. She had once thought him an insufferable, arrogant lord. Her opinion had changed as well. At least she had proven her worth—and research—to him. She took a gulp from her glass.

The whiskey burned her throat in the best of ways. It warmed her from the inside out and quelled the irritating scratch she battled in her throat, the last lingering effects from the fire. She cradled the tumbler between her palms as she stared into the liquid.

"I didn't expect to find the answer so fast." What would she do now? Would she collect her payment from the duke and leave?

She didn't want to. Evelyn had offered her a room in Tenwick Abbey for the winter. She could weather out the worst of the snows and then continue with her life.

She didn't want to do that, either.

"You don't know for certain that we've found the answer." Giddy's voice had a peculiar, sharp quality to it. When she glanced up, she couldn't quite read his expression.

She took another swallow from her glass. It didn't burn as much going down, this time.

"Your mother asked me to stay the winter."

"You should. Stay." He answered so quickly, he tripped over his tongue. He loosened his cravat, his cheeks turning pink, as he added, "The wagon is no barrier against the elements."

It wasn't, hence why she usually rented a room for the coldest months.

Although it might be due to the alcohol, something about the ruddy quality to his cheeks reminded her of when they'd first met. He blushed so easily. A wicked intention unfurled in her chest as she wondered whether or not she could still make him fly his colors. She set her glass on the counter, within arm's reach. Leaning forward, she let her fingers trail up his thigh for the briefest moment as she murmured, "So adamant. Be careful, or I might start to believe that you'll miss me."

His smile shrank as his gaze heated. "Maybe I would rather not find out." He spoke so softly that she didn't hear the words at all, only guessed from the motion of his mouth.

Something hot and potent sank its claws into her. She looked away, not trusting that she'd interpreted his words correctly. Not daring to hope that he might still want her. Needing a change of topic, she stood and reached for his glass. "Another?"

The moment she set the tumbler next to hers on the counter behind her, he caught her free hand. He tugged on it, spinning her toward him. Her head continued to spin, caught up in the effects of the liquor, and she lost her balance. She tumbled onto his lap.

His body surrounded her. Her shoulder was nestled against his chest, her bottom flush on his lap. One of his big hands splayed over her hip—the other traced circles over her back. His hot touch branded her, making her his. Their breaths melded. As he tilted his face down to meet her gaze, his hair flopped onto his forehead. She brushed away the ebony strands.

Their eyes locked. Her body hummed with awareness. He was close enough to kiss, and Lud, did she ever want to. He swallowed audibly as his gaze dropped to her mouth.

Do it. Kiss him.

He licked his lips. "Choose me, Felicia."

His words were spoken in the barest hush. The intimate tone raised goose bumps over her skin. He leaned a fraction closer, the skin of his lips almost brushing hers.

"I love you."

She'd never expected to hear the words laced with such a heartbroken tone. Love was supposed to be light and happy, wasn't it?

He doesn't mean it. It was the whiskey talking. It had to be. She wasn't the sort of woman to make a man like Giddy fall in love.

But, for tonight, she wanted to forget everything that stood between them. She wanted to believe he spoke the truth.

If only for tonight.

She crossed the last inch between them and melded her mouth to his.

Chapter Twenty-Six

Marry me. Two words that were difficult to utter while being kissed.

Truthfully, Gideon hadn't meant to say the first three, *I love you.* But the moment they had left his lips, something inside him had aligned and he'd known it was the right thing to say. He had fallen in love with her. He wanted her, not just now—forever. The moment he'd learned that she hadn't chosen Catt over him, the shields he'd tried to erect to deflect his emotions had shattered. They'd shared two kisses and never spoken of anything further. She hadn't known how he felt. Maybe, now that she did, she would choose him.

She chose to kiss him with abandon. Her mouth moved over his as she shifted on his lap to twine her arms around his neck. He returned the kiss every bit as fervently, trying to prove without words how much he wanted and needed her. He held her tight, not wanting to face the inevitability of having to let her go.

He deepened the kiss, surrendering himself to the way he felt with her. Passionate, yes, but there was an underlying sensation of satisfaction. She was made for him to hold and kiss. Nothing could be more right.

When she shifted on his lap, drawing her skirts up to her hips in order to straddle him and face him fully, he wrapped his arms around her. Her hands trailed over his shoulders, the sensation muted by his shirt and waistcoat as she drew her palms onto his chest. She plucked at the knot of his cravat, quickly unraveling it. He breathed easier without the constriction. Her fingers brushed his front as she sought out the buttons of his waistcoat.

He gulped for air. "Felicia." He didn't know whether her name was a protest or encouragement. He was afraid to do or say anything else. He didn't want to lose her.

Her hair fell into her eyes as she deftly undid his buttons. He tucked the strands behind her ear. She was beautiful. He'd been stunned by that fact from the moment they'd met, but somehow, now that he knew her better, her beauty had only magnified.

He rolled his shoulders back, helping her remove his waistcoat. He wore only his shirt sleeves now, and as she peppered his mouth with quick, soft kisses that he eagerly returned, she attended the fastenings on his collar. Once she undid them all, she slipped her hand inside to encourage the opening to widen. The backs of her fingers brushed his bare skin. His breath hitched. How could such an innocent touch feel so amazing?

When she tugged on his shirt to pull it from his breeches, he lifted his arms to let her strip it from him. The touch of her hands as she returned to explore the contours of his chest was mesmerizing. He burned where they touched, in the best way possible. He wanted more.

Marry me. The words stung his throat, but he swallowed them. She hadn't said that she returned his feelings. He needed to prove to her that he was the man for her, prove that they were meant to be together. Leaning down, he captured her mouth as his hands slipped around to the buttons on the back of her dress. He forced himself not to think, not to question what was happening between them. He belonged with her. That was the only thing that mattered.

That, and discovering how smooth her skin would be.

She wore a maddening number of clothes. The buttons of her dress, the laces of her stays beneath. When he finished with those only to discover the cloth of her chemise still separated them, he almost lost his courage. The warm confidence that had infused him from the whiskey ebbed somewhat as clarity returned.

Felicia had fewer reservations. The moment his hand dropped away from her clothes and he broke the kiss, she pulled her dress over her shoulders and down to her waist. She wiggled on his lap as she tugged her chemise over her head. The moment she bared her skin to the air, she stole his breath.

He traced the contours of her breast with reverent fingers. "You're beautiful." The lamplight gave her skin a golden cast. Her back was to it, so the light stretched rays around her sides, the shadows cloying to her curves.

When he circled her areola, she gasped and arched into his hand. He lowered his mouth to trace the same path with his tongue. She threaded her fingers in his hair, her grip tight. Pinpricks of pain flared to life along his skull. He ignored them as he laved her.

"You have done this before, haven't you?" Her voice was breathless.

He smiled against her breast. "Yes." Once. It had been enough to convince him that when not done with a partner he loved, it wasn't worth doing. With her, it felt better. Her touch was more potent. Her gasps and soft moans rippled through him, building his desire. He wanted to know her body better than he knew his own.

He switched his attention to the other breast.

"Good. I just wanted to make s—*oh*."

He loved that he could render her speechless.

However, speechless did not mean motionless. She writhed against him. Soon, her hand found its way between them to the fall of his breeches. She palmed the ridge of his erection, making him burn. As she found a particularly sensitive spot, his mind blanked and he gasped for breath.

When the spots cleared from his vision, she'd freed him from his breeches. The slide of her skin against his was magic. He leaned his head back on a moan. Her clever tongue traced circles over his neck as she leaned forward. God, he loved her.

Then, without even peeling away the rest of their clothes, she lowered herself against him. The slide of her body felt like coming home. At that moment, nothing mattered but the two of them. Nothing had ever been more right.

Although her cramped wagon didn't allow for much room for him to maneuver, she wrapped her arms around his neck and took command of their passion. He touched her everywhere, craving the feel of her skin. When she shuddered against him, he kissed her deep, her passion fueling his. He joined her in bliss with his arms wrapped tight around her.

Their hearts beat in sync as he continued to hold her. She rested her head on his shoulder. Her breath fanned the skin of his neck, raising chills. He turned to press his lips into her hair. "I love you." He didn't know if she heard his soft words, but he needed to say them aloud.

He wanted to say something debonair or charming, something to solidify her choice. Speaking of a special license wouldn't impress her, and if he tried to propose now, he'd probably end up begging her to have him.

Tomorrow. He would propose tomorrow morning, when he woke with her in his arms. The start of many, many more such days to come.

Chapter Twenty-Seven

Gideon did not wake with Felicia in his arms. Since he had fallen asleep that way, with her head nestled against his chest after they'd snuck into his room, he felt her absence acutely.

He bolted upright. He hadn't shut the curtains last night and the early morning sun drifted through the frosted glass. Leafy green plants—the remnants of the orangery—occupied every inch of space. He usually tended them in the early morning before he left his room. Not today. He had to find Felicia.

As he swung his legs over the side of the bed, flinching as his feet touched the chilly floorboards, he tried not to panic. Too many questions swirled through his mind. Why had she left? Did she regret what she'd done? Hadn't he convinced her that they felt right together? For a moment, he wondered if it had all been an achingly-realistic dream. Her side of the bed was rumpled. Her pillow still smelled like her floral soap. She'd been here.

So why hadn't she wanted to face him this morning?

Maybe she was feeling uncertain of where they stood. The Lord knew he was. A lump formed in his throat as he thought of proposing to her. What if she said no? In his mind, their marriage was a foregone conclusion, but Felicia was a free spirit. He didn't want her to feel as though he were chaining her. Nor did he want to push her away. Lud, he'd never done this before. Perhaps he should read up on the best method of proposing. Some poor sap somewhere must have compiled the research.

He stood, stretching, his mind awhirl and his heart beating fast. Flowers. Women loved gifts of flowers, didn't they? Unfortunately, with his orangery out of commission, his flower supply was limited. Only the hardier plants had survived the toxic smoke and cold, and even they conserved their strength by eschewing flowers. As his gaze passed over the potted plants assembled, he found one small pink flower in the midst. He clipped it away with his pruning shears. Considering that the plant it came from was hanging onto its health by a thread, he wouldn't have let the plant keep the flower, in any case.

Smiling, he quickly dressed and carried his gift as he went in search of Felicia.

Something brushed Felicia's hair as she locked up her wagon. Turning to face Gideon, she raised her hand to her simple coiffure and found something plant-like in her locks.

"Careful," Giddy warned. "You'll crush the petals."

A flower. He'd brought her a flower. Where had he found it?

She searched his gaze. His green eyes sparkled this morning, brighter against the charcoal gray of his greatcoat. He tucked his hands into the pockets, hunching his shoulders almost sheepishly. He hadn't taken the time to shave this morning, his stubble dark against his skin and his uncombed hair sticking up in all directions.

When he opened his mouth to speak, she hurried to say something first. "Thank you."

They'd spent the night together. It had been a wonderful, magical time when she'd forgotten, for a moment, the reality of their situation. She didn't want to hear him retract his love confession—or worse, propose to her due to some misguided gentlemanly notion of manners.

She held up the bottle in her hand, hoping to distract him with that. "I thought we ought to take this to Mr. Keeling to have it tested." After all, if it worked, then her mission was complete. What was the point of speaking of their time together if it was soon to be cut short?

Giddy looked as though he'd like to say something else. After a moment, he ran his hand through his hair and muttered, "What about breakfast first? I don't know if he rises this early."

Nodding, she strode with him back toward the manor. She didn't know how she would survive the morning repast without diverting the conversation away from personal matters. The only thing that might hold Gideon's interest for so long was botany.

Such as the flower in her hair...

With a smile that was much less forced, she asked, "What plant did you find that still had a flower in it? I imagine most would be in a sorry state..."

***

Felicia danced from foot to foot on the rug in front of Mr. Keeling's desk. She didn't dare glance at Gideon. Somehow, she'd managed to keep him occupied for the duration of their meal. Now, with the focus on work, she didn't want to remind him of their time together last night.

Mostly because it rekindled the memory in her, as well. If she were to thrive without his arms around her and the taste of his kisses, then she needed to forget that they had ever been intimate. A task easier said than done. She focused on work.

Mr. Keeling, a thin man with a weak chin and forgettable features, cut the seal on the serum and popped off the cork. He sniffed at the contents and raised an eyebrow. "Are you certain this one will work?" He looked to Gideon for confirmation.

Felicia gritted her teeth. She was the chemist. She should be used to it by now. She tucked her fists behind her back to hide her irritation. "No, we aren't certain. That's why we'd like to test it."

Why did she seem to have this conversation every time they appeared with a version of the serum? Didn't anyone in the Tenwick household understand the scientific process? She took a deep breath, trying to calm herself.

Keeling glanced at her. If he noticed her annoyance, he didn't react to it. He nodded once. "Very well." He swung his gaze back to Gideon again. "Ask me for my mother's name. I was writing a letter to her when you walked in. On the back will have her name and address. So you know I'm telling the truth."

Felicia bristled, even as Giddy loped around the side of the paper-heaped desk to search for the missive in question. To her astonishment, the spy returned his attention to her with a quizzical look.

"How much of this should I ingest?" He hadn't been present for the other trials, beyond finding them subjects willing to imbibe and be questioned.

The hot, prickly feeling in her chest subsided somewhat. She relaxed her hostile pose, her shoulders falling from around her ears. "A small dose will do. A few drops or a mouthful at most."

Carefully, Keeling tipped out a few drops of the serum into his fingertips. He sucked them off. Making a face, he muttered, "Bitter."

Giddy exchanged a wry glance with Felicia as he rounded the desk once more. "Next time, we'll add honey," he quipped, his voice thick with sarcasm. "Are you ready?"

Examining the bottle, Keeling twisted his mouth. "I don't feel any different."

"Give it a moment or two to take effect." It wasn't instantaneous, after all, no more than someone became instantly intoxicated from a sip of wine.

"What is the status of the orangery repairs?" Giddy asked, leaning against the wall as they waited.

Keeling, who apparently wasn't very keen to wait, poured another drop onto his finger and licked it off. "I'm waiting for your brother to sign off on the glass we'll need to purchase. It is an exorbitant sum. I'm not certain we'll be able to have enough delivered before winter sets in. It might be best to wait for spring."

Giddy sighed, but didn't argue. He looked disappointed. Since Felicia couldn't begin to fathom the amount of money that went into building such an edifice, she couldn't think of a way to comfort him, other than to focus on work.

"What's your mother's name?" she asked, her voice casual.

Keeling glanced at her, a small smile playing at his lips, but ignored the question. He licked at a few more drops. She took that to mean that the serum hadn't yet taken effect.

To Giddy, the man said, "If you need a new laboratory set up, I'm sure we can find a suitable room in the abbey to accommodate you. Heaven knows there are enough rooms in this monstrosity."

Privately, she agreed.

"It will have to do, for now. But it won't do as a permanent solution. Plants need sunlight in order to thrive, so I'll need to keep the glass. I'll need to reproduce more of the *brugmansia* plants if we're to replicate the serum in any significant quantity. That will take time."

A lot of time, but he didn't need her for that. In fact, given the way he'd tended to the plants thus far, she would only be in the way.

On the heels of his statement, Giddy added, "It would help if you told us your mother's name."

Keeling's mouth thinned. He shook his head. "I'd rather not speak of her."

Giddy and Felicia shared an excited glance. That was a different reaction than before. Had the serum compelled him to say something truthful? Even if it wasn't the answer to the question they desired, it was a sign that the serum was starting to take effect.

The spy, apparently, didn't think it was working fast enough, because he took a swig from the bottle, corked it, and set it on his desk. Felicia cringed. Coupled with the slow drops he'd been dosing himself with, it might be too much. She didn't know the side effects of the serum yet, aside from those that accompanied the *brugmansia* plant—headache, nausea, dizziness, memory loss, heightened suggestibility.

"How are you feeling?" she asked, afraid to know the answer.

Keeling's color changed. His cheeks flushed, but the rest of his complexion turned waxen. Beads of sweat jumped out on his forehead. He swayed on his feet and groped for the edge of the desk behind him, which he leaned on heavily.

Oh, dear. Would they need to fetch a physician?

"My head tingles." He raised his hand to his forehead. His words were slurred. "I can't think right. There's a fog in my head."

To be expected when he drank that much at once. Felicia pressed her lips together, worried.

Giddy, on the other hand, focused on their task. "Can you recall your mother's name?"

"Caroline." The man gasped for air like a fish. "Caroline Keeling, born Caroline Weston. She came from a big family, but she was the only daughter. I hate my uncles, wretched pigs who would rob their own sister blind, but she doesn't see it and continues to welcome them into her home, feed and clothe them when they're down on their luck. Why, currently—"

Gideon cut off the spy's tirade by clapping his hand over the man's mouth. "That's enough. We got what we wanted. The serum works."

The warm feeling of triumph in her chest fizzled into grief as she realized that her mission had come to an end. She had no excuse to stay.

The moment Gideon lifted his hand, Keeling babbled again.

"Thank you. I have no idea why I told you all that. I thought of my mother and it spilled out."

Giddy pressed his hand to Keeling's mouth again, the most expedient method of silencing him, it seemed. Was it a flaw that the drinkers of the serum couldn't stop talking? Perhaps it was due to Mr. Keeling having ingested so much of it. While irritating, it didn't seem like an adverse side effect from the point of view of the Crown spies. They would collect more information, albeit most of it useless.

As he stood toe to toe with the much shorter Keeling, Gideon's posture stiffened. "Do you work for the French?" His voice was like steel. He lifted his hand.

Keeling's eyes turned as round as saucers. "Of course I don't! What in bloody Hell are you talking about? We work for the Crown, man! *Against* the French."

Gideon silenced the spy once more in order to say, "We've had far too many accidents and close calls, not just in the orangery. The fire, switched labels on dangerous chemicals, and someone tried to kill Miss Albright with a falling brick while we were in Locksley the other day. It's more than coincidence. Someone is trying to stop us from completing this serum and the only people who know of our mission are the household spies."

For a moment, when Giddy lifted his hand and stepped away, Keeling appeared to be too flabbergasted for words. The first ones he managed to splutter were, "I'll handle it." He raised a hand to his head as he tried to stand straight and swayed. "After I sleep this off. It *will* cease after a while, won't it? If it doesn't—"

Felicia cut him off. "It's the same as being intoxicated. You'll probably have a headache when you wake, as well."

Nodding, he leaned heavily on the desk as he rounded it. "I'll make a note to myself then so I don't forget."

Probably a wise decision.

He babbled as he attempted to make the note, but his hand shook to such an extent that he couldn't put the words down on the sheet of paper. He looked to Gideon. "Perhaps you ought to make the note. I would, you see, but..."

Giddy took the pen from him without complaint and bent over the desk to scrawl the note. Neither man paid any attention to Felicia.

This was it. The serum worked. The French spy would soon be ousted by men more capable than Felicia in that area. Gideon could replicate the serum at will, now that he'd watched her do it. He had an impeccable memory for those kinds of things.

And Felicia... she wasn't needed here. It was time to move on.

Ignoring the gaping chasm in her chest, she reached up to pluck out the flower in her hair. A small, pretty pink bloom. She left it on the corner of the desk, a silent goodbye.

She slipped away without drawing the eye of either man.

Chapter Twenty-Eight

Gideon's head ached from Keeling's incessant chatter by the time he finished jotting down the facts as he knew them about the previous sabotage and murder attempts. The only thing Giddy learned in the interim was that the fire in Felicia's room had been deliberately set from the outside. He didn't know how such a thing was possible considering the guest quarters resided on the second story, but he would have liked to have been informed before now. Perhaps he would have believed Felicia and they could have addressed the problem sooner.

Rubbing his eyes, Giddy straightened only to find the room empty save for him and the babbling spy. His heart flipped in his chest, an acutely uncomfortable feeling. Where was Felicia? As he spotted the flower he'd given her lying on the edge of the desk, his entire body chilled.

He had to find her.

"Are you well enough to make it to your room unassisted?"

Keeling, cut off in the middle of discussing his collection of seashells, blinked a few times before he answered, "I think I might take a nap here, in my office."

Unlike Morgan's office, Keeling's was a cramped square space with little room for his desk, lone chair, and rug. There was no place for him to stretch out to sleep. Giddy bit the inside of his cheek as he realized that he couldn't leave the poor man there.

Without asking permission, Giddy hoisted the older man to his feet and bore the brunt of his weight. "No, you won't. Come, let's get you to your room."

He hurried Keeling along even though the man's legs seemed to be made of rubber. He didn't have time to waste. He had to find Felicia before...

He didn't want to think about what she could be doing.

Unfortunately, he was unable to avoid it. As he made his way to Keeling's room, they passed a window peeking out into the circular drive in the front of the abbey. A woman busily hitched Felicia's wagon to a mule. The black spec of her dog romped nearby, spooking the mule and making the task more cumbersome.

She might be going to sell her perfumes in Locksley village again.

Or she might be leaving permanently. He didn't have her direction. If she drove away, he would have no means of finding her again.

I can't. At that moment, everything inside him aligned like the gears of one of his sister-in-law's inventions. He couldn't let Felicia leave, not without a fight—not after last night. He respected her, cherished her, admired her. Damn it all, he loved her and he couldn't let her drive away without so much as a goodbye. She might not react well to a proposal, given her responses to date, but he couldn't let her leave without trying to keep her in his life. She had to feel the same way about him. He didn't know what he would do if she didn't.

He stopped a muscular woman wearing an apron with the Tenwick crest. "Mr. Keeling is feeling ill. Will you see him to his room? And please ignore anything he says. He isn't in his right mind at the moment."

"Ah," she said, a knowing expression on her face. "Got that potion to work, did you? My husband was one of the other testers. Had a nasty headache the next day. I'll take care of Keeling."

That was all he needed to hear. He handed over the babbling man, whose voice had hoarsened until he was only decipherable with considerable effort. The moment the maid had her shoulder braced beneath Keeling's arm, Giddy raced away.

He didn't have much time.

Tearing through the manor and down the stairs, he barely heard anything aside from the thunder of his own heart. He knocked into Lucy along the way, earning a gasp from her and Charlie and nearly getting raked by Antonia's claws as she took to the air. He twisted away just in time, but didn't stop. Not even for the threats Lucy hollered in his wake. He had to reach Felicia.

As he burst into the cold open air, Felicia opened the door to her wagon to usher Chubs inside. She shut it and bounded up to the driver's seat. The second her rear kissed the wood, she flicked the reins. The mule let out a disgruntled groan and lumbered into action.

Giddy's heart turned into a hard knot in his throat. *No.* He couldn't let her get away. Heedless to how it looked, he loped after the wagon. Neat trees, devoid of their leaves, lined the long drive toward the road. There was only space for one vehicle at a time, and the wagon was wider than most carriages. It made for treacherous footing as he dashed around the side. He slipped and skidded but barreled on despite his precarious balance.

As he rounded the front of the wagon, Felicia yanked on the reins, stopping the vehicle short. The mule rolled his eyes and stamped the ground. Giddy laid his hand on the beast's rump and nearly got himself bit for his troubles. He stepped closer to Felicia, out of range.

Her expression turned stony. Lud, he wanted to kiss that look off her face. He shivered as the wind bit through his tailcoat and shirtsleeves. The sweat brought on by the sprint cooled instantly. He fought the urge to cross his arms.

"May I speak with you privately, please?"

Raising her eyebrows, she glanced at the utterly deserted trees and lawn to either side. He had caught the wagon midway down the drive. Perhaps he ought to return to the days when he challenged his brothers to footraces, because it was a pathetic showing considering that her mule didn't much care to be in action.

"In the privacy of your wagon," he amended. "Where it's warmer."

Although she was wrapped in a fur-lined pelisse, she acceded. "Very well." She wrapped the reins around a notch next to the driver's seat and stepped down. Apparently, she trusted her mule not to wander, for she didn't give a backwards glance as she led the way to the door to her wagon. She unlocked it and preceded him inside.

The moment he shut the door behind him, hunching his shoulders so he didn't hit his head on the ceiling, Chubs jumped on him. The mastiff licked his chin, his tail wagging vigorously. Giddy patted him on the chin as he battled him down.

Fortunately, Felicia helped. She wrapped her hands around the dog's collar and hauled him down. Snapping her fingers, she ordered Chubs to return to his bed in the corner. Pinning his ears back against his skull, the mastiff obeyed, his steps slow and heavy.

Giddy took another step into the wagon, closer to Felicia. His chest was burgeoned with emotion, for a moment stealing his voice. He wanted to say too many things, but would she listen?

"St—"

The wagon lurched into motion before he could ask her to stay at Tenwick Abbey and marry him. He stumbled forward, catching his weight on the far wall with an outstretched arm before he crushed her. Her body pressed against his, igniting memories of the night before.

He shoved those memories aside in favor of voicing his irritation. "What in the blazes…?"

Felicia squirmed until she wriggled under his arm. "Rudolph must have tugged the reins free somehow. It hurts his mouth to walk while they're anchored." Without looking at Giddy, she flung out her arms to steady herself against the rocking of the wagon as she approached the door.

When she tried to tug it open, it stuck fast. "What?" She tried again, throwing her shoulder into it.

Giddy had a sinking feeling. The wagon veered. Giddy spread his legs for balance and waddled toward the small window over Felicia's bed. When he unlatched the shutters, the wind blew the rectangular, foot-long and half-foot-wide window open. The passing trees weren't nestled in front of the familiar white steeple. They were headed away from Locksley village, and any help they might hope to find there.

Felicia smacked the palm of her hand against the door in frustration. "Rudolph!"

Was that the crack of the reins? Gideon made his way back to Felicia, hoping to urge her away from the door. "I don't think he's doing this on his own."

As if to punctuate his words, the wagon veered off the road and onto a very bumpy game trail. Giddy and Felicia fell against the door. He struggled to keep the brunt of his weight off her. Chubs whined as he skidded across the floor. The wagon rocked as the vehicle continued down the path.

The light emanating from the open window grew dimmer as the shadow of a tree passed in front of it. The wagon jolted to a stop. Giddy's heart pounded hard against his rib cage. He and Felicia exchanged a wary glance. What now?

The crackle of footsteps over the brush hailed someone's approach. Giddy and Felicia flew apart, searching for weapons. She found the heavy glass bottle of whiskey they'd imbibed from last night in celebration. He found the jar of sodium in oil and readied himself to unscrew the lid if need be.

The door opened, revealing Miss Merewether. Giddy's hands slackened around the bottle. Her? But she'd been friends with the family for years. She still visited his mother and sister weekly.

The daylight glinted off the barrel of a pistol as Miss Merewether mounted the steps. Giddy positioned himself between the angry woman and the woman he loved.

"It looks like I might owe Keeling an apology," he muttered under his breath.

Chapter Twenty-Nine

Miss Merewether never aimed the business end of her gun away from Gideon, nor did she turn her back or Felicia would have clipped her with the whiskey bottle she held. When Chubs growled and launched himself at her, she dodged him with a panicked kind of grace. He soared out of the wagon and she thrust the door shut, barring him there as he snapped and snarled. Although Giddy stepped forward to take advantage of her preoccupation, Miss Merewether regained her faculties in time to aim the gun at him again.

Even now, after Miss Merewether had divested them of their makeshift weapons, forced Giddy to sit on the crate, and directed Felicia to tie his hands behind him and his ankles together, Chubs continued to try desperately to dig his way into the wagon. Miss Merewether winced at the cacophony.

"Silence that dog or I'll silence him for you."

Felicia glared at the villainous woman as she straightened. "Go ahead, waste your shot. I dare you."

She hoped the young woman wasn't quite out of her right mind enough to comply. Felicia loved Chubs with all her heart.

Her shoulders as stiff as rock, Miss Merewether slipped to stand behind Gideon. She pressed the mouth of the gun to his temple. His shoulders flexed beneath his jacket. His green eyes glittered with intent.

Felicia caught his gaze and held it. *Don't do anything rash.* One wrong move and Miss Merewether might pull the trigger by accident. They were smarter than her. They could find a way out, so long as they didn't give in to the panic of the situation.

Giddy's jaw worked. "What do you want?" His voice and posture were surly.

The spinster didn't so much as glance at him. Although he had asked the question, she directed the answer to Felicia. "The love perfume you sold me didn't work. Certainly, it caught a few small fish, but not the one I want. I need something stronger. You will make me a love potion."

She was dicked in the nob. Love potions didn't exist! Lust potions, yes. But not love potions. Only the heart could make someone fall in love. But even if they did exist and even if

Felicia was capable of creating one, she wouldn't.

She had to make Miss Merewether think that she would, if only to buy some time. Slowly, Felicia said, "It won't work the same way as the perfume. You'll have to ingest it."

Anger flashed across the young woman's face. "That makes no sense."

"It makes perfect sense, if you'll allow me a moment to explain."

When Miss Merewether didn't interrupt her, Felicia assumed that she would be granted that moment. Now she had to concoct a plausible lie. She prayed that Miss Merewether didn't have an extensive knowledge chemistry or biology. If she had, it seemed more likely that she would try to create such a potion herself. It was a risk Felicia would have to take.

In a carefully even voice, Felicia explained, "There are certain chemicals in the human body that a person generates when in love. But they need to be associated with a certain person or they will be useless to you. So this potion will essentially do what the perfume did, but on a much more significant scale. To men in the vicinity, you will be the most attractive woman they have ever laid eyes upon."

Miss Merewether nodded. "Make it."

Make it. As if it could possibly be so easy. Felicia moved slowly, explaining to their captor what equipment she would be using and what she would be doing with it before reaching inside the cabinets. She didn't want to startle Miss Merewether into action. The slow progress allowed Felicia time to gauge Miss Merewether's state of mind. She was deranged, beyond a doubt, but would she pull the trigger of the gun if Felicia rushed her? She didn't want to take the chance until she'd decided the answer beyond the shadow of a doubt.

As Felicia listed the ingredients and pulled the necessary boxes and vials from her cabinet, Giddy's hostile stance lessened. He shot her a questioning look, which Miss Merewether thankfully couldn't see. Felicia couldn't answer, even silently, without risking that their attacker would notice, so she turned away.

Silently, she told him, *The serum is the only thing I can think to make. I have all the ingredients on hand.* Hopefully he would puzzle out her plan and not interfere. Judging by the way the serum had rendered Keeling unable to do much more than babble and stumble around, they would soon be able to disarm Miss Merewether.

Although he didn't point out the truth behind Felicia's potion, he did engage Miss Merewether in conversation. "I don't understand. I thought you were a friend of the family."

Unlike Felicia, he didn't bother to make his tone light or welcoming. His voice held all of the animosity and bitterness she felt.

"I am," Miss Merewether said, her voice syrupy-sweet. "You might say I'm like a daughter to your mother. Much closer than that Frederica or, what's her name, Phyllis?"

She reached out to finger-comb Gideon's hair with her free hand. He jerked away. Anger pinched her expression again and she balled her hand.

You could pretend to play along. Felicia bit her tongue. She continued to work with the serum.

When Gideon showed no inclination to continue the conversation, Felicia took up the reins. "You have known the family for much longer, I imagine."

"Indeed." Miss Merewether's voice was clipped, but after that sharp answer and a breath, she warmed to the topic. "Much longer than you, too. Why, I was there to console Evelyn after her husband died. I was there to support Morgan as he bumbled his way through being a duke. I was there to help Lucy shine during her come-out, and if not for that blasted house party, I might have been there when Tristan married."

Felicia exchanged a puzzled look with Gideon. Had Miss Merewether hoped to marry Giddy's brother? She spoke of the family with familiarity. How close were they? Due to her work with Giddy, Felicia hadn't had the chance to acquaint herself with Miss Merewether at all during her visits. Perhaps if she had, she would have noticed something untoward and prevented this.

Felicia hadn't had that opportunity, but she pretended as if they were out to tea now as she worked with the serum. Now that she'd perfected the method of brewing it, it took less time than during experimentation. She filled that time with banal chitchat as she tried to get a measure on Miss Merewether. Unfortunately, her instincts insisted that the spinster was willing to pull the trigger on the gun she held, if pressed. Felicia had best not give her a reason. Although Miss Merewether seemed on the edge, unreachable by reason, her hand was steady as she held the gun to Giddy's head.

For his part, he did no more than shift throughout the interim. If Felicia had to guess, she suspected that he attempted to loosen the ropes around his wrists. They were twine, the same she used to bundle her herbs after she dried them, and she'd only wrapped them around his wrists twice. If he tried, he could probably snap them. She hoped he wouldn't try with Miss Merewether's gun fixed to his head.

As she removed the beaker from the brazier, she held her breath. Would the ingredients separate again? She would feed it to Miss Merewether either way, but it would be satisfying to know that she could replicate the serum at will.

"Is it finished?"

Felicia fought not to make a face at the spinster's sharp words. "It is, but it's hot. Give it a moment to cool."

It was the longest moment of Felicia's life. Once she counted to one hundred and the serum did not separate, she smiled to herself and found a vial. She used a cloth to handle the still-warm beaker as she poured the liquid into the vial. Not all of the liquid fit and she was left with a thin film on the bottom of the beaker. She set it aside, hoping Miss Merewether wouldn't take offense.

Turning, she offered the vial to her captor. "Here you go. Once you drink it, you'll have to wait a minute or two for it to take effect."

The young woman narrowed her eyes. "You drink it first. I want to ensure it isn't poisoned."

Drat. The serum would fog her mind. How would Felicia think of a way out of this situation without her full faculties? She met Gideon's gaze. Given his tense expression, she feared that he would do something ill-thought out in order to save them both.

Wait until the potion takes effect, she begged with her gaze. Hopefully he understood.

"Very well." She tipped the vial and took a small sip.

Miss Merewether waited. When Felicia didn't immediately double over, clutching her neck, she reached out for the vial. She truly didn't understand anything about science, after all. Felicia held the serum out.

At the first sip, the woman made a face at the bitter taste. She choked down the rest of the vial nonetheless. A far higher dose than intended, perhaps even more than Mr. Keeling had ingested. In a few moments, they would be able to overpower her with ease.

Tension hung in the air as the villain waited for the serum to take effect. The silence was broken only by her dog's incessant attempts to break down the door. It seemed the door was sturdier than Felicia would have thought. She started to feel lightheaded and bit the inside of her cheek.

"I'm feeling a bit woozy." Miss Merewether blinked rapidly, as if unable to focus.

"That's how you know it's taking effect."

With a smug smile, the young woman prodded Giddy in the shoulder with the gun. "What do you say, Gideon? Am I the most attractive woman you've ever seen?"

She probably tried for a flirtatious purr, but the slurring in her voice and the unsteady way she shifted on her feet negated the effect.

Alarm flashed across Giddy's face. "You're asking me?"

She walked her fingers across his shoulders. When he flinched, her hand tightened around the gun. A knot formed in Felicia's throat. *Play along, for Heaven's sake!*

"Of course I am." Miss Merewether straightened, an imperious look on her face. "You *are* a man, are you not? I can't very well ask her." She glared at Felicia.

As she surreptitiously slid her hand along the counter in search of a weapon should she need one, Felicia pressed her lips together. *Do not laugh.* But Miss Merewether's attack of Giddy's masculinity was amusing to her, even if not to him, judging by the look on his face.

"Felicia also drank the potion. Perhaps I find her the most attractive woman I've ever seen." His gaze lingered on Felicia as he spoke.

What are you doing? For a genius, he was a remarkable idiot. As if to prove it, Miss Merewether swung her pistol toward Felicia. Felicia flung her hands up in surrender.

"Impossible," she said, starting to babble. Oh, no, would she start to spill her secrets like Mr. Keeling had? She swallowed, trying to tamp down the words but they spilled out anyway. "You had a much higher dose. In comparison, what I drank would hardly have any effect." Felicia clamped her lips shut against the torrent of words bubbling in her throat. *Enough!*

"You could never be in love with someone who is a common gypsy." Miss Merrewether glared at Felicia who struggled to hold her tongue.

"Oh, I assure you Miss Albright is anything but common," Gideon said.

"Still, a lord such as yourself deserves a fine lady. Like me. That's why I tried to save you from making a mistake with *her*." Miss Merewether's gaze darted to Felicia again. "I thought she would have the sense to leave after I changed the labels and ruined your little project."

"*You* changed them?" Felicia shot a look at Gideon. Of course, Miss Merewether had been at Tenwick Abbey for tea that day.

"Naturally. When I saw you with Lord Gideon at church I knew I had to act fast."

"The fire. You set my room on fire," Felicia said.

Miss Merewether scowled. "Well, it seemed like you weren't going to leave so I thought to roust you out. Was quite a trick tossing the lit rags up through your window. And I will have to address the fact that you have servants running about outside at night. I had to do a good bit of ducking and hiding. That just won't do when *I'm* living there."

Giddy frowned at her. "You will not be living there."

"Oh, now, don't be silly." The effects of the serum must have been in full force. Miss Merewether babbled on. "Why, I've gone to so much trouble to save you. I am sorry about your orangery though. The windows wouldn't have had to be broken if you'd just waited for the vapor to dissipate and then you could have retrieved her body."

"And mine," Gideon said.

Miss Merewether frowned. "Yours? I would never hurt you. I made sure you had left before barring the door and setting up the vapor so she would be asphyxiated."

Cat had borrowed Giddy's coat when they'd spilled the solution on his. The coat with the Tenwick colors. Miss Merewether must have thought it was Giddy that left. For some reason the thought of Miss Merewether finding out that she'd killed Gideon by mistake made Felicia want to laugh. An odd effect of the serum, she supposed.

Fortunately, Miss Merewether didn't seem to notice Felicia's inner struggle. She turned to Gideon. "And when you were dancing with this common trollop at the Golden Goose... well a nicely placed brick still didn't even get rid of her. Now. Why haven't you fallen in love with me yet? Are you a sodomite?"

Felicia lost the battle. Laughter spilled from her throat as she slouched against the counter. She was helpless to stop it. At least it wasn't words. Tears leaked from her eyes.

Glaring at her, Giddy said in a clipped tone, "You're wasting your time. I'm in love with someone else."

A stitch bloomed in Felicia's side. She still couldn't stop laughing. "You... idiot... " The words were lost in the torrent of giggles. How was she supposed to get the upper hand if she couldn't stop laughing? She needed to get control of herself.

But she couldn't.

Miss Merewether ignored her and quizzed Gideon on his mysterious love, but no matter how she prodded him, he refused to answer the question.

Felicia's amusement died a quick death as Miss Merewether loosed a frustrated scream. She shoved the barrel of the gun into Giddy's temple—viciously hard, judging by the way he winced.

"It should be me! *I've* whiled away my marriageable years waiting for you Graylocke boys to come up to snuff. I've turned down offers for you, you know. Now I am finally going to get my due, Gideon Graylocke. You *will* marry me or so help me..."

As with Mr. Keeling, Miss Merewether couldn't seem to contain her words. Felicia's jaw dropped as the deranged woman recited every glance the Graylocke brothers had ever given her, the way Tristan or Anthony had occasionally flirted, the way Morgan or Gideon had offered to escort her or carry her bag or open a door for her. By the time she rattled on about Evelyn and Lucy's clear preference of her, Giddy's eyebrow started to twitch.

Heedless to the gun pointed at his temple, he interrupted her. "I will never marry you."

For a moment, Felicia's heart stopped as she feared their captor would shoot him. Thankfully, Miss Merewether seemed to recall that she wouldn't be able to marry a dead man. She aimed her pistol at Felicia's chest.

"It didn't work. Make another."

The nozzle of the pistol wavered. If she pulled the trigger, where would she hit? Felicia tried desperately to swallow against a paper-dry mouth.

She grappled for some excuse, any excuse to stall the threat of violence glimmering in Miss Merewether's eyes. Unfortunately, Felicia's thoughts turned to mist when she reached for them. She couldn't think.

Her gaze lit on the remainder of the serum. Some of it had evaporated, but there were a few drops circling the outer rim of the beaker. Not quite the sip Felicia had taken, but enough.

"You should feed him the rest. Then he'll tell you the truth."

No. That is a terrible idea. Even Giddy, whose response to Miss Merewether's aggression thus far had been suspect, looked at Felicia as though she'd grown a second head. Maybe she had. She certainly wasn't thinking with the one she had. Gingerly, she touched her forehead, hoping that by proving to herself that it still existed and her brains hadn't spilled out that she would regain her faculties. No such luck. She still saw no way out, except to bide her time and overpower Miss Merewether if she found the chance. Her head grew foggier by the minute, so it would have to be soon.

And yet, when the spinster held out her hand, Felicia thrust the beaker into her palm. It nearly slipped out, but Miss Merewether managed to catch it by cradling the beaker between her forearm and her body. She focused on Gideon.

He turned his face away. "I won't drink it."

"You will or you'll die."

The threat had no effect on Gideon save for the clench of his jaw. He glanced at Felicia, something indecipherable entering his green eyes.

Miss Merewether turned the gun on Felicia. "Drink it or she dies instead."

Giddy's chin wobbled before he firmed it. He nodded. When the villain raised the beaker to his lips, he opened them to receive the liquid. Some of it dribbled down the side of his mouth. When Miss Merewether turned away to return the beaker to Felicia, he surreptitiously wiped his mouth against his shoulder.

Had he drank any? Would he lose his common sense as well, the way Felicia had?

Miss Merewether tapped her toe, impatient, as she waited for the serum to kick in. She soon grew tired of waiting. She rounded on Gideon.

Her back was turned to Felicia. What had Felicia wanted to do, again? The wood of the counter felt cool against her palm. She ran her fingers across it a few more times.

Miss Merewether asked, "Why won't you marry me? We were meant for each other."

"No, we weren't."

That was a mean thing for Giddy to say. Felicia giggled. His nickname was Giddy. Did his family call him that because of his walking-on-air personality? She laughed harder.

"Giddy." That was fun to say. No wonder Antonia repeated it so often.

Miss Merewether started to turn toward Felicia again, but Gideon raised his voice and drew her attention. "I was meant for someone else. I love her."

"Who?" Miss Merewether's arm trembled as she levered the gun at him.

"Felicia. I'll never marry anyone but her."

Felicia's hand slid away from the counter as her jaw dropped. He loved her? Actually, truly, deeply loved her? He must, if he was under the influence of the truth serum. He couldn't lie. Her eyes filled with tears as she battled a wash of emotion.

The world seemed suspended for an instant. When she blinked, Miss Merewether turned around, a murderous expression contorting her face as she threw herself at Felicia. The gun dangled in the air between them. Felicia reacted on instinct, throwing herself at her attacker and knocking her arm upward. A shot fired as Felicia grabbed Miss Merewether's wrist to keep it pointing skyward. Their momentum knocked them into the wall. They wrestled for supremacy.

Miss Merewether, a bit taller than Felicia, used her height to her advantage. When she thrust the smaller woman away, Felicia stumbled into the counter. The impact jarred her, but her head cleared somewhat. She grappled for a weapon as Miss Merewether flung herself at her, swinging the pistol as though it was a club. Clearly under the influence of the serum, the young woman swayed and stumbled. Felicia ducked under her arm and raised the weapon she'd grabbed. When she swung at the back of Miss Merewether's head, the glass shattered and the spinster dropped to the ground.

Felicia stared at the jagged edges of the beaker spout still in her hand. Oh. She broke her beaker. Those were expensive, too.

Giddy pulled the broken glass out of her grip. When had he gotten free? He pulled her into his arms, pressing his lips into her hair. "Thank Zeus. I was so afraid." He held her tight.

Moments later, when Miss Merewether started to stir, Felicia stomped on her like she would a cockroach that wouldn't die. The villain lay still once more while Giddy checked her pulse. She must still be living because he said, "Let's find something sturdier than your twine with which to restrain her."

Felicia agreed, but her head was still spinning so in the end, she slipped out of the wagon and endured the kisses and snuffles of her dog as he checked her for injury. She was fine—she thought. Her head swam and her heart... she couldn't begin to decipher that.

Chapter Thirty

Over an hour later, and Giddy was still haunted by the fear that had clawed into his chest when Miss Merewether had lunged for Felicia. For a moment, with the gun flailing in the air, Giddy had petrified with the certainty that he would lose the woman he loved.

Even after turning Miss Merewether over to be delivered to the local magistrate—she had attacked the son of a duke at gunpoint and confessed to acts of sabotage, after all—he still couldn't draw a deep breath. If she had died, he felt certain he would have died with her.

Although he'd mourned his father with the rest of his family, he'd never understood why his mother had felt the loss so acutely that she seemed to lose a part of herself. Now he understood, because if Felicia had died, he would have suffered the same fate. Earlier in the week, he'd been so cavalier about the concept of facing life without her. He'd thought, with time, that he would heal and move on. Now, he knew there was no woman for him but her.

But did she feel the same? With all the matters that needed their attention in the wagon and the wooziness that had gripped Felicia following her ingestion of the serum, they hadn't had a chance to talk. He'd had little enough of the serum that the mind-muddling effects had worn off, leaving him with a throbbing headache. The events in the wagon were a bit fuzzy, but he was certain at one point that he'd confessed his love for Felicia while under the effects of the truth serum. Hell, he'd all but begged for her hand in marriage! Did she remember or were her memories of the time in question slipping away like his?

He had to catch her before they did. He had to know whether she felt the same. Leaving Miss Merewether in the hands of the slowly-recovering Keeling and his trusted underlings, Gideon searched for Felicia. He found her sitting on the front step of the abbey. Chubs had all but crawled onto her lap in an effort to remain near her.

When his shadow passed over her, she glanced up. She huddled beneath her pelisse. Her thick eyelashes fluttered in front of her eyes as she blinked.

He tucked his hands in the pockets of his tailcoat. Maybe he should invite her inside, out of the chill. When he opened his mouth, the only words to tumble out were, "I love you, Felicia. I don't want to spend a day without you. Could you... do you feel the same?"

Her eyebrows knitted together but she didn't speak a word. Instead, she grimaced and touched her hand to her forehead. Not answering the question—the way Keeling had acted while he was under the influence of the serum, but before it had fully taken root. Felicia's dose must have worn off. Her silence spoke for itself.

He took a step back, then another. He didn't trust himself to stay or else he would drop to his knees and beg her to have him. Did he want to marry her if she didn't feel the same about him? She might develop feelings for him over time. They hadn't known each other for that long.

He needed to think. Needed to rid himself of the numb feeling encroaching on his body. Turning on his heel, he strode away to find the farthest, most remote place in Tenwick Abbey. Maybe there he wouldn't feel as though his world was crumbling around his ears.

***

Felicia stared at the spot where Giddy had stood as the sky turned darker and darker. From time to time, Chubs whined and adjusted his position. He was the only thing keeping her warm. Her feet, her hands, her rump felt like ice. It matched her heart.

She hadn't been able to say anything. Her head throbbed, dredged up new, temporarily forgotten memories with each blast of pain. With each ebb, they disappeared, and she was able to breathe again. Until the next pounding brought them back. Giddy confessing he loved her. Giddy holding her. Giddy asking if she loved him. All Gideon.

She could leave. Pack up her wagon, ride into the sunset, and never look back. Running away was what she did best, after all. It's what she'd done when her father arranged a marriage. It's what she'd done when one of her lovers wanted more from her than she was willing to commit.

Like Giddy did, now. Did she love him?

Yes. If that raw, frightening feeling in her chest could be called love. This time, she wanted more. It petrified her. As much as she knew that she should stand and make a decision, she couldn't. There were too many doubts, too many what-ifs.

The click of footsteps hailed a woman's approach. When Felicia glanced up, she met Lucy's gaze. She looked away. The young woman sat next to her and pet Chubs.

For a long time, they didn't speak.

"Are you going to marry my brother?" Lucy's breath puffed out in clouds. They would both catch a chill if they continued to sit out here. Felicia couldn't muster the desire to move.

She stared at her wagon and tried to imagine her future. "I never wanted a marriage. I ran away from one when I was your age, you know."

"You aren't my age anymore."

Lucy delivered the words casually as she scratched behind the mastiff's ear, but they rang in Felicia's ears. She didn't answer.

"Do you still not want one?"

Felicia stared at her hands, fisted in her skirts for warmth. "What if he wakes up one day and doesn't want me?"

"Then you hand him his spectacles, because he'd have to be blind not to see what's in front of him."

A smile ghosted across Felicia's lips. She laughed. As low and hollow as it was, it reminded her of what living was like. Dear Lord, she was going to do this, wasn't she?

Slowly, she stood. She winced at the twinge of pain from muscles stiff from disuse. Wiping her clammy palms on her skirts, she muttered to herself. "This is ridiculous. I've stared down highwaymen. I just grappled with a madwoman. I can do this." She swallowed and admitted, "This is the scariest thing I'll ever do." But she could do it—she would.

Lucy beamed as she got to her feet. "I've seen the change in my brothers since they've found their wives. It will be worth it."

Felicia hoped so. What if she'd hesitated too long? She squared her shoulders and started walking.

It was only when she reached five paces that she realized that she had no idea where to look.

"Giddy is in the orangery," Lucy called, her hands cupped around her mouth.

Felicia waved in thanks. She couldn't speak.

Trembling, she marched toward the ruined hothouse. Chubs nearly tripped her several times, with his unwillingness to move away from her for even an instant. His presence calmed her, settled her. No matter what, she would always have his love. Even if it wasn't quite the same as Gideon's.

Her heart quickened, thundering in her ears. The flutters in her stomach increased as she approached the jagged silhouette of the orangery. She found Giddy plucking dead weeds out of the mounds of dirt that had once held thriving plants. When her shoe crunched on a stray shard of broken glass near the gaping hole by which she entered, he raised his head.

He didn't say anything, not even hello. Just as well. It was her turn to speak.

"I've never been in love," she confessed. "Until you."

Tears stung her eyes but she blinked them away. She balled her fists. She could get through this.

"I can't stop thinking about you. I can't leave you. I—" She swallowed. "I want a life together and that scares me." Her chin trembled but she didn't break eye contact with him as he unfolded his frame and wiped his hands on his breeches.

He stepped toward her and in an instant, they were in each other's arms. Her fears melted away, replaced by the warmth that infused her with his touch.

"You don't have anything to be afraid of, I promise. I will love you until the day I die."

She drew away to look him in the eye. "What if I waited too long and can't have children?

What if word gets out about my past and it disgraces your family? What—"

He placed a finger over her lips, silencing her. "It doesn't matter." Gathering each of her hands in his, he lifted them one by one to his lips. Then he kissed her on the mouth, long and lingering.

When he drew away, he whispered, "None of it matters, as long as we have each other."

Epilogue

One month later

"What is this supposed to say?"

"What do you mean?" Giddy asked. He spared her a brief glance as he checked on the progress of their *brugmansia* clippings. With winter setting in, it didn't seem likely that their shipment from South America would arrive before spring. That left them with nothing to do but try to grow their own and tend to their own research.

Felicia waved the sheaf of papers in her hand. The rustle of the page echoed against the stone walls of the room they'd been temporarily allotted until the orangery could be repaired come spring. Long wooden benches ate up the space in the narrow rectangular room, two long rows facing the bank of windows at the end to allow the sun to shine onto the pots clustered there.

"This," she said, pointing to a line near the top. "This chicken scrawl right here."

He barely glanced at the page. "That reads 'Rate of Growth.'"

She examined the page again. "It does not."

"It does." Wiping his fingers on a handkerchief, he stepped closer. He pointed to the line in question. "It's clear as day right next to these numbers, the results."

"You call those numbers? It looks like you doodled a pumpkin."

He raised his eyebrows, the corners of his mouth twitching as he fought not to laugh. "That is two zeroes and the number two."

She squinted. "It looks like a pumpkin to me."

Wresting the notes from her grasp, he laid them on the tabletop and wrapped his arms around her. She squealed as she was enveloped by his embrace. He lowered his mouth to her ear, placing a tantalizing kiss there.

"Remind me never to write you a love letter."

She chuckled, but twisted her head to give him greater access. "From now on, I'll take the notes."

"Whatever my beautiful wife wants."

The moment was interrupted as Catt and Rocky, huddled across the room near the pots, burst into one of their many arguments. She gestured madly as she spoke, inching closer and closer to him all the while. He gave as good as he got, his expression intense.

"Do you think they have feelings for each other?" Felicia mused, her voice soft.

Giddy laughed. "Of course not. They always rubbed each other the wrong way. Once they let off some steam, they'll be fine for a while."

She shrugged, her shoulders brushing his chest as he adjusted his hold around her. "I remember when we used to fight that way." She tilted her head to smile at him. "Am I wrong in thinking you wanted to end one of those arguments with a kiss?"

With a fond smile, he pressed his lips to her forehead. "You're delusional, my dear."

She scowled at him.

At least until he added, "I wanted to end them all that way. But Catt and Rocky are not us."

The spat reached its crescendo. Rocky turned on her heel and stormed from the room, her skirts swishing.

Felicia extracted herself from her husband's hold. She bent to open a cabinet built into the bottom of her work bench. The bench had been commissioned as a wedding gift from Gideon.

When she plucked out one of her perfumes, her husband sighed. "What are you doing?" He sounded resigned.

She flashed him a flirtatious smile. "Maybe I might go put it on."

His gaze darkened. "Perhaps you'd best hold off until after supper." He looked as though he might pull her back into his arms for a more thorough kiss.

She grinned and danced away from him, out of reach. "I'd rather drive you wild beforehand."

He flashed her a devilish smile. "You always do, my dear. Perfume, or no perfume."

After blowing him a kiss, Felicia scampered into the corridor. She had no intention of putting the perfume on, at least not from this bottle. She spotted Rocky just as she was about to turn the corner. Hiking up her skirts, Felicia ran to catch up.

"Felicia," Rocky said as she stopped short. She blinked owlish eyes behind her spectacles. "Is something amiss?"

"Not at all." She thrust the perfume into her friend's hand. "This is for you."

Rocky frowned. "That's sweet, but I'm afraid I don't wear perfume."

"This is worth wearing. It drives men out of their minds. Just a few dabs." Felicia mimed splashing some on her pulse points. "For when you want to render a man speechless."

"Oh." Rocky examined the perfume, then hid it against her skirts, covering it with her hands. "Thank you."

Felicia grinned, satisfaction running through her. When Rocky wore that perfume, Catt wasn't going to know what hit him.

Also By Leighann Dobbs

Regency Romance

***

Scandals and Spies:

Kissing The Enemy

Deceiving The Duke

Tempting The Rival

The Unexpected Series:

An Unexpected Proposal

An Unexpected Passion

Dobbs Fancytales:

Dobbs Fancytales Boxed Set Collection

———

Western Historical Romance

***

Goldwater Creek Mail Order Brides:

Faith

American Mail Order Brides Series:

Chevonne: Bride of Oklahoma

Contemporary Romance

***

Reluctant Romance

Sweetrock Cowboy Romance Series:

Some Like It Hot (Book 1)

Too Close For Comfort (Book 2)

Witches of Hawthorne Grove Series:

Something Magical (Book 1)

About Leighann Dobbs

USA Today Bestselling author Leighann Dobbs has had a passion for reading since she was old enough to hold a book, but she didn't put pen to paper until much later in life. After a twenty-year career as a software engineer with a few side trips into selling antiques and making jewelry, she realized you can't make a living reading books, so she tried her hand at writing them and discovered she had a passion for that, too! She lives in New Hampshire with her husband, Bruce, their trusty Chihuahua mix, Mojo, and beautiful rescue cat, Kitty.

Find out about her latest books and how to get discounts on them by signing up at:

http://www.leighanndobbs.com/newsletter-historical-romances

Connect with Leighann on Facebook:

https://www.facebook.com/leighanndobbshistoricalromance/

About Harmony Williams

If Harmony Williams ever tried her hand at being a chemist, she would probably wind up blowing something up like Giddy almost did. Instead, she lives an explosion-free life in the middle of the Canadian countryside with her enormous lapdog, Edgar. In her spare time, she likes to sip tea, read too many books (if such a thing is possible) and dream up funny new ways for characters to fall in love in Regency England. Join her newsletter at www.harmonywilliams.com/newsletter and get a free novella!